Katie~

Hope you enjoy pride and have a great day. Happy Reading

(signature)

↑ Seattle Pride 2022

Under the Sitka Sky

By: Violet Morley

D1738064

Cover Artist: Cath Grace Designs

Editor: Kat Jackson

Copyright © 2021 Violet Morley

Acknowledgments

I wouldn't have gotten nearly as much done without the constant corralling my wife did while I tried to find any project under the sun to do instead of a session of writing. She is also my champion, cheerleader and the best damn thing that's ever happened to me. Thank you for forever being my Goose.

To my beta readers, Conny, Julie and Emily, you took this document and made it readable. Thank you for your suggestions, critiques, and lovely notes. The book is stronger because of your input and I'm eternally grateful.

I'll forever be appreciative to have grown up in such a unique place as Sitka, Alaska. Thank you for picking such a cool place to live and raise kids, mom and dad! Oh, and also for helping me with endless questions about Alaska, berries and flight information. I think we found a good balance of technical and relatable which was extremely helpful.

Kat brought out the polishing rag to make the book shine, and to deal with those no-see-ums I like to call commas, thank you for going on this journey with me.

Lastly, but certainly not least, Cath, one of my favorite parts of the process is working on the cover. It brings the book to life, and such a fun process to work through.

Dedication

To all who read this and want a dog, I feel you.

Chapter One

Rain pummeled the windshield as the Cessna dipped suddenly, causing Cam's stomach to meet her throat in a swoop. Her grin reflected off the side window as she looked to her left, trying to see through the storm. She was startled when a talon-like grip on her upper arm pulled her attention to Eric, one of her passengers.

"You okay there?" Cam asked through her headset, side-eyeing the man as she tried to dislodge his death-grip from her arm.

She peeked behind her to make sure the second passenger, Amber, was doing okay. She noticed Amber's face had a sheen of sweat, and her jaw muscles jumped in exertion as she stared out the window.

"Fuck. Do you even know how to fly in this weather?" Eric's whiny voice came over the headset before he slammed the palm of his hand over his mouth. His other hand moved from Cam's arm to the flight panel.

Cam glanced at Eric and her eyes widened before she started looking for the air-sick bags she usually kept in the side pocket of the seat. She mentally slapped her head when she remembered the last charter passengers had gotten sick and she had forgotten to replace the bags. At this point, all she could hope was that Eric held in his lunch until they landed and he was far from her plane.

"God, you're going to kill us!" Eric screeched before swallowing hard a few times.

Cam leaned back in her seat to stretch out her back, not bothering with a response. She needed to concentrate as the plane jerked to the left with a gust of wind. Over the horizon, Cam could see the harbor. Her heart quickened when she keyed the mic to let Flight Service know she was inbound for the channel and had listened to the Automatic Terminal Information System (ATIS) recording, which provided helpful information when landing. Even after flying thousands of times, the exhilaration never dimmed. Pointing the nose towards the strip of water that made up the harbor, she smiled at seeing her hometown of Sitka, Alaska.

A large gust of crosswind pushed them further to the left, and another screech came through the headset. "We're going to crash!" Eric pawed at her arm while screaming. "Why is the window rattling? Do you even maintain this plane?"

She grabbed his hand and pushed it away from her body. "Stop touching me and shut the fuck up." Even though she could practically fly in her sleep at this point, she still wanted to concentrate, especially while landing. Having Eric's voice in her head wasn't helping matters. She flicked off the control to his headset before continuing towards the water.

Cam relished in the relative silence that followed. The wind was pushing the rain off the windshield, but visibility was still poor. Without screeching in her ear, though, she was able to focus on the task at hand. She tightened her hand around the yoke, rubbing her thumbs against the plastic grip, finding the solid material comforting. As the plane approached the water, Cam rolled the yoke to the right, causing the tip of the wing to dip on the right side towards the water. This action kept the plane from drifting sideways to the left from the fifteen-knot crosswind. At the same time, her left foot pressed down on the rudder pedal, which counteracted the adjustment on the yoke. The pedal controlled the tail, which kept the plane's nose straight ahead. While dealing with crosswinds was like second nature, it still took coordination to get everything aerodynamic and facing forward for landing. She eased the yoke towards her, bringing the plane's nose up to create a smooth landing on the floats as they kissed the water.

Holding back a fist pump at the smooth landing on the water's surface, she guided the plane towards the dock. She was almost to the destination when she heard a gurgle. Cam looked to her right and saw the passenger door was open. Eric's body was leaned over the side, heaving his lunch. She saw the chunks coat the side window before a gasping yell met her ears. Wind from the propeller had caused most of the mess to splash back into the cabin and now covered Amber.

Making it to the dock, Cam quickly killed the engine, but the damage was done. It wasn't the first time someone had upchucked their lunch, but it was a first to have it splattered around the plane's interior. She quickly hopped out and secured the plane to the dock before helping her passengers out of the aircraft.

Cam could hear heaving and a slight splash as Eric continued to empty his stomach's contents into the harbor. All Cam could do was roll her eyes. Wiping off the aircraft, she cursed her luck at having seen their distress signal. If she had stayed home as her brother had suggested, there wouldn't have been a need to clean up the mess in her plane.

Eric's skiff had gotten stuck at high tide after he lost track of time. He was lucky she had happened to fly over where they were and saw him waving an orange life vest wildly around, or Eric and Amber would have been stranded for the night. It was quite a surprise when she saw he was with Amber, a woman who was certainly not his wife.

Cam finished the post-flight check before grabbing her gear and patting the top of the hand-carved wooden eagle attached to the plane's dashboard as she whispered a 'thanks' for the safe flight. As she rounded the corner of the aircraft, she had to hold in a laugh that was threatening to bubble up. Eric was on his hands and knees, dry heaving, while fat raindrops were hitting his head. Had Eric been a decent person in high school, she might have felt bad for him, but small towns and long-held grudges ensured they would always have strained interactions.

Ready to get out of the rain, Cam scanned the dock for Amber, who was peering over the edge, looking at a couple of birds pecking at the tainted water. The rag had done an okay job of cleaning off her face, but her hair was going to need a good wash. The frown on her face matched the stormy weather. Cam reached into her backpack for the hand towel she kept and silently handed it over to Amber, who accepted it with a slight nod.

"Come on, Eric. I'm ready to get home. Do you or Amber need a lift somewhere, or are you all right?" Cam asked, her hands on her hips.

"Nah, I'll call Suzy to pick me up. My car's at Sealing Cove." Eric had finally stood up but was still bent slightly at the waist. "You know you're a pretty shitty pilot, right? I've never been sick before." He swayed on the dock, and Cam shoved down an urge to push him into the water.

"She saved us from getting pneumonia, Eric." Amber finally spoke up. "Who knows how long we would've been stranded on that island." Amber was trying to catch Eric's eye, but he was doing everything in his power to keep from looking at her. Finally, sighing, Amber turned to Cam. "Thank you," she said before continuing up the ramp from the water.

4

"Well, I still think she could have flown better," Eric mumbled as they reached the top of the ramp where it leveled out to the parking lot. "Umm, listen, we were just going for a hike, okay," he added, glancing sideways at Cam.

Things were left unsaid, but it wasn't anything Cam wanted to get involved in, so she just shrugged and turned to Amber. "Do you need a ride anywhere?"

"She'll need a ride home, yeah," Eric stated before taking a step away from her, presumably to create distance now that there were potential eyes around.

Amber's eyes bore into Eric, who had found an intriguing pebble on the ground and was studying it intently. Her shoulders slumped before looking back at Cam and nodding once. "That would be great. My place is a little past Sandy Beach."

With only fourteen miles of road from one end of town to the other, all homes were within driving range. "Sounds good," Cam replied as she hiked her bag further up her shoulder.

After dropping off a subdued Amber, Cam headed to her brother's house. She parked in front of his house, taking a moment to center herself after the intense flight. As soon as she opened the door, Cam heard heavy footsteps on the wooden floor. Her younger brother Micah rounded the corner, and when he saw her, relief smoothed the worry from his face. He extended a hairy arm towards her and lightly placed a hand on her shoulder, knowing she didn't like much physical contact. His beard moved slightly as a large smile peeked out from the hairs. She weakly patted his arm before shrugging out of his grip and struggling to take off her shoes at the front door.

As they parted, Micah said, "I'm glad you got home safely, Cam. We were concerned with how quickly the weather turned." He was rubbing his hands together in front of him, a clear sign of his anxiety.

"Nothing to worry about." She patted his arm as she walked further into the house. There was a two-year age gap, and Cam hated for him to worry, even if he did all the maintenance on her plane.

Where Micah was stocky and scruffy with light brown hair from their mom, Cam had favored their dad. She was taller with thick dark black hair she usually kept in a ponytail and warm brown eyes.

"Hey, Cam." Lily's muffled voice came from the garage. Through the open door leading to the garage, Cam could see a crab pot set up in front of her that she was repairing. The flame from the torch reflected off the welding helmet that Lily wore.

"Dinner's almost ready," Micah called from the kitchen.

"Need any help?" Cam asked as she leaned against the counter in the kitchen.

Steam billowed out of the oven, fogging Micah's glasses. "No, I've got it." He put down the transparent casserole dish on the stovetop. "I'm trying the lasagna with zucchini noodles this time."

Every Saturday, they had a family dinner at Nana Winnie's house. Since Cam's diet was plant-based, Micah tried to learn new dishes for everyone to try out. That way, Cam didn't need to bring her own food and instead could partake in the shared family meals.

Cam's mouth filled with saliva as the smells of the dish hit her. "If it's as good as it smells, we are in for a treat. Need me to grab anything for Nana Winnie's house?"

"It's all packed and on the table," Lily said from behind her as she placed the welding helmet on the counter.

"Hun, why?" Micah asked, staring pointedly at the sooty helmet. "We have a perfectly functional garage, which you were just in, I might add." His hands were on his hips, but a smile threatened to blossom on his lips. This wasn't their first argument over the offending object.

"We're going to be late. Come on!" Lily grinned as she tried to hurry them out the door.

"Every Saturday," Micah murmured as he grabbed the casserole dish. "You'd think we would have learned to manage time better by now."

Cam held in a giggle as her feet pounded down the porch stairs. "Well, at least you're around now, Lily. I had to deal with his" —she nudged her head in Micah's direction— "shenanigans for twenty-eight years, *alone*. Those two years before he came along were bliss." She put an arm around Lily's shoulders and sent a teasing grin to her brother.

"Come on." Micah laughed as he carefully maneuvered down the porch steps with the casserole in his hands. "Nana Winnie is waiting."

They walked in relative silence three houses down the street, not bothering with knocking when they got Winnie's.

"We're here," Micah called out as all three of them removed their mud-covered shoes inside the front door.

Micah had his arm around Lily as she whispered something in his ear. As they walked through the door, Cam followed behind, trying not to look closely at the loneliness radiating from her. The comforting smells of laundry, wood, and spices filled her nose as she stepped into the house.

Nana Winnie wasn't their grandmother by blood, but the friendship Micah had forged as a child with Skyler resulted in an endearing and close relationship with Skyler's grandmother that had lasted the test of time.

"Come in, my little bugs," Winnie said from the couch. Her coloring looked a bit better from the previous week, but Cam's heart clenched in concern. Winnie held her arms out, waiting for the parade of hugs.

Cam wrapped her arms around the woman, bending at her hips to accommodate her short stature. Willowy arms wrapped around her shoulders as a breath of air puffed around her hair. "You're not eating enough," Winnie said as they parted. She tried to pinch the skin around Cam's forearms. "It's all that plant food you've been eating, made for the rabbits." Spit flew everywhere as her dentures loosened. "Where's Goose?" Winnie asked as she pushed her dentures up further.

"He's sleeping at the house." Cam settled on the couch. "Your carving saved me from crashing today." She pulled a pair of Nana Winnie's reading glasses out from under her butt and placed them on the side table near the couch. "I'm convinced the only reason I made it home in one piece was that eagle watching over the flight." She winked.

"Oh, psh," Winnie said as she dropped her foot to the ground. "You can fly out of a storm with a blindfold on." Her phone rang at a volume not suitable for young ears, making everyone younger than eighty wince. "Oh, it's Skyler." Her face lit up at the display.

Cam smiled and wandered to the kitchen as Winnie talked to her granddaughter. "Need any help?" She leaned against the fridge, watching Micah and Lily as they fussed around the kitchen.

"No, we just needed to warm up the bread," Lily said, turning and squeezing Cam's arm on her way to get the dishes.

"Yup, Lily and Micah's older sister, Camryn." Winnie's voice carried from the living room. "Yeah, Cam. You remember her, don't you? Of course you do. You and Micah were joined at the hip. It would be odd if you didn't remember her."

Cam shook her head. Memories of school flooded her brain: Skyler's braces and bright eyes. Her lanky body and

8

devilish grin. Skyler and Micah had gotten in such trouble before she moved away between sophomore and junior year, seldom to be seen again, although Micah had kept in close contact with her over the years.

"Dinner's ready." Lily's voice floated to them, shaking Cam out of the past.

"Got to go, Sky-Tie, talk next week, love you." Winnie ended the call on her way to the kitchen.

"How's Skyler doing?" Micah asked as he grabbed plates for everyone.

"Good, she sends her love."

Cam tried not to give extra thought to the long look Winnie gave her as she dug into the comfort of the veggie lasagna.

***

Skyler ended the phone call to her grandmother with a smile. She could hear the hum of multiple voices in the background and it warmed her heart that Micah had stayed close with her Nana after she had moved to Portland twelve years prior.

The only time she'd been back to Sitka since she'd moved was when Micah married Lily seven years ago. Thoughts of the past flooded her mind. As the wedding photographer, it was a busy weekend for her, and Skyler had only gotten glimpses of her childhood crush, Cam, through the camera lens. However, it was enough to set her heart fluttering before the last memory filtered in from when they were in high school—flying papers and silent tears.

"How's Winnie doing?" Skyler's mom, Maggie, asked while pouring water from a Brita pitcher.

"Good. She says hi and sends her love. She is sounding tired as the years go along." Skyler went to pick up her glass when she noticed a ripple on the surface of the water.

She looked around to make sure the big earthquake that was due to hit the west coast wasn't occurring right then.

Skyler's aunt Abby's flushed face came barreling around the corner at a run.

"And what do you think you're doing, Abs?" Maggie scolded as she grabbed for the tipping vase in the middle of the table.

"Got to get my steps in, you know when you're our age" —she indicated with a sweaty palm between her and Maggie— "you'll be sorry for not getting your steps in while you could." She stopped in front of her chair and started high stepping while looking at her exercise watch. "Got to close all my rings."

Skyler chuckled into her water as she watched the twins battle back and forth. Separated at birth, Maggie and Abby had only found out about each other fifteen years prior. Now, they were inseparable and currently lived in a duplex, although even Skyler didn't know who lived in which house.

"Words to live by, Aunt Abs, thank you." Skyler cheered her with her glass and let out a sigh of relief when Abby settled in her chair. "How're things going at the library, Mom?" she asked while scooping lettuce onto her plate.

"Did you take your meds?" Maggie asked, completely ignoring Skyler's question.

"Mom, I've had a few seizures since I was eleven, and they've only occurred when I'm stressed," Skyler said, as if that was a perfect answer to her question, while cursing at having indeed not taken her Antiepileptic Drugs (AEDs) yet. She wanted to get food in her first and didn't want to give her mom more ammunition to fuss over.

"You know I worry." She shrugged. "How's work going?"

Skyler tried not to grin at her mom's deflection, and she suddenly understood where she had learned her diverging communication technique. "It's good. I've got a couple of baby announcements and one graduation shoot. Business is steady, but you know I'd much rather take pictures outside. At least one of the announcement sessions will be in a park."

"When I lived in Colorado, I saw a wolf standing upright." Abby took a large bite of mashed potatoes. "But then I turned around, and it was just a guy wearing a coat." Abby bent down, her head disappearing from view.

"That was a random story. I always thought it was funny that the Sitka High mascot was the wolves, but Baranof Island, which is the island Sitka is on, doesn't have any wolves. What are you doing, Abs?" Maggie asked as she grabbed the table to peek underneath.

Skyler bent for a look and hit her head when she straightened, her shoulders shaking in silent laughter. Below, Abby was placing the exercise watch around her cat's tail.

"There. Live long and get me those closed rings," Abby said, sitting up again. Her face was flushed.

"Need any help at the library, Mom?" Skyler asked through a chuckle, her knife shaking as she cut off another piece of flank steak.

"Sure, if you wouldn't mind reading for the kid's corner event on Monday," Maggie replied as she gathered up the dishes.

"Yeah, I can make that work. Don't have anything until Wednesday."

"Can someone help me wrestle the cat? I think my watch is being dragged through the litter," Abby said, looking towards the laundry room. Skyler tilted her head. She could hear the distinct scrape of litter over the clatter of dishes.

"You're on your own, Aunt Abby." Skyler laughed, grabbing more plates.

"So, how are things, Skyler? Seeing anyone?" Maggie asked as concern shone through her grey-green eyes, so like Skyler's own.

Skyler paused, trying to think when she last went on a date, before shaking her head. "Nothing has changed since the last time I saw you two days ago. I'm trying to get my business off the ground. You know I don't have time to see friends, let alone date."

Maggie chuckled, shaking her head. "I suppose two days doesn't give you much time to find someone, but the rest is just an excuse, and you know it. If your dad hadn't decided he wanted to fish more than he wanted to be a part of the family, he'd hit you upside the head."

Skyler ducked from the incoming attack, laughing. "You can't tell me what attack you're going to do. It loses its effectiveness." She put her arms around her mom. "I know you're just watching out for me, but I promise I'm fine. I've got my cat, you two crazy ladies, and my camera. There isn't much more I need out of life." She leaned down to kiss her mom's cheek.

"I just—you have so much to give. There is more to life than watching the world pass through that camera lens." Maggie's sad smile brought a film of mist over Skyler's eyes.

"I know. I'm okay for now, though." Skyler squeezed her mom's arm.

The moment broke when Skyler saw Abby crouching low, trying to grab the cat that was zigzagging along the floor. The cat's tail was flopping around as if trying to flick off the watch. Skyler had to hold onto the banister near the front door to keep upright as tears of laughter streamed down her cheek. "Never a dull moment in the Callaghan house," she said as she reached for her coat and keys.

Skyler said her goodbyes to her family and started walking to her house. The evening was clear, and the stars were beginning to peek through. Thoughts turned back to high school when she and Micah had climbed into the bed of her dad's truck and talked about their future. She had come out to Micah that night after he tried to kiss her. The sputtering apology cemented their friendship. Her heart tried to fast forward to the images of Micah's older sister while her mind told her to shut it down.

Sighing, she opened the front door of her house and was met with painful silence. She'd never tell her mom this, but she was lonely. Settling down on the couch, she smacked her hand down on the cushion next to her. An indignant meow on the opposite end of the sofa caused her to look up. Raven's eyes opened, providing a contrast she hadn't seen before sitting down. He was lucky she hadn't sat on him as his black fur blended in perfectly with the dark microfiber fabric.

Skyler scratched the top of his head, murmuring apologies before Raven settled his head back down on his legs and went back to sleep. Then, humming softly, she grabbed the sapphic romance novel she was currently reading and tried to drown out the memories of the past trying to sneak through her barriers.

Chapter Two

"Can you hand me that wrench? Earth to Cam... Come in, Cam."

Micah's voice finally permeated the thought bubble over Cam's head. She was thinking about a conversation she'd had with Nana Winnie the week prior while helping pull carrots from her garden.

"Sorry, here you go." She handed the wrench to her brother and started pacing the shop. She did her best thinking while putting a rut on the shop floor, never one to sit still. "Do you ever regret not getting out of town?" she asked, turning to her brother and leaning against the small aluminum skiff her brother was fixing.

The weather was warming up as Sitka moved from the rainy April and May months into June and even though it wasn't that hot, the lack of air moving in the shop made sweat pool along Cam's back.

"I know you were close to getting out your senior year, but why would I want to leave? This place has everything I want: my business, my wife. It's the perfect place to grow up." He paused and looked into her eyes. Matching dark eyes met as the moment stretched before he continued. "Or raise a family." His eyebrows raised up and down while wrinkles showed up at the corner of his eyes as he grinned.

Cam blinked rapidly, replaying what he just said before slamming a foot down and shouting, "NO! Are you serious? I'm going to be an aunt?" She started bouncing around the garage pumping her fist in the air, knowing they had been trying for years to get pregnant, and everyone had slowly given up on it happening. "I'm so happy for you!" She grabbed Micah's shoulders and started shaking them back and forth.

Through laughter, Micah responded, "We just hit the three-month mark, and I officially got the permission to tell you this morning." He sniffed, trying to keep back tears. "You are going to make a kickass auntie."

Cam straightened her shoulders with the newfound responsibility. "That kid will never want for anything in this world."

"Let's not get too crazy there, Cam. We don't want a spoiled kid. Come on, let's finish up this boat. I need to get home soon. If I don't cook, Lily will just eat chocolate, and she needs nutrients right now."

Cam started picking up the shop while Micah finished the skiff's engine. "Mom and Dad would be proud, you know. They would have made great grandparents." Cam's words were almost a whisper, but the concrete flooring carried the words efficiently.

"Do you ever talk to them?" Micah asked after a moment of silence. He used his pointer finger to push his glasses back up his nose.

"Talk to them? What do you mean? Why would I talk to them? They're gone." Cam fussed with the tools so they lay in a perfect line.

"You know, like when you're flying, or doing a project, or showering, like, just *talk* to them."

"Why would I talk to our dead parents in the shower? Mike, you need to get your head checked. You might have a case of baby brain. I heard that's a thing."

"Don't call me Mike. You know I hate shortening my name. Our parents named me Micah, and that's what I want to be known as." He seemed to have just barely held back a foot stomp.

Cam grinned, holding her hands up in front of her. "You're right. I know you hate it. But it's hard when there is always such a reaction. I can't help but poke. What are siblings for anyway?"

Micah grabbed her in a headlock and started messing up her hair. Cam tried to wiggle out of the grip, but her foot ended up slipping, knocking into the table, and with a crash, the perfectly lined up tools came tumbling to the ground.

Micah let go, and they both slowly straightened before looking at each other.

"Hun, are you okay?" a worried voice shouted from the front door of the shop.

"Yeah, Lily, we're fine. Cam just kicked all the tools down like the bucking bronco she is."

Lily's worried face came into view when she rounded the corner. Right away, Cam noticed her holding her belly and wondered how long she'd been doing that.

"I can clean this up and close up shop if you want," Cam offered when Lily's stomach growled almost as loud as the falling tools.

"Thank you, that would be great," Micah said as he wrapped his arm around Lily's shoulder.

"Oh, and before I forget, the plane is due for its one-hundred-hour inspection. Can I bring it into the shop tomorrow?" Cam had to look away from the love-eyes that her brother was giving Lily.

"Sure, I'm just finishing this skiff, but I can fit the inspection in tomorrow. So when's your next charter

16

flight?" Micah asked, looking at the grease stained schedule taped to his desk. Cam had been trying to drag him into at least the twentieth century, but Micah refused the technology for some reason.

The charter comment brought an unexpected pain as the conversation with Nana Winnie popped into her head again. "Sure, let's set something up for this week." She stepped closer to Lily and nudged her shoulder. "Congrats, Lil! I'm over the moon excited for you two."

Lily grinned, then blushed when her stomach yelled at them again.

"Get your wife home and cook her a meal, you bum." She shoved Micah's back towards the door.

Cam stepped away to clean up the fallen tools. When she looked back, Micah was holding his wife's belly, and Lily was radiating love. She had to blink back tears that were threatening to fall at the display. Her brain was ecstatic for her brother, but her heart wished it had someone to hold onto that tightly.

The gravel crunched under Cam's brown and muddy Xtratuf boots on her way up the driveway to her trailer. The boots were a Sitka staple and a must-have in the wet climate. The tough material lasted forever and kept your feet dry when traipsing on hikes up the different mountain trails that Sitka had to offer.

With the inheritance from her parents, she'd bought the land which sat outside of town when she was twenty-one. After spending most of the money on her Cessna and flying lessons, there was enough left over for land and a refurbished double-wide trailer. She hoped to build a house someday, but the materials needed were expensive, so the dream was on hold for now.

Micah had gone to the University of Alaska Southeast and became a certified mechanic. While Cam got the flying bug, Micah was a natural with the inner mechanics and workings of the engines of boats and planes. He bought the shop near a harbor downtown with his share of their inheritance. It worked out well for Cam to have someone in the family who could work on her plane and deal with the upkeep and maintenance needed to support her air charter business.

Wrapping her hand around the handle of her door, Cam smiled when the excited yips of her golden retriever, Goose, turned into a whine when she didn't open the door right away. Finally, she swung the door open and quickly ducked to the side.

Goose shot out of the door with his tail wagging. He ran down the steps to the porch before doubling back in search of his pack leader. Cam had hunched down and was waiting for his vibrating body to wiggle onto her lap.

"Ready to go visit Nana Winnie, Goose? Come on, slowpoke," she cooed into his ear as he tried to lick her face. "Alright, alright, down, Goose."

She reached into the house and grabbed the leash from a hook. She draped the object around her neck before shutting the door and calling Goose from the fascinating blueberry bush he was sniffing around.

The weather was slightly overcast, the sun trying to poke out through the clouds, matching Cam's mood perfectly. Walking up the steps to Nana Winnie's porch, she paused and turned around, taking in the sights of the house her brother had practically grown up in. It wasn't until after high school that Cam had started coming over and getting closer to Winnie.

Goose's tail started thumping on the wooden slats of the entryway before Cam turned around at the squeak of the door opening. Winnie stood in the doorway, her body framed like a picture, a sunken smile on her lips.

"Did you misplace your dentures again, Nana?" Cam turned fully and stepped into waiting arms. Winnie was one of the only people she'd hug without hesitation.

"I know exactly where they are, but currently they're out of reach. This is a pleasant surprise, Bug. What are you doing here? Come in." She moved to the side, petting Goose as he raced into the house.

"I was going to do some grocery shopping and was wondering if you needed anything," Cam said as she took off her muddy boots.

"My list is somewhere. Hold on." Winnie shuffled some papers on the counter by her telephone, one that still had an old-style cord. The objects in her house hadn't changed since she bought the place in 1956, and it was like looking through a museum at times. "Ah, here we go." She held the piece close to her nose.

"Where are your reading glasses?" Cam chuckled softly.

"Probably having a party with my dentures. You might be able to make a full human using my inanimate objects. But no, this appears to be my list of people's perfumes I don't like." She flipped through more paper and mail.

Cam's face was red from holding in laughter. "We can make a new list if you want, that wa—"

"Here it is." Winnie's victorious smile cut off the rest of what Cam was going to say. "I would never have remembered dill on a new list."

"Dill? What are you cooking with dill?" Cam took the list and scanned it over. Her confusion mounted with each ingredient.

"I was on the Pin thing and saw this recipe, but I didn't have any of the ingredients. I bet the spice industry made that site to have people buy all the obscure ingredients for their spaghetti dinners. I remember a day that working with salt and pepper was just fine, thank you very much. My son was a shit father to our Sky-Tie, but he grew up with delicious meals of venison and seafood, spiced only with salt and pepper, without any other fancy ingredients thrown in the mix." She nodded once before turning to head to the couch.

"Hmm, that's an interesting theory," Cam said as she noticed Goose wedging himself between the wall and the end table. She bent over laughing when Goose came out with a complete set of human dentures in his mouth.

"Come on up here, Goose." Winnie patted the couch next to where she was sitting, and his body wiggled before he settled his head in Winnie's lap. "That's a good boy." She plucked the teeth from his mouth.

Cam saw a light reflect off the lost glasses and bent over the end table to grab them. Winnie thanked her with a nod while rubbing the dentures with the sleeve of her long shirt before popping them back in her mouth. She tested them with a few gashes of her teeth, causing Goose to look up in alarm before settling down again.

"Skyler would have a fit if she saw me put dog drool dentures back in my mouth." Winnie grinned. "Have you thought any more of what we talked about last week?" she asked after settling her glasses near the edge of the end table.

Cam looked at the teetering object and refrained from pushing them back towards the middle of the table. "Yes, a little. I hate talking about what you want after you die, but I'd gladly take your ashes to Kinky Island." Her cheeks reddened at the word. "I can't believe we have an island called Kinky," she mumbled, shaking her head.

"I want to pay for your charter plane to take my granddaughter as well." She was blinking a lot, trying to keep from taking a nap.

Cam settled in the rocking chair next to the couch and began slightly rocking, finding the motion soothing. "How do you even know she'd come? She's been away a long time."

"She'll come. I don't think it will be long now. She'll come, and you'll fly her to where my Eddy proposed all those years ago. I want that to be my final resting place, and you and Skyler will take me there." Winnie's voice was scratchy from fatigue.

"I'm not charging you for the charter, and I'll only do it because you're my best friend, and I can't deny my best friend her last wish. But I'm not sure why we are even talking about this. You're a long way from dying." Cam's smile didn't reach her eyes.

"You're a good one, Bug. You could leave Goose here if you wanted to run to the store." Winnie's hand rested on Goose's head as Winnie's breathing deepened to match his slumbered breaths.

Cam tiptoed out of the house, taking a final look behind her before running to the store.

***

The rain had soaked Skyler's auburn hair. She tried to swipe the errant curls away from her face as she walked through the doors of the library. Whoever had decided to put tiled flooring in the first quarter of the building needed to be fired; her squeaky sneakers yelled across the quiet room. She tried high stepping but just ended up looking like the Pink Panther sneaking around.

Reading to the kids had become a weekly occurrence over the past couple of months, and she was enjoying the questions and discussions the kids brought up.

Spotting her mom with a cart full of books, she stepped beside her and threw an arm around her shoulder. "Mom, can I use your locker to put my bag in? I need to keep it safe from all the sticky fingers around these parts."

"I don't think anyone would steal your stuff, Skyler," Maggie said, scooting around to place another book.

"No, not sticky fingers as in stealing, but actual sticky fingers. You don't know where those kids' hands have been." Skyler shuddered.

"If you ever have kids, you're going to have to deal with a lot of sticky situations. But yes, go ahead and put your bag in the locker." Maggie shook her head with a smile.

"Thanks, I only have a few more days of my meds left and don't want anything to happen to them. The stuff is more valuable than gold." Skyler patted her shoulder bag on the way to the employee break room before heading to the children's corner for reading hour.

On the way, her phone buzzed, requesting a last-minute photographer for an engagement party in a few hours. She confirmed with the prices, silently cheering at the extra money she'd make.

Settling on the little stool in front of a bunch of wiggly kids, she began the story. The kids laughed at her goofy voices and cried out when they thought the witch had won. One little boy scooched so close to her knee that she could see the snot bubble form on his nose. Skyler wanted to back away, but the floor surface wouldn't allow it. She had to try to hold back a gag when the bubble popped.

"The end," she finished, putting the book away. "Do you have any questions?" Tiny hands shot in the air, and with a smile, she pointed to a small girl towards the back.

"Why are witches always girls, and why are they always bad?" Her quiet voice carried over the heads of the children and smacked Skyler in the heart.

"Hmm, that's an interesting question. A lot of witches in fairy tales have been unfairly portrayed. That doesn't mean they are bad; it just means their stories were never told. More books and movies are coming out now, telling the witch's side." Skyler sent a radiating smile, hoping to cultivate creativity for the little girl.

After wrapping up with reading, Skyler ran to her bag for her hand sanitizer. She winced when the sting of the liquid touched a previously unknown cut.

"Heading home?" Maggie asked when she walked into the break room.

"No, I have a last-minute photoshoot but should be home after. Need me to pick up anything?"

"Abby's running some errands, although I should probably have you pick up some veggies. If Abs had it her way, both our kitchens in the duplex would only have bread and candy. Thanks for coming by today."

With a wave, Skyler headed to her next appointment.

When she arrived, Skyler almost turned her Subaru around. Nicole, her ex, stood at the park entrance with her hand on her hip, a foot tapping anxiously. The extra money didn't seem worth the pain this would bring up. Her sweaty palms slipped from the steering wheel as she tried to regulate her erratic breathing.

After parking the car, Skyler took deep breaths before grabbing her camera bag and trying, but failing miserably, to get out of the car gracefully. "Nicole. I didn't realize the engagement shoot was for you. Didn't recognize the number."

"Changed my number after we broke up. Your crazy aunt kept sending me weird voicemails and texts."

"She's not crazy, just protective." Skyler left it at that.

The night they broke up, Skyler had knocked on her mom's door with tears streaming down her cheek. She couldn't handle Nicole's controlling nature anymore. Abby was the one who answered, and it took both Maggie and Skyler physically sitting on Abby for twenty minutes before she calmed down enough not to go out and hurt Nicole for breaking her niece's heart. Without Skyler's knowledge, she harassed Nicole in other ways. When Skyler finally found out about it, she had to hold back a barking laugh.

"Well, you're the only photographer who was available on such short notice. We're this way." Without seeing if Skyler was following, Nicole turned down and headed towards a trail.

Skyler had to bite back a retort at the dig to her schedule, but she was nothing if not professional.

For a second, Skyler wondered if this was a trap before shaking her head at the paranoid thought. Nicole might have been controlling, but she wouldn't do something like that. Soon, the trees thickened, which kept the sun from shining through, and Skyler almost screamed when a tree branch brushed her shoulder. Maybe she hadn't shaken off the thought as well as she should have.

They rounded a bend, and a breath of relief left Skyler when she saw a few other people.

"There you are. Thought you'd run off with your ex for a second," a shorter woman said when she saw them. "Hi, I'm Tammy. Thank you for coming on so little notice." Tammy held her hand out to Skyler with a beaming smile that helped put her at ease.

"I'm Skyler. Nice to meet you. You've picked out a great place." Skyler painted on her professional smile as she observed Nicole with her fiancée.

"I would never leave you." Nicole wrapped her arms around the shorter woman while giving her a soft smile—a smile Skyler had never seen before from her ex.

Well, they do seem happy, Skyler thought. As she looked around, some of her anxiety lessened.

"Where should I set up?" Determined to get through the shoot, Skyler had her mask in place, even if it was slightly seeped in discomfort.

"Over there." Tammy waved in a general direction.

Skyler looked around and saw a place where the lighting would look great with minimal shadows. She pulled out her camera and started taking a few test pictures, trying hard not to look at the couple who honestly looked happy.

"Are you done yet? We don't want to be stuck here all day," Nicole said, breaking free and tapping her foot on the mossy ground.

"Sure, if you two could stand here." Skyler pointed to an area framed with pine trees that had excellent lighting.

Of course, Nicole had to fight Skyler on every little direction. Just as Skyler's frustrations were about to bubble over, Tammy asked to see the shots before having a quiet conversation with Nicole. Afterward, Nicole had reined in her controlling nature, and it was smoother sailing.

Even though Skyler got some dirt under her fingernails, the shoot didn't turn out half bad. The couple seemed genuinely happy with the work, and Skyler hoped the chapter of Nicole was now forever closed.

On the way back to her car, her phone rang. A smile formed on her face when she saw the display.

"Micah, it's been a while. How's it going?"

The smile faded when she heard what he was saying.

"Okay. No, thanks for letting me know. I'll be there as soon as I can."

They talked through plans and next steps, but Skyler's mind had scattered in the wind.

Skyler relied on her muscle memory to get her safely home. Still in shock and not quite believing Nana Winnie was gone, she called her mom to see if either she or Abby could take Raven for a few days while she went back to Sitka to help with funeral arrangements. During the phone call with Micah, they had started plans for the celebration of life, and they decided Micah, Lily, and Cam would work on getting the service together for the day after Skyler would get into Sitka.

She'd found out from Micah during the phone call that Nana Winnie had set her up as executor of the estate without her knowledge, and the weight of responsibility was falling heavily on her shoulders. She shook her head. She could deal with that later. Skyler packed up a few things at home and tried to coax Raven into the cat carrier without incurring any wounds from her angry cat.

Her mom had a hug waiting when she opened the door. Skyler was surprised when she saw the red-rimmed eyes. Maggie and Winnie had been close while she was married to her son, but they drifted apart after the divorce.

"Don't worry about Raven. We'll take care of him. Won't we, you delightful little shadow," Abby cooed into the carrier before opening it up to let the cat come out when he was good and ready to do so.

"I'm sorry about your grandmother. I wish I could have met her," Abby said, gently pulling Skyler into a tight hug.

Skyler's eyes widened in shock at the low and soft volume she didn't know Abby had access to.

"Thanks for watching him and letting me park in your driveway. Feel free to use the car whenever you need." She put the car keys on the counter, knowing Abby would lose them in thirty minutes.

Both Maggie and Skyler were silent on the way to the airport, immersed in a slideshow of memories.

Chapter Three

Cam stood in the middle of Winnie's living room. Her breath caught when she saw the glasses still hanging over the edge of the end table, knowing she would never again fish them from odd places. The thought almost brought her to her knees. Wrapping her fingers around the delicate frames, she cradled them in her hand before hooking the arm on the collar of her shirt, letting the frames dangle near her heart.

She knew Skyler was flying into Sitka to pack up and clean out the house but figured she'd be neighborly and help pick up a little before she got there.

Cam sneezed. At the very least, she would dust.

It was times like these that she wished she had a best friend to call as she plopped down on the ground, completely overwhelmed. Goose sensed her turmoil and nudged her with his wet nose as grief washed over her. Times of hugs, laughter, and memories circled on repeat, and Cam wrapped her arms around Goose's neck, hiding her tears in his fur.

A loud rumble caused Cam to look around, seeing if Goose's tail had thumped into something. At the second sound, she placed her hand on her stomach, trying to muffle the noise. While rummaging through the cupboards, her eyes landed on daunting proof that Winnie hadn't been okay. The only opened packages were some bottles of

Ensure and anti-nausea meds. The food from Cam's past three grocery trips remained unopened.

She grabbed at her heart but only managed to graze the hanging glasses as thoughts flitted past on why Winnie had felt the need to keep her sickness a secret.

Another loud rumble and Cam closed the cupboards. She told Goose to stay and that she'd be right back. Then, with shaking hands, she climbed into her truck to go to the store. If nothing else, it would be good for Skyler to have more than spices and Ensure. Maybe she'd get her a Sitka welcome package with Theobroma chocolate and Alaska Pure Sea Salt. Cam loved the different flavors of salt to sprinkle on the chocolate.

Cam put her truck in park after pulling into the parking lot of one of only two main grocery stores. She pushed the visor down to try and tame her shoulder-length hair. There wasn't anything she could do for her red-rimmed eyes or the fact she was emotionally raw and felt like she'd been hit by a truck. A light mist of rain dusted her dark hair, causing it to twinkle in the low light as she made her way inside. Grabbing a basket she hung on her elbow, she took three steps before Ms. Hamilton, her third-grade teacher, stopped in front of her with her arms open wide.

"Camryn, my favorite student. How are you doing?" Ms. Hamilton held her hands up, waiting for a hug, and slowly walked towards her while Cam tried to think of a way to maneuver her open arms into a handshake instead.

Not seeing another feasible option, she smiled tightly and pivoted her hip a little to try and maneuver into a less invasive side hug. "Ms. Hamilton. Hi, it's good to see you."

Of course, the one time when she'd just wanted to keep her head down and get through a grocery run without talking to anyone, she'd run into someone right away.

"Oh, please, you can call me Grace. I've been done with teaching and retired for ten years now."

Cam was trying to figure out why it seemed like Ms. Hamil—Grace—had planted in front of her. "That might take some getting used to. If you'll excuse me, I've got to get a few things." She tried to step around the shorter lady but felt a hand land on her arm.

"I'm sorry to hear about Winne. She was a pillar in this community and a loss to everyone." Grace's eye contact was intense, and Cam was the first to look away, trying to hide the tears that had sprung in her eyes.

She swallowed a few times to clear the frog that had burrowed into her throat. "Thank you," was all she could manage.

A sigh of relief left her lungs when she could walk away with only a nod. Not looking for any conversation, she kept her head down as she worked her way through the aisles. She wanted to text Micah to see if he remembered some of Skyler's favorite foods but didn't want to explore too closely why she seemed to want to make a good impression for the return of the prodigal friend.

"Cam, it's been so long!" a voice screeched, echoing off the cereal aisle and landing in her ears with a bang, making her wince.

Turning to see who the offending greeting came from, Cam's eyebrows met her hairline, surprised such a petite woman could produce a volume that shattered her eardrums. The woman barely came up to the third shelf and had a baby on her hip. "Bailey, hi, it's been a while."

"How the heck are you? Are you still down Halibut Point Road? Don't tell me you're still flying the plane? Are you seeing anybody? Oh my God, we need to catch up!" Bailey's little boy was fussing, and she looked down at him with a small smile before looking back at Cam, who hadn't responded to the whirlwind of questions. "Okay, we'll catch up, tootles."

And with that, Bailey was bouncing her kid down the aisle while Cam was still frozen, unsure what had just occurred.

Her eyes slipped to the Lucky Charms near her and smiled when she remembered rounding the corner to the kitchen one morning and seeing Skyler and Micah chowing down on the cereal while making up stories of the different marshmallow shapes. It had warmed her heart to hear their giggles fill up the ordinarily quiet house. It had been nice to see the darkness from her brother's eyes lift a smidge. Cam shook her head, trying to dislodge the memory as she reached for the cereal before going down the juice and snack aisle.

By the time she reached the refrigerated section, Cam's face muscles were twitching so badly from holding fake smiles and platitudes with the different parents, school friends, and charter clients that she was almost ready to drop the basket and walk out the door without anything.

"Oh, hi." A timid voice had Cam looking up, where she caught the slightly panicked eye movement and someone who looked a lot like Eric slink to another row.

"Amber, how are you doing?" Cam said with a nod.

"I'm doing good. Just work and stuff." Amber was picking at a string from her shirt and looking everywhere but at Cam.

"Glad to hear it. Well, I'm almost done." Not wanting to prolong the fun, uncomfortable silence that had filled up around them, Cam tried to make a quick exit.

"Oh sure, it was good seeing you. Thanks again for the other day." While scanning the other customers' faces, she gave a small wave as if afraid to take up too much space.

As Cam was walking up to the front to pay, her eyes landed on the sign for the liquor store next door, and she decided to swing in for a bottle of Jameson. It was one of those times she'd need help numbing her sorrows.

After entering Winnie's house and taking Goose out for a final walk of the night, she blasted music and got to cleaning.

Each item she touched brought a new wave of memories and tears. A large gulp of the alcohol Cam had been sipping on caused a burning trail down her throat when she came across Winnie's carving knives and a half-finished project. It was still a reasonably solid wood block. However, the blob looked like a camera and something was etched in the lens. She couldn't make it out, and knowing she'd never get to ask Winnie about the project, she downed the rest of the drink in her glass.

Cam was starting to feel the effects of the alcohol. With each sip, she slipped further into oblivion. Finally, tired of crying, she tried having a dance party in the living room. Blasting the music, she swayed her hips with each song. She even got Goose to dance on two legs before they both fell in a heap on the ground. Goose started jumping on her and wiggling his body, thinking it was playtime.

By the third try of heaving herself off the ground, Cam had found the drinking giggles. Finally finding her feet, she stood hunched over with her hands on her knees, trying to find a counterbalance to the spinning room. Squinting, Cam tried to focus on only the objects in front of her, having gotten a case of drunk tunnel vision. She reached for the bottle and was surprised to see how much she had consumed. *One more*, Cam thought, which was every drunk person's famous last words.

The world spun while Cam danced. The world spun, and Cam cried, the world spun, and Cam ping-ponged her way through the halls. Finally, she landed in the guest room, a room where she had spent many nights just like this one. Tripping into the covers, she was almost asleep before her head hit the pillows.

***

The leg from Portland to Seattle was uneventful, and Skyler vibrated with nervous energy during the two-hour flight to Sitka. She'd been kicking herself for not visiting more, but life got in the way. Of course, it didn't help that the plane tickets were more than she could afford, but the video chats had helped make up for the lack of physical visits.

She leaned her forehead against the plane window after she wiped the surface down with a disinfectant wipe. It wasn't until she got a view of Mt. Edgecumbe, the iconic Sitka landmark of the dormant volcano, that the large drops of tears started running down Skyler's face. As the jet began its descent to the place of her childhood, she struggled to keep a sob from escaping, but there wasn't enough oxygen reaching her lungs.

She'd always assumed there would be more time: more time to visit, more time for conversations. But instead, questions she never got to ask of her grandmother's childhood flooded her mind like a tsunami. Pair that with landing in Sitka. It was no wonder she couldn't catch a full breath.

Skyler's stomach dropped as the plane descended lower. Little islands were sprinkled through the ocean. The closer they got to the landing strip, the stronger the pang of loss seemed to stab. Even though the plane was about to touch down, she didn't feel the excitement that she usually felt when coming home, knowing one of her favorite people wasn't there to greet her. All she could see was water, and it was coming up fast. The closer the plane got without a visual on the landing strip, the stronger Skyler gripped the armrest. At the last second, the ground appeared, and the jet hit the runway hard. Skyler's body slammed forward as the brakes instantly engaged. There wasn't much room to slow down on Sitka's short runway. The plane made it to the end of the runway and turned to make its way back to the gate.

Loosening her hold on the hand rest, Skyler looked out the window, trying to find the off button for her tears.

"That wasn't the worst flight I've been on," the passenger next to her commented. "This one time, there was a gust of wind so strong the plane's wing touched the ground. I thought we were done for."

Skyler gave a watery smile and nodded, glad the passenger decided not to impart that story until after landing.

"Hey, are you okay?" The person tilted their head.

She had to swallow a few times before answering. "Yeah, the flight just brought up memories, that's all. I'm fine." She discreetly sniffed, not wanting to wipe her nose on her shirt.

"Well, nothing like landing on this little slice of heaven. Should clean those sinuses right up." The passenger started moving down the aisle.

Skyler grabbed her bags and followed her landing companion down the jetway. The twists and turns it took to get to the terminal made her dizzy, but finally, the tunnel opened to expose straining necks trying to get a glimpse of loved ones disembarking.

Her Nana would have been in the front row, pushing little kids out of the way to get to her. A wave of sadness gripped her heart. As she looked around the small airport, trying to find someone she recognized, she kept getting jostled as people rushed to get to their loved ones. Finally, Skyler maneuvered towards the one luggage belt in the airport as she checked her phone to see if she had missed a call or text from Micah, who was supposed to pick her up.

Finding a pillar to lean against, she pretended to be on her phone while people-watching. People's faces changed from sad, worried, or indifferent to happy as they saw their loved ones disembark. Her fingers itched to grab her camera.

"Are you looking for a good time?" a voice said from behind her.

She startled, whirling around in time to see Lily slap Micah's shoulder. "You can't sneak up on women, dick," Lily scolded with a smile.

"Hi, Skyler. How are you doing?" Lily's voice was soft, and her arms were open, ready to deliver a hug, which Skyler gratefully settled into and rested her chin on the top of Lily's head.

She went for Micah's hug next and almost screamed when he picked her up but settled when he squeezed tightly before placing her down, but not letting go of the bear hug.

"I can't believe she's gone," they said at the same time before parting.

Mirrored, watery eyes reflected at each other before they wiped them and smiled.

"Let's not do this here. We have plenty of time to reminisce and cry," Skyler said, wishing she had grabbed extra napkins on the flight.

"Now that is a game plan." His eyes were still red, and he wrapped an arm around Lily's shoulders. "Let's get your stuff and roll." Micah checked his watch. "Just in time for dinner. Would you mind terribly if we grabbed some food at a bar and had a few drinks to catch up?" He turned to his wife with puppy dog eyes and an exposed lower lip.

"Of course not. I'll even be your designated driver," Lily said with a smile, rubbing her belly.

Skyler looked at the motion before whipping her head to Micah, then looking back at Lily's belly, her eyebrows raised in question.

"Oh, did I forget to tell you? We're having a little peanut." Micah's shoulders straightened with pride.

Skyler squealed and jumped up and down, knowing the heartache they had gone through trying to get pregnant. "I'm so happy for you two." She stopped jumping and held Lily in a loose hug, not wanting to hurt the baby.

The alarm started buzzing, letting everyone know the luggage belt was about to begin. "I'll grab my bag and meet you back here. Just a second." Skyler tried to elbow her way through when she spotted her bag. Unfortunately, nobody let her through, and she had to wait for it to go around another loop.

Skyler walked back up to them. Both had their eyes closed and matching small smiles on their lips. Lily leaned against her husband while his hands wrapped around her and rested on her belly. Not able to resist the opportunity, Skyler pulled out her camera and took a picture of the domestic bliss painted on their faces.

"Alright, let's go," she said quietly, sad to have disturbed the tranquility.

Micah grabbed her bag while Skyler rolled the carry-on.

"Time for some shots." Micah grinned. "Tequila for us, and water with lemon for you." He waved between the group.

"Why did I even get married?" Lily asked to the sky, her hands over her head.

"Couldn't resist all of this." Micah laughed while wiggling his hips as he put the luggage in the trunk.

Skyler's tears had dried, and she was grateful for her best friend. It seemed they slipped into a comfortable role no matter how much time had gone since they last saw each other. Their playful banter from childhood always fell around them.

Hours later, Skyler saw double. She tried to keep to a one drink, one water ratio, however, everyone knew Micah and he was forced to drink for two when people found out about the upcoming baby. People also were buying them condolence drinks. Skyler knew the Porter siblings were close to Nana Winnie, but it warmed her heart to see how many patrons also sent a cheer to Winnie. It was nice to know the community was as affected as she was about the loss.

Even with Micah passing every other drink to her, Skyler was feeling the effects. She was also dodging a few people trying to hit on her since a few regulars were excited to see a new face. Lily helped run interference to keep the unwanted attention away. She was already practicing her mom instincts while Skyler's inhibitions were lowered.

"You're my best friend. You know that, right?" Micah slurred as he slung his arm over Skyler's shoulders.

"I'm so glad we've stayed close all these years," Skyler said with a sob.

"To Nana Winnie. Even though she wasn't my real grandma, I loved her just the same." Micah tipped the glass in the air.

"To Nana. Even though we didn't live in the same state, I'm glad we were able to stay close. You were always my biggest supporter." Skyler clinked her glass with Micah's and downed the rest of the drink. The alcohol had numbed the track down Skyler's throat hours ago, and she almost didn't feel the burn anymore.

Lily chuckled through a yawn. "I hate to be this person, but I'm hungry for some chocolate and pickles. Do you mind if we head home now? You can stay with us if you want, or I can drop you off at Nana's house, Skyler." She started scooting out of the booth.

"Lily! You. You. You're the best person I could have ever imagined for Mike Attack over here. You are just wonderful, but I think I'd like to stay at Nana's house." Skyler followed with swaying steps and threw an arm around Lily's shoulders, playing with her silky hair.

"Hands off my wife. Get your own and don't call me Mike. You know I hate that." Micah tripped as he tried to snuggle up to Lily's neck while his glasses slipped askew.

"Oh boy, time to go, you two. In you go." She tried herding them inside the Rav-4 but was shaking with laughter when Skyler decided to climb in headfirst. With her feet dangling out the side she screamed, "There's no traction!" while miming a swimming motion with her arms and legs.

"Skyler. Hun. We're here." A soft voice made Skyler lift her head and she saw Nana's front door. It was just like she remembered.

"Okay, thanks for the ride, Lily," Skyler slurred as she tapped the glass that currently had Micah's face squished against it. Not getting any reaction, she gave a wave to Lily and swayed up the porch with her bags in hand.

Stumbling up the final steps, Skyler dropped her bags on the porch and from her pocket she wrestled the keys that Micah had given her. It took a few tries, but she finally got the door opened, and when she did, a little yelp of surprise escaped her as a dog she wasn't expecting came barreling towards her in a full wiggle.

She dropped to her knees, giving her full attention to the excited pup. "Well, who do we have here?" She dug her fingers into the dog's fur, almost cooing at the soft texture. "I'll have to deal with you tomorrow. Right now, a bed is calling me." She kicked the front door closed with her foot without looking back.

Squinting her eyes to try and focus the spinning room, Skyler watched the dog settle back on the couch as its tail thumped against the cushions. Exhaustion pulled at her eyelids as she walked through the house. Making her way to the guest bedroom, she pulled off her clothes, preferring to sleep completely in the nude, and snuggled into the warm bed where sleep found her quickly.

Chapter Four

On the cusp between dreaming and wakefulness, Cam found herself at peace. She burrowed herself deeper into the pillow. She felt a warm presence behind her, loving the feel of breasts pressed against her back. Her sleeping conscience reached for the hand wrapped around her body and pulled it closer to her chest.

The hand rubbed and gently squeezed along her breasts, causing her nipples to harden, and Cam felt her lower body respond to the action. Her back arched, which grinded her ass deeper into the other body. She exhaled a light moan as their fingers, still intertwined, started sliding down her stomach. A throbbing started in her core as she felt deep, even breaths on her neck and the tiny hairs stood at attention.

She moaned as the dimmer switch to her wakefulness was slowly turning on. Her head turned, seeking out the woman's lips, before everything came rushing back. She blinked rapidly as her eyes adjusted to the body in bed with her that most definitely hadn't been there when she'd fallen asleep. A scream escaped her lips as she flung the covers off, startling her bedmate awake.

Cam and the woman scrambled from the bed, mirroring each other on opposite sides of the room. The woman was very naked and very much now recognizable as Skyler, her little brother's best friend. Skyler, who had indeed grown into her own very womanly body.

Skyler looked around the bedroom in confusion, rubbing the sleep out of her eyes. "I'm sorry. I didn't know you were here. I just woke up. Are you okay? I didn't mean to touch you like that. I honestly thought I was having a dream. I'm sorry." Skyler's face darkened in embarrassment as her chest heaved with deep breaths from her rushed words. "I'm sorry," she repeated when Cam didn't respond right away. Skyler's brows furrowed in confusion.

"What?" Cam responded, trying to process the morning's events through her pounding whiskey headache. She shook her head. "I'm sorry, I've got to go," she added before bolting out of the bedroom.

She called Goose and tore open the door before tripping over damp luggage that had been left on the porch. She went skidding along the wooden surface before tumbling down the stairs. Her knee slammed into the step, which stopped her forward motion.

Sitting on the bottom step with Goose licking her face to make sure she was okay, Cam felt the sting of tears, thinking it was the perfect exclamation point to the morning. Skyler Callaghan. She needed to put a pin in her thoughts to unpack why she had felt so comfortable being in Skyler's arms, but first a shower. Grabbing the railing to haul herself up, Cam almost cried out when she put weight on her knee. She stumbled to her truck, ready to lick her wounds and hopefully find the will to look Skyler in the eye again sometime within the next decade.

She pulled out her phone to call Micah as she kicked rocks before opening the door to let Goose in the cab. Goose settled in the front seat, his tail wagging happily. Cam was slightly jealous of Goose's blasé attitude toward her plight.

***

Skyler stood, pacing the strip of floor by the edge of the bed going from one end of the wall, pivoting, then stalking to the far side as she mumbled to herself. The faint sound of a crash outside couldn't pull her out of her existential crisis.

"I had Camryn Porter in my arms," she mumbled to the empty room. *It's like my dream since I was fourteen came true then turned into my waking nightmare. Am I so horrible that she had to run out of the room looking horrified?* Her internal dialogue took over as she paced the room before sitting down on the bed in a huff, startling when a cold object hit the back of her bare thigh.

Sitting up slightly to grab the phone, she could see her face's reflection on the dark screen. The image showed that her hair was tangled in every direction, and mascara streaks ran down her face.

Standing up, Skyler looked down at herself, seeing her flared hips and the small scar on her side from when she'd tried following Micah up a tree once and got punctured by a branch on the way down. Cam had found her first, and she helped calm down an eight-year-old Skyler while putting pressure on the bleeding wound. She eventually slid Skyler's hand over the wound and talked her through holding the pressure. It was pretty impressive how calm and collected in an emergency ten-year-old Cam had been. Once she saw the bleeding subside slightly, Cam told her she'd be right back before running to Nana Winnie's house for help.

Frowning at the onslaught of feelings and memories, Skyler's shoulders slumped as her brain went over the feel of Cam's body. Her hand started tingling from the memory before Cam's panicked scream had jolted her from what she thought was a dream, one she never wanted to wake up from. Her sleeping mind had put Cam as the body she was holding, and her years of suppressed feelings took over without Skyler's conscious permission.

Well, not much I can do about having her run out the door. Sighing, she looked around, trying to remember where she had left her luggage. Her eyes fell on the pile of crumpled clothes she had crawled out of the night before and she wrinkled her nose at the thought of putting back on the airplane-germ-infested and bar-crusted threads.

Not seeing her luggage in the room, she grabbed her phone and wrapped a sheet around her body before wandering the house. When turning the corner to the living room, her foot landed on a squeaky chew toy, and she wracked her brain, trying to remember if Nana Winnie had a dog before recalling the one she met the night before. Skyler wanted to smack herself in the head and mentally vowed never to drink again.

The vibration from Skyler's phone buzzed, and Micah's face flashed on the screen. She answered, half distracted from still not finding her missing luggage.

"Hey," she said, looking under the kitchen table, even though she had no memory of going into the kitchen the night before.

Only deep laughter met her ears. "Micah, I've had a pretty crappy morning. Do you need anything?"

She peeked through the front door and scoffed when she saw her luggage strewn across the porch.

"I just had the most enlightening phone call with my sister," Micah said as she tucked the phone between her shoulder and ear while simultaneously wrestling bags and trying to keep the sheet around her chest.

"Oh, God, no," she groused. "I'm not sure I want to hear." Skyler kicked the front door closed and wheeled the baggage through the house.

"Were you feeling a little, uh, frisky this morning?" His cackle made Skyler pull the phone from her ear.

"ME?" Skyler shouted but quickly winced when her pounding head screamed back. "She was—we were—it was nothing," she finished quietly.

"Well, that's about her side as well," Micah agreed. "And before you both decide to try and avoid each other until the end of time—on a tiny island, I might add—we are all going to lunch before the memorial, so get your butt into gear, and Cam will pick you up in an hour."

He hung up without another word. All Skyler could do was look dumbly at the now blank phone. She idly wondered what Cam and Micah's conversation had been like before taking a steadying breath and steeling herself to see Cam a lot earlier than she had planned.

Looking at the clock on her phone, she jumped up to get ready. If Cam was picking her up, she'd at least put effort into looking presentable. Not that it mattered, not one bit.

After her shower, Skyler rummaged through her carry-on for her AED meds. Unfortunately, there were only enough for four days in the container. With everything going on, she had forgotten to get the refill done in Portland. Skyler quickly sent a message to her neurologist for a new prescription to be sent to White's Pharmacy in Sitka.

***

Cam was tapping the side of her leg rapidly with her left hand while she went to reach for the door handle with her right. Turning the knob, she frowned before her eyes widened in embarrassment. She was so used to walking right into the house that her muscle memory took over and she almost barged in, which would have been a perfect way to reacquaint herself with Skyler after almost kissing her in a fog between sleep and wakefulness.

The conversation with Micah hadn't been helpful. After she'd explained what had happened, she'd had to wait what seemed like thirty minutes before he stopped laughing. She had been close to throwing the phone down and walking away. Although in a small town on an island, that probably wouldn't have done any good.

On the porch, she lifted her fist to knock and glared at her shaking hand. Her knuckles landed in three quick raps before she shoved her hands in her jeans pockets. A timid smile developed on her face when Skyler's head poked between the crack in the open door.

"Hey," Cam said with a head bob. "Umm, Micah said we were all going to lunch. Are you ready?" She was proud her voice projected at its usual steady volume. Sometimes when she was nervous, her voice shook.

"Yeah, let me just grab my bag. You can come in if you want." Skyler opened the door wider before disappearing back into the house.

Cam shuffled from one foot to the next before placing her hands on the porch rail while looking out to the front yard.

Hearing the door click shut, Cam turned around and almost choked on nothing when she saw the bright white blouse Skyler was wearing. Cam looked towards the sky and saw the storm clouds forming. "Do you have a jacket?" she asked, glancing back at Skyler who had a backpack dangling from her hand.

"A light cloth hoodie in here, but it's warm out." Skyler lifted the pack slightly before shrugging.

"It looks like it'll rain. You sure you don't want something heavier or waterproof?" Cam asked, not moving out of the way when Skyler stepped closer.

"I'll be fine." Skyler waved off the concern.

Cam wasn't in a place to push further, so she just threw up a shrug with "Suit yourself." She let Skyler walk ahead of her, trying to come up with a topic of conversation.

Skyler walked to the passenger's side and waited. Cam bent, glancing inside the truck to see if there was anything in the seat blocking her from getting in. Not seeing anything, she said, "It's open." She waved her hand to the door.

"Oh, right. No one locks doors here." Skyler palmed her forehead while Cam got a kick out of the light dusting of red showing up on her cheeks.

"No, not like you city folks," Cam joked as she started the engine.

"Locking doors is just common sense," Skyler pushed back.

"True, but even if someone did steal a vehicle, it's not like they can take it very far, us being on an island and there only being fourteen miles of road and all." Cam shrugged with a smile as she navigated to the restaurant on the outskirts of downtown.

Skyler nodded, and soon the silence filled the truck almost like a third passenger. Cam wasn't sure how to break the awkward barrier. When they reached the stoplight, Cam inwardly cursed when it took two lights to get through a turn, not able to move past the tourists who seemed to not remember the rules of the road while on vacation.

Finally making the turn, Cam groaned when she had to stop and wait for multiple people to finish taking pictures of the church in a roundabout downtown. People coming off the cruise ships tended to forget about silly things like traffic while they stood in the middle of the street to find the optimal photos. Her hand itched to blast the horn, but right as she hovered over the wheel, the tourists started moving on, pointing at the giant carving of a bear while squealing in delight.

"I forgot about the craziness of the town when the cruise ships are in port." Skyler broke the silence as yet another person stopped in front of them, taking pictures of the mountains surrounding the town. "I used to work there during the summers." She pointed to the New Archangel

Trading Co. they were passing as Cam cut down a sidestreet. "People kept asking if we took American money or tried to pay with Canadian bills since the stop prior was in Canada. Oooh, or when they asked what the elevation in Sitka was. That was always fun, looking out to the sea, then looking back at them with a confused look." Skyler continued to throw out more tidbits from her stint at the store.

Cam laughed as the buildup of panic seeped from her. She was grateful for the tension breaker. Skyler had always been easy to talk to when they were kids, and she was glad they didn't have to dissect the events of the morning. "A tourist once stopped me to ask if Russia was that little island over there." She pointed and smiled. "But it feels nice to swap stories about the tourists. They help the town out, even if I don't like going anywhere near downtown when they're here." Cam grinned as she pulled into a parking spot.

Walking up to the restaurant, fat drops of rain started pelting them. Skyler began to jog to the restaurant while the rain fell around them. Cam limped along behind her as her knee stiffened from the morning fall.

"After you." Skyler held the door open when Cam walked up.

"Thank you," Cam said, walking up the stairs gingerly.

***

If Cam wasn't going to bring up this morning, she sure as hell wasn't going to, Skyler thought as she watched Cam take the wooden steps, concerned at the slight limp she witnessed.

"Is your leg okay?" Skyler asked as they got to the top of the steps.

45

"Yeah, nothing a little Ibuprofen and an ice pack won't cure," Cam said, waving when Micah and Lily, seated a few tables away, came into view.

Cam pulled the chair away from the table, motioning for Skyler to sit. Skyler gave her thanks with an arm squeeze before settling down. She had to tell her heart that sitting near Cam wasn't a cause for extra beats. Scooting in closer, she looked down and blushed when she saw her white shirt was now a tad see-through and felt slightly foolish for her testy outburst toward Cam when she mentioned the jacket. She twisted in her seat to pull the hoodie from her backpack, not wanting to give her tablemates a show.

"How are you two doing? Micah, you're looking a little green around the gills." Skyler grinned as she finished zipping up.

Everyone already knew what they were getting, so Skyler asked to go last when the waitress came by with some water, and quickly settled on a club sandwich, her go-to meal for new places.

"Yeah, he's sworn never to drink again," Lily said, reaching for some bread knots the waitress placed on the table. "We'll see how long that lasts. My guess is by the weekend."

"I'm not sure why you are all yelling, but please, tune it down a few thousand decibels," Micah whined into his glass of water.

"This lunch was your idea!" Cam yelled from across the table. "That yell was a bad idea," she finished, holding her head.

"Alright now, calm down, everyone." Lily settled into mom mode. "Are the plans set up for the celebration of life this afternoon?" She looked between Cam and Skyler.

"Yes, everything should be ready. The town rallied together to help plan." Skyler nodded before thanking the waitress who dropped off their food. "And we'll go up tomorrow to spread the rest of her ashes?" Skyler asked, turning slightly to Cam.

"Yeah, I'm hoping to leave around ten if that works for you?" The reply rippled the top of the spoonful of vegetable soup near her mouth. Skyler just nodded her response, unable to take her eyes away from the huge window overlooking the ocean.

"Are you sure you don't want to go with them, honey?" Lily asked Micah as she tore at her bread before dunking it in her soup.

"Yes, you know I'm not a huge fan of flying, and I need to get the Millers' plane done. Plus, I'll have said my goodbye today," Micah responded after taking an audible gulp of his water.

Skyler watched the people below them walk around as the conversation blended around her. She could spot the locals versus tourists by seeing if they had an umbrella. For some reason, most locals didn't carry one, even though it rained more than in Seattle. She smiled at the toddler wearing tiny Xtratufs who jumped in a puddle.

The weather gods were looking over Winnie's celebration of life when the sun appeared through the clouds as everyone traded Nana Winnie stories. Some were hilarious, a few were sad, but most were hopeful. It seemed the whole town was there. The sea and mountains provided a backdrop of the setting sun while the forest at the beach's edge provided cover for the fire pit. When the group spread most of the ashes into the ocean, even the sky couldn't hold back tears as the rain started coming down again. But it didn't stop people from paying their respects or the drinks from being poured in Winnie's honor.

A nose bumped into Skyler's hand, and she looked down at the beautiful golden dog who didn't seem to want to leave her side. Earlier, Cam had run home to grab Goose, so Skyler officially met the mystery dog from the night before. Since Micah, Lily, and Cam were about the extent of people in Skyler's Sitka bubble, she stayed close to them but shook hands and exchanged hugs with more people than she had in a long time and had to refrain from using hand sanitizer after every interaction.

Skyler would never tell Cam this, but the light hoodie she'd brought was definitely not strong enough to hold off the evening chill, and she was soon shivering near the fire. She felt a weight of something warm land on her shoulders and looked up in time to see Cam's retreating form. Skyler found herself snuggling into the jacket and smiled when she was able to catch Cam's eye again and give her a thank you nod, and she received an 'it's no big deal' shrug in return.

The hugs of greeting soon turned to squeezes of goodbye as the group slowly dispersed. Skyler's voice was cracking from too much use, and the emotionally intense day was catching up to her. People helped clean up, and it wasn't long before she felt a warm hand on her shoulder. "Ready to go soon?" Cam asked, leaning in close.

Skyler just nodded and tilted her head back as a sigh escaped. The day had been emotional, and she was grateful for Goose and Cam's calming presence. She wanted to put her head on Cam's shoulder but refrained, remembering her aversion to hugs. What she did get was a hand on the shoulder and a squeeze, which made her smile.

In the truck, Skyler rested her temple against the cool window and closed her eyes. She felt the weight of Goose's head land on her shoulder, and she reached to the side to pet his soft fur and coo quietly in his ear. Much too soon, Skyler felt the truck drift to a stop and the click of the gear going into park. She opened a tired eye and looked over at Cam, whose hand hovered over her shoulder. When Skyler turned, the hand quickly retreated to Cam's side of the car.

"Thanks for the ride," Skyler said as she wiggled out of Cam's coat. "And thank you for this. You were right."

"You should listen to me more often. I know things," Cam responded with a smile. "See you tomorrow around ten."

Skyler kissed Goose's head then waved goodbye before hopping out of the truck. She waited on the porch to make sure Cam got out of the driveway before heading inside. The silence enveloped her as her body adjusted to the quiet rooms.

Chapter Five

A strip of sun fell between a sliver in the curtains while Cam slowly entered the waking world again. A dream was still playing in her head as she woke up. She rarely felt such safety from the presence of another person like she had in the arms of a mysterious dream woman. A whining dog pulled her further into reality as Goose licked her face to be let out.

"Come on, boy," Cam called as she flung the bedding away from her body and swung her legs over the side of the bed.

She smiled at the full-body wiggle that greeted her knees. After checking her smartwatch, she stretched her hands over her head before calling Goose to follow her outside. "Ready to fly today, boy? We're taking Skyler to spread the rest of Nana Winnie's ashes." At the mention of Winnie's name, Goose looked up at her, then towards the path that would take them to her house. He took a few steps towards the house a few doors down, then sat down dejectedly when Cam didn't follow. "I know. I miss her too." She patted his head. "Come on. We've got a few things to pack up."

As Cam got ready for the flight, her mind wandered back through the years. Breakfast the day before had shown how well they all got along like no time had passed, and Cam tried not to focus on the fact that she felt at ease with

Skyler. The morning before had proven it when she'd woken up with arms around her, and she hadn't immediately shrugged them off. Yes, she had run, but it wasn't because she was uncomfortable—it was because she was too comfortable, and the feeling scared her.

Reaching for the Lärabars, a smile developed on her face when a memory filtered in of twelve-year-old Micah and Skyler mashing protein bars into their teeth while pretending to be toothless. Nana Winnie had come to pick up Skyler and howled in laughter when she saw the duo's grinning mouths. She popped out her dentures and opened her mouth, showing the dark and gummy cave. Skyler and Micah's eyes went wide in shock before everyone started laughing.

At the memory, a small stream of tears fell, both in laughter and sadness. It had been an emotional couple of days, and this trip was the final chapter of Nana Winnie's story. With a heavy heart, Cam double-checked she had everything before grabbing a few Nalgenes full of water and calling Goose to hop up into the truck. It was only eight, but she wanted to get down to the plane to make sure everything was ready and pack up the supplies before picking up Skyler.

At the dock, Cam used a hand cart to carry food for later and the gas jugs to fuel the plane. She kept camping gear and other supplies in the plane, always ready for an adventure. Getting to the gate, Cam sighed when she saw one of the other pilots had forgotten to close the lock on the coded gate. Shaking her head, she kicked the gate open and maneuvered the supplies down the ramp of the floatplane dock.

After a bit of tinkering on the plane and laughing when Goose chased seagulls off the dock, she looked up at the overcast sky. The weather seemed like it would hold and was what she had expected when she'd checked this morning. It wasn't a terrible day to fly. As she poured gas into the plane, Cam thought back to the memorial and how Nana Winnie would have enjoyed being the center of attention, especially hearing all the stories about her.

A text vibrated on her watch. Looking down, Cam smiled at the words.

Want me to bring anything? I can make some sandwiches, and apparently there are three containers of dill. Not sure why Nana needed so much dill.

Cam laughed when reading the text, shaking her head before responding.

No to food. Doing the final checks now. Pick you up in 30.

After doing one final pre-check and being satisfied with the outcome, she called Goose back from the dock. He was paying particular attention to the area where Eric had lost his lunch. She tried not to gag at the thought as she watched Goose lick at something on the dock.

"Come on, Goose," Cam called as she walked back to the truck. "Time to pick up Sky and head to the skies." She chuckled at herself before starting the truck.

As Cam pulled up to Winnie's driveway, Goose started going bonkers trying to get out of the vehicle. He was pacing back and forth and barked when Cam left him in the truck while she got out to knock on the door. Before she got to the porch, the door flew open, and Skyler stumbled out. The light hit just right, and Cam watched her smile develop.

"Hi," Skyler said with a wave. "I'm excited to get to fly. Thank you for taking me up there."

Cam grabbed the ever-present backpack and went to put it on the small bucket seat behind her.

"Oh, actually, can I keep that up front with me?" Skyler asked, seeing its destination.

Cam just shrugged, handing it back to her as Skyler made her way to the passenger side.

"Hi Goose, the best boy in the world. That's right, you are." Cam could hear Skyler cooing through the closed window.

Cam slid into the driver's seat, mumbling to herself, "Someone's going to get spoiled on this trip."

"Is he coming with us?" Skyler asked, scratching his hindquarters as he stood on the middle seat of the truck. His enthusiastic tail greetings were whacking Skyler in the face.

"Goose, sit," Cam commanded and waited until he had settled, sitting up proudly in the seat. "Yeah, he's great with flying. You don't mind, do you?"

"Of course not," Skyler said, scratching the top of his head. He had maneuvered until he sat in the exact middle, between them.

"Always the trouble-maker," Cam joked, but felt a burst of love for her goofy pet. She chuckled when Skyler grabbed his paw and held his hand like a person.

"Do you think we'll have some time to take a few pictures around the island but be back in time to pick up my prescription from White's? Unfortunately, I only have a few pills left."

"Sure, we'll have time for both. Are the pills for your seizures? How are things going with that?" Cam asked, remembering their one art class together.

The elective had allowed for seniors and sophomores to mingle in the same class. One hot day Skyler collapsed near the front of the class and started convulsing on the ground. Cam rushed to her side, trying to block the view from the other students with her body. Unfortunately, most of the people in the class had seen what happened and started poking fun about it, thinking she was faking. Cam had wanted to punch her classmates, but especially Eric, who had teased Skyler relentlessly for the rest of the year. She'd felt a surge of protectiveness for her sibling's friend.

"It's better. The doctors got me on the right dosage of AEDs, and I haven't had an episode in a few years. I was even able to finally get my driver's license." Skyler's grin lit up the car.

"Congrats! I'm happy for you," Cam said as she pulled into the parking spot for the second time today. She called Goose and waited for him to jump down. "Right this way." Cam waved Skyler to follow. "Want me to grab your bag?" She put her hand out in an offer.

"No, it's okay. I'll hold onto it." Skyler held the bag closer to her chest.

They walked down to the plane, and Cam couldn't hold in a grin after seeing the wide-eyed wonder as Skyler took in the aircraft.

"Skyler, meet Jane. Jane, meet Skyler," Cam said, pointing between the aircraft and Skyler.

"Nice to meet you, Jane." Skyler patted the aluminum side. "Haha, I get it, Plane Jane. That's a good one, Cam."

Cam looked up, shaking her head, her face warming slightly. "Damn, I didn't even put that together. Well, technically, it's 51*JN*, but Jane is close enough, and Plane Jane henceforth." Cam helped get Goose and Skyler situated and gave Skyler the rundown. "If you want, while we're in the air, I can let you fly for a second. It's pretty easy." Cam gestured to the controls on Skyler's side of the plane.

Laughing at the face Skyler was giving, she shook her head and reached up to grab a headset and handed it to Skyler before saying, "This will help cut out some of the noise and allow us to talk during the flight."

"Thanks." Skyler situated the headset over her ears. "Testing, testing."

"They don't work until the plane is running and the radio has to be turned on." Cam smiled while pointing to a switch.

After ensuring Goose was comfortable in the backseat and Skyler's harness was secured, Cam untied the plane from the dock before jumping into the pilot seat and clicking in her own shoulder harness before starting the engine. The propeller started, and she felt the familiar thrill of getting to fly buzz through her body as the plane slowly taxied out toward the middle of the harbor. Cam maneuvered the aircraft with the rudder pedals to stay clear of several boats also navigating through the harbor. Cam then listened to the ATIS weather recording and radioed Flight Service to announce her intention to depart the area to the north.

Flight Service came back on the radio asking if she wanted to file a flight plan. She declined, which gave them more flexibility in not rushing back home. This would allow Skyler time to take pictures and enjoy their day.

When the take-off lane was clear of boats, Cam pushed the throttle to full power while pulling the yoke close to her chest. Then, as the plane got on step, gathering speed, she relaxed her pull on the yoke. Within a few more seconds, the aircraft was in the air, headed north to Kinky Island to spread the rest of Nana Winnie's ashes.

Cam gently turned the plane before straightening it out as her thoughts turned to Nana Winnie. She couldn't help thinking this was exactly what she had in mind when she had asked Cam to take her ashes with Skyler: The two of them with Goose, the sun at their back, and the plane's vibration causing a cocoon of comfort.

***

Skyler's stomach settled once they leveled off. The morning fog had burned off, leaving a clear view of the sea and mountains, including the infamous volcano, Mount Edgecumbe. The plane rattled with loud vibrations, but the headset cut out most of the propeller and engine noise.

There were a few bumps in the air as Cam flew along the ocean.

"How are you doing there?" Cam's deep voice was amplified through the headset.

"Good. It's a beautiful day." Skyler couldn't decide where to look. Every direction provided a unique view. She briefly thought about taking her camera out of the hard case to take a few pictures but ultimately decided to do that on the way back.

"Look, there's a bear." Cam pointed to a flat grassy area between the water and forest.

"Where? I don't see it." Skyler angled her head towards the ground.

"There—see the boulder, near the water? It's to the left of that. A little past the grassy area." Cam indicated again.

Skyler giggled in delight when she caught a glimpse of the brown bear standing on its hind legs with its nose in the air. It seemed like it was looking directly at them.

She glanced to the left where Cam's profile caught her eye, and she found it hard to look away. Cam was someone she'd started feeling something for when she was fourteen. One day she and Micah had snuck up behind the unsuspecting older sibling, and an epic wrestling match commenced in the middle of the living room. Lamps had crashed to the floor, bruises popped up and lasted days, but mostly laughter filled the room. At one point, Cam was on top of Skyler, and her world tipped into the unknown. Skyler's body reacted in a way she didn't understand. From that moment, she started paying even closer attention to Micah's older sister.

In the air, Cam lost the heaviness on her shoulders and the semi-permanent bundle of concentration between her eyebrows. A small smile played at the side of her lips, and Skyler's heart skipped a beat. She wanted to reach over and squeeze her arm, or run a hand through her dark hair, just to have a connection with her. Goose crawled from the back of the plane, wanting to be close to the two passengers up front.

"Look, there's a whale." Cam pointed in front of them.

Skyler just barely caught a glimpse of the tail of the humpback as it dived. She was thinking again about getting her camera out and held the backpack near her chest as she felt a rattle of turbulence. She sighed at the thought that most likely the pictures would be out of focus.

"There is a little burble here. So I'm going to head a little east to see if it clears some," Cam said, making a slight adjustment to the nose of the plane.

Not wanting to sound silly by asking what a burble was, Skyler pointed to the wood carving attached to the dash. "Did Nana Winnie carve that?"

"Yes, it was the last thing she gave me." Cam nodded, smiling sadly at the eagle.

"It's beautiful. I wish I'd asked her to teach me how to carve." Skyler pulled her hand back before touching the head. Her arm was wobbling with the plane's movement, and she didn't want to accidentally damage the intricate woodwork of the bird.

"Same," Cam responded.

Skyler looked out her side of the window, lost in thoughts of the past.

"Want to try flying for a second?" Cam asked, looking over to Skyler with her eyebrows raising up and down.

"No! Are you crazy? I'll crash the plane!" Skyler's auburn ponytail whipped back and forth as she shook her head.

"I'll have control here the whole time if something goes wrong. You won't crash, I promise."

"Alright, I'll try it, as long as you're not going anywhere."

"Nope, I'm strapped to the seat. Grab the steering handles in front of you. It's called the yoke. Turn it left to go left and right to go right. Just pull back on the yoke slightly before leveling off if you want to climb a little higher. Try and stay away from pushing forward too much. Easy peasy. The mountains are far away, and I have this here if anything goes wrong." Cam patted the yoke in front of her.

Skyler's hands were shaking when she reached out in front of her. She wrapped her fingers lightly around the thin U-shaped handles of the yoke but had to wipe the sweat that had gathered on her palms. Settling back on the wheel, she took a deep breath and tried not to scream when the plane went silent. Eerie was the word that came to Skyler's mind. After more than thirty minutes of buzzing engines and a moving propeller, the quiet was compressing into the plane's cabin.

She looked down at what button or switch she could have hit to have caused the plane to shut off but didn't see anything. Cam's curse cut into her thoughts, and she saw her head start to turn in all directions.

"I'm so sorry—I don't think I hit anything, but why did the engine stop?" Skyler asked, frantically scanning the foreign dashboard.

"Just a second, Skyler, something's not right."

Well, those are the worst words to hear from your pilot, Skyler thought as she tried to keep down the bile rising from her stomach.

One of Cam's hands was whirring from one switch to the next trying to get the engine to restart. With each failed attempt without the engine turning back on was a louder scream of silence. Her other hand was guiding the yoke forward. Skyler was lifted slightly out of her seat as the plane adjusted to a glide. Cam's calm demeanor helped keep some of the panic at bay, but just barely.

"We're going down. Clip Goose into the harness and then brace yourself for landing. Oh, and get the life vest under your seat." Her voice was calm, and her eyes never stopped scanning, but the bundle of tension was back between her eyes, and she was taking steadying breaths. "Mayday, Mayday, Mayday, Cessna *Five one Juliet November* lost all power, headed for landing in Davison Bay," she continued in a calm, almost monotone voice. "Shit, they aren't responding."

I was wrong, 'Mayday, Mayday, Mayday' is a way worse phrase to hear from your pilot, Skyler's inner dialogue helpfully provided as she snapped Goose's harness into place. He was looking straight at her, small whines rumbling from deep in the back of his throat. He sensed something was wrong and didn't seem to be enjoying the lack of mobility the harness caused. "It's okay, Goose. We're going to be alright." Skyler was ninety percent sure the information wasn't just for Goose's benefit.

Turning around, Skyler saw the water fast approaching and felt the floats glide along the water. She slumped in her seat in relief at the relatively smooth landing.

"Oh, shit," Cam said under her breath.

That can't be good, Skyler thought as she tried to cram her rising panic back into the pit of her stomach. She looked around to locate what Cam had seen. From her view, everything seemed okay.

"Hold on, where did you come from, fucker?" Cam screamed, breaking through her monotone pilot speak. A wide range of emotions showed in those few words, which didn't help Skyler's panic.

There was a loud screech that could be heard over the dual screams from both women as the plane's metal floats met a rock that was inches below the water's surface. Skyler's body slammed forward into the shoulder harness, jostling her head before the plane flipped.

As the plane settled upside down, with the front of the plane dipping underwater, Skyler couldn't figure out the view. Hanging upside down, she watched the crack in the windshield slowly create a longer trench in the glass while she peered out the window towards the depths of the ocean. The only thing her mind could focus on was the symphony of dog barks and her own panicked breaths. Everything else was like a sonogram, vague and hard to figure out.

"This isn't good." Cam's shaky voice filled the cabin before she fumbled with her seat belt.

Skyler couldn't see what she was doing but heard a thud and a howl of pain. Blinking, she looked over to Cam, who was hunched over, holding her head. Skyler was still having a hard time getting her brain to adjust to the reality of being upside down. It was tripping her out to watch Cam limp along what she knew as the ceiling of the plane. The view was like watching a stop-motion movie as she processed Cam reaching under the seat that was now above her head but then was suddenly in front of her.

The plane was tilting, and Skyler could see water streaming under her head. She watched her hair dangling as she stayed buckled in and upside down.

"We don't have much time. I'm going to help you down, and I need you to grab Goose and get out to the wing." Cam helped with Skyler's seat belt before guiding her right side up.

Skyler looked down at the seawater that was licking at her calves. She gulped at how quickly the plane was taking water. She stood clutching her backpack and looked around, trying to figure out what was happening. "Skyler, get Goose and get out now!" Cam's sharp voice brought in some focus.

Flinging her backpack over her shoulders and tightening the straps, Skyler then felt herself lunge forward and fumble with the clip of Goose's harness. His legs were dangling as he tried to find purchase with the air. The shock and cold water weren't helping the delicate actions needed to flick open the clip, but she braced an arm under Goose and finally released the hitch.

Goose was more solid than she thought, and she gently put him on the ground and looked around again. Cam was digging towards the back of the plane, throwing a few bags up towards Skyler. She stopped and looked behind her, sighing at seeing Skyler just standing there. "Skyler, grab a bag and get out to the wing!"

Skyler nodded but didn't compute the words. A bit on autopilot, she reached out to push open the passenger door. She had to sit in the seat and use her legs as leverage to get the door open, but once she did, the water filled up fast around them. She noticed Goose grab Cam by the pant leg as he tried to drag her to the open door.

"Grab Goose and any bag you see. The plane is taking on too much water. I don't think it's going to stay afloat much longer." Cam's authoritative voice filled the cabin.

In shock, Skyler blinked rapidly, still trying to process how her feet were walking along the ceiling of the plane. She lifted a foot and shook her head before Cam's screaming voice pulled her out of the brain fog she was trapped in. Her head was pounding, and she couldn't hear anything over the beat of her rapid heart rate.

"Skyler, get your shit together and help me!" Cam gently pushed her towards the open door. "Try standing on the wing. I'm going to open this raft and toss a few things to you."

Cam threw something in the water but held onto the long rope before yanking hard. There was a hiss outside as a small raft magically appeared from a bag. Skyler would have been more impressed if she had two brain cells to rub together at that moment.

Skyler pulled Goose tight to her leg. The rocking of the sinking aircraft made it hard to walk and she struggled to keep Goose close before she grabbed a red bag coated in plastic that was floating near her knees. *Dry bag*, Skyler thought to herself, naming the bag usually used for camping around Sitka. Her brain wasn't connecting things, but this she remembered. Throwing the strap of the dry bag over her shoulder, she grabbed Goose by the collar and worked her way out the door of the plane.

She gently placed Goose on the aircraft wing and tried to edge along the narrow walkway to the boat. Goose kept looking back towards the plane, but Skyler kept him moving forward. When they ran out of space to walk, Skyler jumped into the sea to swim the rest of the way to the boat that was floating a few yards away. From the wing, it didn't look that far, but freezing Pacific water shocked her system as she struggled to make it to the sanctuary of the raft. The large bags jostled against her arms as she fought the cold water. Finally, her frozen fingers wrapped around the edge of the raft, and she let out an involuntary whoop of excitement at having made it. First, she shrugged the bags off her shoulder and flung them into the raft before looking at her personal Everest she'd have to climb in order to get to relative safety. The sides looked daunting, but Skyler dug deep and heaved herself over the side before landing on the rubbery bottom as a shivering mess. Everything in her wanted to curl up and sleep, but Goose's whines forced her on her knees to look over the side.

Looking around for Goose and Cam, she saw Goose's head bobbing near the boat as he tried to climb the slippery surface to get in. Grabbing his harness, she used both hands to wrap around his body and drag him into the boat. His fur stuck to his sides, making him look like he'd lost forty pounds before he shook, causing water to spray everywhere.

Skyler looked around for Cam, who was finally out of the plane. However, the wings were now submerged, and she had to swim to the raft. It looked like she was struggling, and the raft had floated even further away, making matters worse. Skyler's heart clenched at the pained grimace that seemed permanently etched on Cam's face. Looking around for something to use to paddle the boat closer, she groaned when her eyes landed on the paddle in Cam's struggling hands. It looked like the one that was attached to the float.

"Try passing me an end," Skyler yelled, leaning as far as she could over the side of the raft. Her arms screamed in protest, not wanting to do any more work, but she ignored the pain as Cam tried to ease the paddle towards her outstretched hands.

It took a few wobbling tries, but the end finally hit her numb fingers, and she started dragging Cam into the small boat. The raft was barely big enough to hold the three of them.

Cam slumped against the edge of the raft. She had been in the water a lot longer than Skyler had, and her shaking body and unfocused eyes were spiking Skyler's heart rate. The ordinarily stoic pilot was shivering and not responding to Skyler's voice. She couldn't be sure, but it seemed she was turning a concerning shade of blue.

The plane groaned as it tipped further to the side before slowly sinking underwater. Watching the plane get sucked into the vast ocean like it was a little toy in a tub was more than either of them could handle. The bubbles from the plane provided the last signs of life before the tail disappeared.

The last thing Cam did was look around and point a shaking hand and say, "Hhhead fffforrr that iiiisland over there," before slumping over the bow of the raft.

"Cam?" Skyler said timidly. "Camryn?" she asked again, louder. "Camryn!" she screamed, throwing the oar down in the boat before sidestepping Goose on her way to Cam.

Frantically looking around, she saw an emergency blanket tucked into a pocket of the raft. She quickly shook it out and crawled back to the unconscious Cam as she wrestled with the crinkly fabric in the light breeze.

Skyler held her breath as she gently twisted Cam to lie on her side and scooted her along the bottom of the boat. Her arms were yelling in protest at the continued strain. She watched Cam's chest and sobbed out in relief when she saw it moving. She swept Cam's hair out of the way of her eyes, murmuring that she was there as she tucked the silver fabric around her. She knew it would be better to get her out of the wet clothes, but Skyler's energy was at zero.

Goose was lying on Cam's legs, and they locked eyes. "She'll be okay, Goose. She has to be."

Tears formed in Skyler's eyes as an indescribable feeling fell over her, one she hadn't felt in a long time. Goose started whining and inching towards her. "No, no, no, not now." She looked around, not registering anything before her body seized up, and all went dark.

Chapter Six

Day 1

Raindrops fell on Cam's face as she rocked gently in the slight wind. She was trying to remember why she hadn't left the hammock in her backyard before the events of the crash started flowing over her mind. With a gasp, she sat up, the silver emergency blanket slipping from her torso. She winced at the pain radiating from most of her body. Goose had his head on Skyler's legs but lifted it when he saw Cam moving around. The echoed thunk could be heard as his slightly wagging tail hit the raft.

Blinking, she tried to put together the sequence of events that had landed them there, but all that got her was a pounding head. Squinting, she looked around and felt the scrape of the raft along the beach. Peeking over the raft's side, she saw they were half beached, the waves gently pushing them further to shore.

Cam looked around for her cell phone before remembering the object flying from the holder when they hit the rock. She crawled over to Skyler and saw her eyes were open, but they weren't focused on anything. Cam reached over and gently held her hand. Goose's tail started wagging more forcefully, but he stayed near Skyler. He barked once before looking back at Skyler.

"Skyler, are you okay?" Cam swiped the wisps of auburn hair that had fallen from Skyler's ponytail away from her eyes before using the back of her hand to check her forehead. It felt clammy, although that could have been from the rain. She saw Skyler blink a few times, then look around. Cam wasn't sure if she had a concussion and her heart lurched at the possibility.

Cam looked around. Pulling up a mental map of where they'd gone down didn't help any. She twisted in the raft, trying to locate recognizable landmarks, but she couldn't pinpoint the islands littered in front of the bay or the strip of land they were on. An increasing panic set in when she saw nothing that looked familiar in any direction.

She had no concept of how long they had been floating before the current played matchmaker with their destination. The sun showed about four, but that didn't help to determine how far they'd drifted from the crash site.

Cam's head swam when she sat back in the raft, making the world tip. She tried taking a few deep breaths when the edges of her eyes went dark before sharpening. Her neck popped when she whipped it fast to the side at the sound of Skyler's moan. The motion made her head feel like it was going to crack in two, but it was worth it when she saw Skyler's gray-green eyes were clear and focused.

"Hey," Skyler said, sitting up gently. "What happened?" She continued looking around.

"How are you feeling?" Cam maneuvered her arm to Skyler's shoulder when she saw her shiver, pulling the discarded blanket over them for extra insulation.

"Where are we?" Skyler asked, snuggling up to the extra warmth.

"I'm not sure," Cam answered honestly. "What happened? I don't recognize anything around here. What happened to navigating us to the island I pointed out, and how long have we been beached?"

"Beached?" Skyler turned in Cam's arms to look around. "I don't know. I had a seizure when we got into the raft, and it always takes me a while to shake off the exhaustion and confusion afterward."

Well, I feel like an ass. Nothing about this is Skyler's fault. It was my plane that quit flying which put us in this situation, Cam berated herself. She felt Skyler try to push away from her. "Shit, I'm sorry, Skyler. Are you feeling okay?"

Skyler's eyes softened somewhat. "I'm a little weak and embarrassed that my first seizure in a while happened at a time like this, but I'm feeling a little better. A few hours must have passed, huh?" She waved her hands to the area around them.

Cam's eyes flicked to Skyler's wrist. "I think so. Does your watch work?" she asked, nodding to the object, seeing Skyler struggling for a topic change.

Skyler twisted her hand towards her face before shaking her head. "No, the battery died. I forgot to charge it last night."

"What about a cell phone?" Cam asked as she pet Goose, who was sitting between them.

Skyler sat up and patted her pockets before triumphantly showing Cam the wet object.

Cam took it from her. "Shit, I think the battery is dead as well," was all Cam could muster as a response as her eyes took in their surroundings. On any other day, she would have found the view peaceful. Now she felt the crushing responsibility for her passenger. The guilt of being the pilot and putting them in this predicament churned her gut as Cam handed the phone back to Skyler, not able to look her in the eye.

Cam moved her arm to look behind them. Seeing the lining of the forest, she sighed. "We should try and get to the forest for some protection and make a shelter. Also, I'm not sure if they heard the mayday, so who knows how long we'll be stuck out here." She pulled her leg to sit cross-legged before grunting in pain and quickly stopping the motion.

"What? What's wrong?" Skyler asked, sitting up.

"Nothing, I'm okay." Cam tried to sit on the raft's edge but collapsed back down when a zap of pain flared from her knee. "Fuck," she exhaled.

"What?" Skyler leaned in, hovering her hands over Cam's body as if not sure what to do or where to touch.

"My knee," was all Cam said before trying to roll her stretchy pants up. She was struggling to reach the bottom of her pants when she felt Skyler's gentle fingers slide against her leg as she tenderly started working the pant leg up. "Thank you," Cam mumbled, not used to letting people help her out.

"Sorry, almost there," Skyler said after Cam grunted. "Goose, no, it's okay. She's okay."

Goose's nose pushed up against the exposed skin, tickling the hairs along her shin.

"There you go. Hmm, it looks a little swollen." She cupped the knee. "And a smidge warm to the touch."

"I can't seem to bend it much, but I don't think anything broke."

Cam tried to think of a way to help, but she was going to need Skyler, who was recovering herself.

Skyler looked around, her eyes not focusing on anything. Cam noticed her breathing increase in short bursts and leaned in with an arm to her back. "Are you okay?" It scared her that the normally fun-loving Skyler had such a wild look in her eyes.

"What. Are. We. Going. To. Do?" Skyler asked through shallow panicked breaths. "We're on an island. Crashed. Just a little water, barely any food." Her breaths were coming even quicker now, which Cam wouldn't have thought even possible thirty seconds prior.

68

Turning slightly, she winced at the pain that shot in her knee, but this was important. "Skyler, look at me." She waited until she got skittering eye contact that lasted a few seconds each pass. It wasn't perfect, but it would have to do for now. "Breathe in. Slowly, now out." It took a few minutes to get Skyler to match up with her breathing, but when she did, Skyler visibly relaxed.

After Cam was confident she could speak again while Skyler kept the calming rhythm, she said, "We take it one thing at a time. You like lists, right? You're Nana Winnie's granddaughter after all." That got a smile which brought an unintentional sigh of relief out of Cam. "Let's get inside the tree line. It should help protect us a little while we inventory our stuff." She looked at her leg. "I'll need you to help me up there. Can you do that?"

Skyler stood in the raft, teetering left and right on the unsteady surface, and held out her hand for Cam to grab. Taking a deep breath, Cam prepared herself the best she could for the jarring movement. Her head swam at the effort as she inched her way to sit on the edge of the raft. She used Skyler's steadying hands, but even with that, getting up was going to have to be done in phases. Of course, it helped that Goose stayed near the whole time, providing stoic comfort knowing she was in pain.

"Keep it straightened and let me come around," Skyler said, stepping out of the raft.

Cam heard a splash as Skyler worked her way towards the front. She tried grabbing the rope but missed it before shaking out her hands. "Damn numbness," Cam heard her whisper before taking the rope with both hands and heaving the craft from the water. There was scraping against the bottom, and Cam had to brace herself as the movement almost unseated her.

Goose looked over the edge before barking once, then jumped out and tried to grab the rope with his teeth to help Skyler.

"Alright, let's try and swing your legs over this way," Skyler said, putting a hand on Cam's shoulder.

"I got it." Cam's testy tone was a way to protect her ego as she struggled to maneuver her legs over the side.

A bubble of success quickly popped when she stood then immediately crumbled under the pain.

"Are you ready to let me help you?" Skyler asked, watching the display with a frown and arms crossed in front of her.

Cam could only nod but kept her eyes away from Skyler's. She was pretty sure the rain was causing steam to billow from her hot cheeks as she felt Skyler's hands wrap underneath her armpits like one would when picking up a child.

Once upright, Skyler snaked her hand around Cam's waist and grabbed Cam's arm to sling over her shoulder. She waited for a beat while Cam adjusted to the position. "You ready?" Skyler asked quietly.

"Lead the way," Cam said, wincing with each limping step.

The work was slow going. The gray, muddy sand sunk deep with each step as they walked the short trek to the forest. Pain shot up Cam's leg as she hobbled along. Skyler was taking most of her weight, and the knowledge was eating up her independence.

"Just a little further," Skyler said, pointing to a large tree a few yards inside the tree line. For now, it was a good spot, providing a little cover from the rain and space to go through their inventory.

Cam grunted her agreement while Goose ran ahead but looked back every couple of steps. Once they got to the coveted tree, Cam slid down the bark, her shirt riding up on the way down. She didn't care about the scratches, she was just glad to get off her leg. Even though it was only twenty yards, it felt like they had run a marathon. She smiled when Goose's nose pushed into her sweaty hair sticking to her face. She reached up to run her hands through the soft fur near his ears.

"I'm going to grab the supplies. Will you be okay?" Skyler's face was flushed with exertion, and Cam's heart squeezed in sympathy.

"Yes, I'm fine. Thanks," she mumbled, hating being put on the sidelines while knowing Skyler was exhausted and hurt.

She watched Skyler turn and head towards the beach. Goose was sitting between them, looking back and forth. "Go on, she needs you more than I do right now," Cam said, and flicked her head to Skyler.

Goose took off after her, bounding in long strides to catch up.

The ground was spongy, and her fingers found a pinecone to play with as she sat idly, thinking. Thoughts of the plane flooded her: going over what she could have done differently, berating herself for not seeing the rock in time, wondering if there was anything more she could have done, more she could have grabbed. Tears stung her eyes as her nose tingled. There on the forest floor, Cam allowed herself to shed them. Her shoulders shook silently as she thought about what could have happened, at the loss of her plane, but most importantly, at the relief they were all safe.

Her tears fell, and the trees listened. Soon the dam dried up, and Cam was left raw and tired. Her head wobbled as she leaned her head against the bark and closed her eyes.

***

Skyler sat at the edge of the raft, looking out towards the water. Her arms shook from practically carrying Cam the short distance to the trees. Observing the rain patter along the ocean surface was mesmerizing, and Skyler split her attention between the water and Goose as he examined all the smells the beachfront had to offer. Emotions that

71

threatened to run over were knocking hard on her door as the rain continued falling around her.

Soon Skyler didn't know where her tears began and the drops of rain ended. Panicked thoughts turned back to the crash, and she could feel her heart slamming against her chest as if trying to crawl out and get away from the situation. Instead, her breaths turned short and shallow as another panic attack gripped her body. A wave of nausea rolled into her stomach as the taste of metal filled her mouth along with extra saliva. Her measly breakfast came up as her forehead coated in a layer of sticky sweat.

While trying to find the technique Cam had used to calm her down the first time, she looked down when she felt a heavy pressure on her leg. Goose's soulful eyes looked back directly at her. Avoiding the pile she'd just created, Skyler scooted down and plopped her butt into the wet sand before burying her head into his fur. When nothing else was working, the comfort of a dog worked magic, and Skyler soon found her breathing returning to normal and the pressure in her head lessen.

"You're such a good boy, Goose. Do you think when we're out of this, I can take you home?" Goose tilted his head at the words and started wagging his tail. Then, he looked towards where Cam was stashed. "No, I suppose you're right. Cam might have a few words about that." She chuckled before standing up.

"Let's see." Skyler looked at the few bags in the boat. "Let's keep everything in the raft and see if I can drag it up to the forest," Skyler said to Goose as she grabbed a handle at the front of the raft and started pulling it while walking backward. Instantly, she felt the strain in her overtaxed arms but ignored the pain as best she could.

Skyler almost couldn't go on when she looked behind her and saw Goose holding on to the dangling rope between his teeth, 'helping' pull. The image made her stomach clench in laughter. It seemed she needed all types of emotional releases today.

They made it to the trees when Skyler had to stop and try to find the correct opening from where she'd left Cam. She used the break to look around while stretching her lower back muscles out and shaking her arms. It was Goose that saved her from panicking again. He put his nose to the ground and started working his way into the forest. His tail wagged, and he looked back at Skyler and barked as if to say, 'come on, what are you waiting for…'

The trees provided unique obstacles in dragging the raft with the bags, so Skyler pulled out the bags and placed them on the ground before stuffing the emergency blanket in the pouch of her hoodie. Then, with her hands on her hips, she looked around while deciding what to do with the raft. Finally, her eyes landed on a tree that seemed to be reaching out to her. If anything, it was better to leave the craft on the beach until they could get a signal or something built.

Once Skyler secured the raft, she eyed the bags on the ground before sighing at more manual labor for her already strained body. She dug deep and grabbed the three packs, slinging them over her shoulder. Hunching over, she followed Goose to where they had left Cam.

Parting the bushes, Skyler sighed in relief when her eyes fell to her sleeping pilot. She observed for the first time a knot near Cam's temple that was turning a dark blue. Goose ran up to Cam and started licking her face. Skyler witnessed a small smile form before confused eyes opened.

"Goose, come on, bud, knock it off." Cam reached out to push his wandering tongue away.

Skyler noticed the bloodshot eyes and black rings taking residence under Cam's lower lids. "I brought some goodies," she said, flinging the bags to the ground before looking around to locate the cleanest patch of moss she could find before she just ended up tucking her legs under herself near Cam and settling on the damp ground.

"I hope the matches aren't wet. We're going to need to start a fire soon before the sun goes down. And hopefully, get out of these clothes," Cam said, pulling her stiff shirt away from her body.

"Let's see what we have, shall we? Hopefully, a set of clothes because I know I only packed a sweatshirt." Skyler waved her hand around the bags like a gameshow host showing the audience what they could all win. "Would you like to start with curtain one, two, or three?" Skyler asked, indicating the different bags. She knew what was in her backpack and was secretly dying to see if her camera survived the crash, slightly kicking herself for not checking at the beach.

"Let's do two," Cam said, playing along with Skyler's silly game.

"Two it is." She nodded once in Cam's direction before pulling the bag towards her.

It was the red dry bag Skyler remembered vividly from the plane. The bag had a clip at the top then rolled a few times down, providing a protective layer for the supplies inside.

"It's like opening stockings at Christmas," Skyler remarked before pulling the first item out, a sleeping bag.

"Oh good, I thought I took that out. I'm glad it's still here," Cam said when she saw the sleeping bag.

Skyler investigated the bag as she bit her lower lip. It was already mostly empty without the bulky fabric. Sticking her hand in, she pulled out a square container with a large red plus sign. "This should come in handy." Skyler glided the zipper open. Her eyes widened at the first aid stuff. "We can use this to get a brace on your leg." She pulled out an ace wrap.

"That's not a bad idea," Cam replied, holding her hand out for the wrap. She looked around and extended her pointer finger to the left. "There might be some sticks over there that could work."

"Sure, sounds great, but let's finish our inventory first," Skyler said, returning to the bag.

Cam slumped against the tree, and Skyler hid a smile behind the lip of the bag. A pouting Cam wasn't a face she knew very well, but damn, if she didn't think it was a little cute.

Rummaging through the first aid kit again, Skyler grabbed what she was looking for. "Here, take these." She handed Cam two over-the-counter pain meds. "Your leg has got to be killing you."

"Thank you," Cam said, popping the pills into her mouth and chewing them with a grimace.

A few more trips into the bag, and everything from curtain two was laid out on the forest floor.

"Not much, huh?" Cam remarked, swishing her pursed lips from side to side, staring at the objects. Her concentration was so intense, Skyler wouldn't have been surprised if Cam was trying to multiply the few measly items with sheer will. There was a handheld satellite radio, but they weren't hearing anyone and decided to check in a few hours to preserve the battery.

"It's better than nothing," Skyler helpfully provided. "Let's check the next bag." She leaned over to grab it, brushing Cam's foot on accident.

The next bag wasn't waterproof, and that's where they found a few matches in a plastic bag, a tiny saw, a water purifier, a flare, and a flashlight. There were also two pairs of pants, two sweatshirts, and a few pairs of socks, all soaking wet. For food and drinks, they had a few bottles of water, four Lärabars, and a couple of bags of trail mix. Seeing the food made Skyler's stomach growl.

"Damn it!" Cam exclaimed, slamming her fist into the soft ground. "I don't know how long we're going to be stuck here." She gazed up at the canopy of trees, looking for answers. "Why did this happen?"

"It's okay. We're alive, maybe a little banged up, but alive. That's because of you. I was a pure bundle of panic and completely froze. You kept a calm head and got us out of there." Skyler was unconsciously rubbing Cam's leg near her ankle. She pulled her hand away when she saw Cam staring.

"What about your bag?" Cam nodded to it with her chin, her voice tight. Skyler could tell she was trying to get herself under control.

It took a few tries to get the zipper to work with her cold hands. Finally, the zipper caught, and the loud clicks filled the forest around them.

Skyler reached in and took out the hard case for her camera, and put it on her lap. Goose, who had been sniffing their surroundings, now came near and investigated the case before giving it one snort of approval and moving on. Reaching in again, her fingers wrapped around the plastic tube that held her medicine. The rattle sounded hollow with only three days of pills. Skyler closed her eyes and hoped they would be rescued before her AEDs ran out.

She pulled a soaked book with the pages already warping.

"*Backwards to Oregon*?" Cam read the book cover upside-down. "Is it any good?" She reached for the book.

"Any good?" Skyler grabbed the book to her chest in horror. "It's only one of my favorite sapphic books," she scoffed with a teasing smile.

"If it dries out, maybe we can read it?" Cam said, putting it on top of the sleeping bag after reading the back. "Sounds interesting. I've never read a sapphic novel but have always wanted to try one out."

Skyler nodded, only half-listening as she pulled out some beef jerky, a pack of ruined gum, and the wet sweatshirt. It was time to see if her camera worked.

Pinching the clips to the case, she held her breath as she opened the hard case. It was a little damp but not too bad. She took out the soft camera bag that was holding her livelihood and lifted it out. Then, with bated breath, she flicked on the power button and waited.

When the light came on, Skyler whooped out loud before looking guiltily at Cam. "Sorry, that was probably insensitive of me. I'm just glad the camera still works."

Cam gave a small smile. "We were due for some good news. I'm glad your camera still works. You have a great eye for color and light." Skyler looked at her as a bundle of wrinkles formed between her eyes. She caught Cam's eye before it skittered away again. She shrugged. "I looked at your website a few times. Nana Winnie talked about it a lot, and I wanted to see what she was yammering about. You're good."

If Cam had said she could sprout wings and fly them out of there, Skyler would have felt less surprised than she did after Cam's actual words. Not only had Nana Winnie talked about her work, but Cam was curious enough to check it out. She hugged the device closer to her chest, finding warmth in her words.

Skyler cleared her throat and swallowed the sudden lump that had formed. "I'm not sure we are going to find a better place right now than this area." She looked around, seeing at least a little protection from the trees. The raindrops weren't horrible, with the tree branches above absorbing most of them. But now that the first steps Cam had come up with were done, panic-bile started rising in her throat again. "What are we going to do? There is so much to do. How long will we be stuck here?" she almost shouted.

"Hey, hey, it's okay. Take a few breaths." Cam's calm voice washed over her. "We are going to take this one thing at a time, remember? We'll probably want to clear out an area around here and put some branches that have a lot of leaves down on the ground. We're going to get cold at night, so the trees here will help protect us, but we'll want some insulation on the ground and maybe some branches to lean around us. That will take care of the shelter for now." Cam started looking around, but a frown soon formed as she reached over for some branches. They were just out of reach. The twisting motion must have tweaked something in her knee because she yelped before sitting back against the tree.

"Alright, I'll grab the branches. You try not to move." Skyler stood up and brushed off her pants, liking having a goal.

"Here, this might help." Cam dug into the side pockets of one of the bags and handed her a knife. "I'll clean up this mess." Cam then waved to their supplies. "We'll want to ration and most likely forage. I won't be of much use." She frowned at her knee. "Can you try and not bring any cedar? I accidentally wiped myself as a kid with one of the leaves from a cedar tree and had hives in unmentionable places." Cam looked down, her face reddening at the confession.

"Sure, if you can point out which one that is. I'm a little rusty in my plant knowledge." Skyler had her hands on her hips, looking at the different types of trees lining the skyline.

"It's the one with droopy green branches like the leaves are melting." Cam pointed to one a little further into the forest behind them.

"Gotcha, no droopy leaves." Skyler headed to gather branches for their bed while trying to ignore the flush of excitement at the thought of sharing a bed again with Cam, even if it was mostly made of dirt. *Not the time*, she scolded herself.

When Skyler came back, Cam had cleared the area. Goose was curled up and had his head on Cam's leg. Cam was shaking with cold, but luckily, the no-see-ums were not out because of the breeze and rain. Aptly named, the tiny mosquitoes were impossible to see and came out at dusk to wreak havoc on campers. It would almost be impressive that the itchy bumps were usually twice the size of the actual creature, but no, they were mostly just a nuisance.

"I can try and get a small fire going, but we might need to preserve the matches," Skyler said, putting the bundle of branches down. She had to ignore the leaves caressing her face and tried not to think about how many bugs might be hidden in the foliage. "Oh, damn, I forgot this was in my pocket. I'm so sorry." Skyler reached into her pouch and pulled out the blanket, mentally berating herself for taking so long. While she had been working up a sweat, Cam had been stuck getting progressively colder.

"You should probably get into the sleeping bag as well since it's dry. Try to get warm. It most likely would go faster if you take off your clothes." Skyler's face reddened at her words but knew it was true. "I'll get you a few sticks for your leg tomorrow." She looked around for some large rocks to create a rim for the fire pit.

Cam didn't protest as she cuddled with the silver blanket. Goose got up, grumbling at the crinkly sound. "Ccccan you hhhellp mme with the bbbbag?" Cam's shaking voice sounded small as she struggled with the zipper of the sleeping bag.

Skyler kicked herself again for forgetting to give the blanket. She'd been moving around, but Cam's body was probably pulling heat at an alarming rate.

"Okay, hold on." Kneeling on the damp ground, she arranged the branches for a little bed, then helped Cam pull off her shirt. If she weren't half-frozen herself and dead on her feet, she would have had a stronger reaction at seeing her crush since childhood half nude. As it stood, her three brain cells left were huddled together, trying to stay warm. Skyler flicked the bag open and helped Cam scoot into the comfy looking cocoon.

"I'll be right back," Skyler said, moving the hair out of Cam's eyes. The whole sleeping bag was vibrating with her shivers.

Skyler grabbed thick sticks and put them near their supplies, then found some rocks and placed them in a small circle. Next, she found some relatively dry moss and sprayed it with bug spray found in bag two before flicking the match and watching the flames catch. Slowly she added a few twigs and leaves for kindling, and with a sense of accomplishment, Skyler watched the small fire grow.

There wasn't much wood to keep it going, but hopefully, it was enough for now. Skyler stood with her hands on her hips over the fire as a smile spread across her face.

"That was pretty impressive." Cam's voice was muffled through the sleeping bag drawn near her mouth.

"Haven't forgotten all my Alaskan skills they taught us in school. Plus, I camped a little in Portland. Here, you should drink some water and eat something," Skyler handed Cam one of the water bottles. She was now debating if she should ask if she could crawl into the bag with her. *Would that be a weird thing to ask or just something that was assumed? I mean, we are stuck here. Am I overthinking things?*

Skyler's panicked inner rambling was interrupted when Cam flicked the bag open. "We should use body heat to stay warm." Cam's shivering was easing slightly.

The wind rushed from Skyler's lungs in a relieved sigh. "Let me just take my meds, hold on." Skyler ruffled through her backpack and popped her medication, and swallowed it down with a few swigs of water. The liquid cooled her parched lips. She ate a few nuts from the trail mix, knowing they would have to look hard at their food and water situation tomorrow.

Stripping down, she crawled in the bag and nuzzled into Cam's body. "Can I put my arm around you?" Cam asked

80

as her breath tickled the hair on Skyler's neck. If she weren't so dead on her feet, it would've been torture.

"Sure." Skyler hadn't meant for her response to be as breathy as it was, but the events were catching up with them, and her filters were lowered.

Goose settled near their feet, and after sitting still for thirty seconds, the day pressed into them as sleep claimed them fast. Skyler tried not to think of the strong arm around her middle or the warm body that she fit perfectly into. Finally, the crackle of the fire lured her into sleep.

***

Lily watched Micah rut a track into their floor with his pacing. She rubbed her belly, trying to self-soothe the heartburn she was feeling.

"Where are they?" Micah said, pacing and looking at his phone every few seconds.

"Well, maybe Nana Winnie's prediction came true. They probably had a stellar time out on the island and are now cooped up in the house, continuing their date." Lily's smile practically grazed her ears as she wiggled her eyebrows up and down.

"What do you mean, prediction? What prediction?" Micah asked, finally halting in his march.

"The one where Winnie was sure at some point those two would get together. My bet is Skyler finally got the nerve to grab Cam along the neck of her shirt and kiss the crap out of her." Lily giggled at the mental picture.

"Careful, that's my sister and my best friend. So she predicted they would get together?" Micah said, his ears turning pink.

"Loads of times. Didn't you see the drawings for the last carving she was going to do? It was a camera with an etching of a plane in the lens. Get it? Cam the pilot, and

Skyler, the photographer." Lily stepped to the kitchen to make some ginger tea for her stomach.

"So, you think they are back at the house, um, talking?" Micah quietly asked as he grabbed the cups and tea bags for them both.

"Sure, talking. If that makes you feel better, hun." She patted his stomach on the way to lean against the counter. "You know how lesbians are on a date. Lots of… talking." Lily hunched over in laughter at seeing his face.

"How would you know?" Micah questioned, wiping the already clean counter with a rag.

"I've been with women before, Micah. I'm bisexual, remember?" Lily shook her head.

"Well, you used to be. Not anymore." Micah turned and puffed out his chest.

"Oh no. That's not how it works. Just because I married you doesn't mean my sexuality is erased." Lily rolled her eyes at him on her way to the now boiling water.

"No, you're right. That was insensitive of me. I'm sorry." Micah kissed her on the cheek. "So you think they're okay for now?" Lily noticed furrowed lines of worry firmly back between his eyebrows.

"If something happened, we would have heard about it by now, don't you think? I'm sure they are just shacked up. Skyler is probably unleashing years of pent-up lust for your sister."

"La la la." Micah grabbed his ears and started singing, and Lily's laughter trailed into the living room.

Chapter Seven

Day 2

Cam woke up gradually. Her body screamed with discomfort from her head, knee, and stomach, but the loudest scream came from her bladder. She felt Skyler wiggle into her, pressing into the area that was now sounding the five-alarm bell. She let out a groan, which a sleeping Skyler seemed to mistake for something else as she ground into her again.

"Skyler, wake up. I need your help." Cam felt Skyler stiffen, then prop herself up on an elbow.

She was facing away from her, but Cam could see her disheveled hair and could picture the confused look on Skyler's face, which was something she remembered from their childhood when she was awoken suddenly out of a dead sleep.

"I need some help. I've got to pee, but I'm not sure how I can manage it." Cam waved to her knee. A test bend had caused Cam to wince in pain.

Skyler stepped out of the sleeping bag and pulled on still slightly damp pants and a sweatshirt. Without her warm body in the sleeping bag, the material cooled quickly. Cam reached for the sweatshirt Skyler handed her, which she battled over her head. Of course, Goose didn't help matters; his nose was up in Cam's face, ensuring she didn't get lost.

When Cam's head finally popped free from her sweatshirt war, she saw Skyler take her morning dose of AEDs. Cam's heart clenched in worry, hoping for a swift rescue.

"Alright, I think there is a log over there. Maybe you can sit on the edge of it, allowing your leg to stay straight in front of you? That might work while you pee, you think?" Skyler said, pointing to an area to their right.

Cam tried to picture it but reddened at the help she'd need. "Sure, let's try."

Skyler was already bent down to help her up. Trying to swallow down the fact that she needed help, Cam leaned heavily on Skyler as she hobbled the short way to the log. It was a perfect height for what they needed to do, and Cam nodded her approval.

Wrapping her arm around her hip, Skyler helped lead Cam down towards a log before turning away. "Umm, just call me when you're done." Skyler walked to the left and stepped behind a tree. Cam settled on the log before shimmying her underwear down a bit and out of the way.

A slight case of shy bladder took up residence as Cam tried not to focus on the branches stabbing her in the butt. Finally, the seal broke, and a steady stream trickled down the log she was sitting on. Relief was instant, and after taking care of one bodily thing, it was time to work on some food and water. She shimmied the underwear back up but was having a hard time getting it over her hips while balancing on one hand and one leg.

"Skyler? Can I get some help, please?" Cam waited and only heard the chirps of different birds. "Sky?" she asked again.

"Just a sec, finishing up," Skyler said from a few yards away. "Eww, no, Goose, stay away." Cam chuckled at Skyler's dialog. "I'm going to need buckets of sanitizer when we get back home," Skyler continued as she made her way to where Cam was perched.

Goose came to sniff the log and deemed it boring before moving on to the next tree. Skyler grabbed Cam's shoulders and hauled her up. "Hold on," Cam said as she adjusted her underwear higher.

They made their way back to camp, and Cam got settled back at her tree. "Can you hand me those sticks and the ace bandage?" Cam gestured to the items.

Skyler grabbed them and sat next to Cam, laying the items on the ground. Cam's previous embarrassment flared when she saw Skyler start to place the sticks.

"I can do it!" Cam yelled. It was louder than she meant, but she didn't like the inadequate feelings she was having.

Skyler stood quickly. "Sorry, I was just trying to help." She turned. "I'll see what we can have for breakfast."

Cam sighed as she watched Skyler walk away. Goose bounded near Skyler's side, and the quiet of the forest was hard to take. Even the birds had stopped chirping at her outburst.

Banging her head back against the tree, Cam closed her eyes for a second to get her emotions under control. She'd never lashed out, usually preferring the strong, silent method. Not sure where it came from, Cam decided to work on the task at hand by creating a brace for her leg. Murmuring her approval at the strength of branches that Skyler picked only plummeted her mood further.

She got the first two branches braced along the sides of her legs, and then she placed the third behind her leg to keep the knee from bending. The start was slow going and would have been a lot easier with four hands, but eventually, the brace was on and the bandage was wrapped around her leg.

Resting back against the tree again, she was grateful it had stopped raining. There appeared to be a small fire still going. New waves of guilt washed over her when she saw the pile of wood that Skyler kept near the sleeping bag, keeping the fire going through the night, not sure when she had found the time or why Cam hadn't woken up when Skyler moved.

Cam's head was pounding from the bathroom excursion, and it was still only an hour into their morning. Her body screamed for coffee, but instead, she chewed on a pine branch and laid her head against the tree and closed her eyes to let her mind wander.

Rustling branches woke Cam up from a light nap, but she wasn't sure how long she'd been out. She heard Goose's panting before she saw him busting through the underbrush. "Hey, buddy. Have fun with Skyler?" Cam smiled at his whole-body wiggle as he tried to get into her lap.

Skyler's body came into view a moment later. She looked flushed, and Cam could see the rapid breaths escape her mouth in little puffs of fog. "We had a blast. I picked up the items, mainly sticks, and he told me where to put them or tried to steal them," Skyler said with a small smile. "Looks good." She nodded towards Cam's leg.

"Thanks. Sorry I was short earlier." Cam's mumbled apology was muted in Goose's fur as she was having difficulty looking into Skyler's eyes.

"One of us snapping was bound to happen. Probably won't be the last time either," Skyler said, squatting down near the food.

"What were you doing? It seemed like you were gone for a while," Cam said, trying not to stare at the meager pile of food. They had enough water for a few days, but it would be helpful to find some extra food.

"Made an SOS sign using some driftwood and stuff. I'm not sure it's big enough, though, and the high tide might wash some of it away." Skyler pulled a bite of jerky forcefully with her teeth. "You don't eat meat, right?" she asked, handing Cam a Lärabar.

86

"Right, I went plant-based a few years ago and have loved it. I'm surprised you know that, though." She tilted her head as she bit off part of the bar.

"Nana Winnie talked about it sometimes. 'That Cam of ours is going to blow away in the wind, eating that rabbit food.'" Skyler's voice was a dead ringer for Winnie's, and Cam wasn't sure if it was laughter or a sob that escaped.

Wiping her eyes, Cam smiled at Skyler. "Well, as you can see, she was exaggerating a little at being a strong wind away from blowing over." She looked down at the supplies. "Skyler, I'm not sure how long we are going to be stuck here, and we'll run out of food and water quickly." Cam started picking at the seam of her pants. "I won't be of much help for a few days but can help determine what is edible. Also, we didn't file a flight plan because I wanted to give us some flexibility. That means I'm not sure when they will find out something's wrong. I'm sure Micah will figure it out soon, but still, we could be here for a while."

Skyler blinked before looking around, nodding. "I can try and explore a little. We got lucky last night when the rain stopped, but we probably won't be that lucky every night. Maybe there is a better shelter a little further, and I'll look for some berries and such."

Cam hated feeling useless but wasn't in any place to suggest something else. "Just be careful and mark your way. It's easy to get turned around in the woods all alone."

"Good idea. If Goose wasn't around yesterday, I might not have found you after grabbing the supplies." Skyler looked around. "We don't have anything to mark with, though."

Cam thought for a second before saying, "Find sticks and jam them into the ground, or pile rocks. You could even mark an X in the tree with the knife, but make sure to make lots of noise to scare off any bears and take Goose with you."

Skyler visibly relaxed at the mention of Goose. "Alright, it's a game plan. I'll bring a sweatshirt to gather berries in and Goose as a guard dog. Are you going to be okay? Need anything?" Skyler picked up a sweatshirt and tied the arms around her waist. The hood hung in her front, which easily created a cradle.

"I'm fine for now. I'm going to try to make each of us a toothbrush using these soft branches," Cam said, tugging at a branch a little to her left. That way, she wouldn't have to move far, and at least she'd feel like she was contributing something.

***

Goose bounded a few feet ahead as Skyler hiked an overgrown path. The natural curves of the trees and branches created an easy track to follow, but she stopped and gathered a bundle of sticks and shoved them into the ground every couple of minutes.

On the fourth stop, she pushed Goose back for the tenth time. "No, these aren't sticks for you." A final shove and Skyler stood up, examining her handiwork. "Not bad if I do say so myself." Goose was sniffing the sticks and went to grab one with his mouth.

"Come on, Goose, no." She looked around before spotting the perfect distraction for the excited dog. "Here you go, boy!" Skyler waved the mossy stick around while Goose jumped almost to her knees. "Let's see what you can do. Sit." Goose sat immediately, although he was inching forward, and his eyes were focused on the stick. "Stay." Skyler flung the branch into the brush as Goose watched the trajectory over his shoulder before looking back at her. "Fetch." Goose tore through the brush and trees, disappearing in the direction the stick was thrown and came back moments later with not one, but three branches.

Skyler doubled over in laughter. "Always the overachiever, huh? Just like your Uncle Micah." She scratched his ears in acknowledgment while murmuring, "Good dog." Goose's shaking tail showed he was enjoying the moment.

Continuing the walk, Goose found a few bear scats, at which Skyler began to sing. She couldn't sing to save her life—although in this instance, it just might scare off the bears. The thought of coming face to face with a bear was too much to handle on top of everything else that had happened.

She was trying to keep a brave face, seeing how embarrassed and self-loathing Cam was being, but that didn't mean she wasn't tired, hungry, and close to breaking down every moment. When they were together, Skyler wasn't going to let it show how much Cam's outbursts were affecting her. One of the reasons she retreated to the beach was to keep from bursting out her own angry retort, knowing that wouldn't do any good at that moment.

After a half hour of walking, Skyler's throat was getting raw from singing, and a light layer of sweat coated her limbs. She stumbled on a stump and skidded down a slight hill. Branches scraped along her skin as she searched for something to grab to stop her fall. Finally, her fingers tangled in the twigs of a bush a few feet down.

Goose was barking as Skyler fell, and when she came to a stop, his tongue was in her face, making sure she was okay. He even shoved his nose in her hand, which helped her find the balance needed to get her back to her feet. Skyler took care not to put weight on him but instead used his head to steady herself when she pulled herself up. Back on her feet, Skyler made sure to scratch behind Goose's ears before giving him a strip of jerky, which he tenderly took between his teeth.

Taking a sip of water, she looked at her surroundings. She hadn't meant to go down this path. She put her hand over her eyes to shade the sun and looked around. In the distance, something caught her eye. Goose looked up at her, then started wagging his tail and trotting down the hill.

It was a slightly different direction than before, but Goose seemed to catch something in the air, which was fine by Skyler.

Goose stopped with his tail in the air, and Skyler gasped. In front of her was a crudely built cabin, but it had four walls and a roof. She wanted to kiss the ground where it stood.

Goose was still checking out the perimeter as Skyler walked up the creaky wooden steps. "Hello?" she called out. Nobody appeared to have been there in a while, but calling out seemed like the neighborly thing to do. "Hello?" she repeated, getting to the door. She pushed it open, and the rusty hinges screeched in protest, revealing a dusty plywood floor.

"I'm coming in," Skyler announced, pushing the door open fully.

Goose was by her side and ready for the new adventure of smells once the door was open. The cabin was drafty, dark, musky, and she didn't want to know what bugs had their PO boxes set up here, but it didn't matter. To Skyler, the place was a perfect shelter from the elements. There was a roughly built counter lining one wall, with a cast iron pot and some matches sitting on it.

There was a small wooden picnic table along the far side, and along one wall was a shelf that looked like it could either be used as another seating area or a place to sleep off the floor. It was wide enough for two people to scrunch together, but just barely. Along the bed, there was a dirty-looking foam pad. Skyler tried not to think about the germs that had sunk into the mat.

"Well, this would do nicely, don't you think, Goose?" Goose had no qualms about the germ-infested dirty mat and curled right up on the bed. He looked up at her with half-closed eyes in acknowledgment. "Figures, you did walk four times the amount I did, going back and forth the whole time. So I'm just going to check out back."

Skyler slipped out the door, making sure it was open enough for Goose to get out if he wanted, before looking at the rest of the area. There wasn't a place for a fire in the cabin, but the sleeping bag would help keep them warm, and the thought of being out of the elements made Skyler's shoulders shake in excitement. She found a fire pit, a few cut up logs, and a rusty axe for splitting wood out towards the back. Whoever had built this little cabin had been prepared for a few days, at least.

"Now, we just have to figure out how to get Cam here." Skyler had her hands on her hips and looked down at Goose, who was now sitting beside her with his head tilted.

Skyler went back to the cabin to grab the pot before coming back outside to pick some blueberries she found along the way. It took a few hours to fill the container halfway, but it was because she was eating the profits as well, filling up on the juicy berries.

Skyler looked around one more time before calling Goose to make the thirty-ish minute hike back to Cam. She felt accomplished bringing the axe and a pot filled with berries back to camp.

***

Micah was driving along the street that swooped around from the store along the waterfront to downtown. He was hunting for more ginger tea because apparently, their little peanut was making it hard for Lily to keep anything down. Tea seemed to help, and Micah was determined to help in any way possible. He looked up in the rearview mirror and caught his own small smile in the reflection, still overcome at becoming a dad and knowing Lily would be a great mom.

A little worry niggled at the back of his brain from still not hearing anything from his sister or Skyler, but Lily seemed adamant that they were just releasing steam and hadn't come up for air yet. Micah's hair flopped into his eyes when he shook his head. It sounded odd at first, Skyler and Cam, but the more he thought about it, the more he wondered how he hadn't picked up on Skyler's crush from the start.

"They would make a cute couple." Micah's voice filled the empty car. "Maybe Skyler will move back. She can be an aunt. Hell, I already think of her as a sister." His smile grew as he thought of wedding plans for the two of them, the idea of their relationship already solidifying in his brain.

He slowed the car down as someone tried to back out in the small side street. While he waited for the car to straighten out, his eyes fell on a familiar truck in the parking lot of the harbor. All thoughts of matrimony went out the door as he felt the color drain from his face.

"No, no, no, no." He inched forward and saw the window decal of the outline of Alaska and a floatplane in the middle of it. Micah remembered the care he'd taken to place the object on Cam's window, ensuring it was perfect since it was a gift when she'd paid off her plane.

There weren't any parking spots, but he was beyond caring right now, and quickly pulled up behind a few parked cars, threw on his hazards, and ran to the truck. Not seeing anything out of order, he looked to where the plane was usually parked, and it was as if the empty space taunted him.

A few pilots were huddled near the bottom of the dock, so Micah started running to ask them if they had heard anything. Skidding to a stop in front of the men, he placed his hands on his hips and bent over.

"Micah, you okay?" Hank Reeves, one of Cam's flying buddies, asked. He had his hand on Micah's back.

"Have any of you heard from Cam?" Micah finally wheezed out.

All three men shook their heads in unison and looked out to the sky like synchronized puppets.

"Heard she went out yesterday, but it doesn't look like she came back." Hank played with his long beard. "We were just talking about that. Wondering if she was camping."

Micah looked around, trying to figure out why there suddenly wasn't enough air in the open outdoors.

"Hey, come on, sit down a second. You look like you're going to faceplant into the ocean." Hank took him aside. He seemed to be talking, but Micah couldn't make out individual words. It was all a muffled tone in his brain.

The sharp ring of Micah's cell finally snapped him out of his panic when he saw Lily's smiling face on the screen. Taking a breath, he waved the phone to Hank before stepping away and answering.

"Hey hun, have you left the store? Is it possible to add a few more things?" Lily's voice carried through the object in his hand and provided the grounding necessary to think of next steps. "Micah, are you there?"

Micah cleared his throat, "I'm here. Lily, I'm at the dock. Cam's plane never made it back." He closed his eyes and gripped the phone tighter. His shaking hands caused the phone to nearly slip from his grasp.

"Okay, come on home, we'll figure out what to do together." Lily's tone was soft and comforting but left no room for argument, not that he wanted to argue with her.

He stumbled through an explanation to the concerned pilots, and Hank said he'd make some calls. Hurrying back to his car, he mumbled an apology to a person who had wanted to back out but couldn't because of Micah's car. In the safety of his vehicle, Micah cried for the first time since his parents had died. Fear gripped his heart as he worked his way back home.

Chapter Eight

Day 3

Cam sat staring at the fire. There were still embers burning from their fire the previous night, and with small pieces of wood and careful coaxing, Cam was able to get the flame going again without using another match. The elbows on her sweatshirt were wet from when she'd crawled a few feet to get some young leafy branches which created a lot of smoke. It wasn't much, but it was her contribution to the SOS signs needed for rescue.

It had been a long day of sitting and staring. Skyler had told her about the cabin when she got back yesterday, but they decided to stay on the beach for a little longer, especially since Cam was practically immobile. There was nothing from the radio, and the fact that nobody had responded to the mayday call was making her a little crazy. Cam was mentally back in the pilot seat, going through what had happened.

Picturing the moments after losing power, she remembered pushing the yoke forward to dip the plane's nose down to keep the wings flying in a glide. There were a few spots to choose to land, but the strip on the bay seemed the easiest. If only she had seen that damn rock under the water. She shook her head, reliving the moments of joy when they landed on the water to the terror when the hidden rock came into view just under the surface of the water.

She was staring at the little fire as her fingers idly slid through the moss she'd collected from the tree she'd spent most of her day nearby. There wasn't much she could do, but the moss had provided excellent insulation and a springy surface to lay on at night. Her thirty-ish-year-old back was protesting the current bed, plus she wanted to help make Skyler as comfortable as possible as a thank you for her doing all the manual jobs. As she made a more suitable bed, Cam reviewed the facts of the hard landing, turning them over and studying every micromovement in her mind.

The new sound took a second to register. At first, she thought it was part of her memory from before the plane lost power, but the *whoop whoop whoop* was a different sound from her aircraft. Lifting her head towards the sky, she tried to get a visual. The sound was faint but there—the steady and exciting sound of helicopter blades.

Cam looked down at her chest, sure she would see the flutter of her pounding heart through her shirt. Her arms scraped along the ground as she tried to scramble upright, using the tree as a perch to inch along the surface like a worm. She kept her leg outstretched and used her good leg as an anchor as she scratched her back against the bark. Then, after what seemed like forever, she was finally upright. The sound was still there, but she wasn't sure if it was from her imagination or not.

With one step and a hop, she became reacquainted with the forest floor in a crumpled mess as pain shot up her leg. It had been a long time since she had felt this hopeless. Walking into the kitchen after her father's funeral was the closest to this feeling she could remember. The fact that she and Micah had gone through losing both their parents close together, and at a young age, meant they could get through anything. But now, lying on the ground, hope flickered in the wind.

"Cam! Are you alright?" Skyler's worried voice carried to her. She hadn't seen or heard her come back from the beach, and she wanted to burrow her face deeper into the spongy floor.

But first things first. "Skyler, I think there is a helicopter. Run to the beach and check. Take the flare!" she called when Skyler had already turned and started running. Skyler stopped and pivoted before running back to the bags.

"Good call." Skyler dove for the bags in search of the flare.

Cam heard the yell of excitement as Skyler rummaged through the bag, then the rhythmic thudding of Skyler's running sneakers. Goose's nose twitched against her face, and Cam could feel the puffs of air cool down her overheated skin. If anyone could help pull her from the fog of depression, it would be Goose.

Waiting wasn't her strongest suit but waiting without being able to pace felt like torture. Dragging herself back into a seated position, she gently ran her fingers through Goose's fur. He seemed tuckered out, no doubt from running back and forth between all the smells. Cam smiled into his fur as he laid his head along her legs, his tail thumping softly into the ground.

"I've missed you, buddy. I feel like I haven't seen you in forever. Having fun gallivanting around with Skyler?" Her rambling tapered off as she stared at the place where Skyler had disappeared. Cam was willing her to return, hopefully with the cavalry in tow.

Cam's heart sank when she finally saw Skyler's dejected face through the trees. Before slowly resuming her morose walk back to the camp they had set up, Skyler stopped to pick something up. Goose's tail started thudding against the ground quicker as Skyler neared.

"I didn't see anything and didn't want to waste one of the flares on nothing," Skyler mumbled as she walked up to camp. Cam watched as she tucked the gun back in the bag and set the pot half-filled with berries down near Cam before extending her hands over the warm fire. Every few seconds, she blinked rapidly, and Cam wasn't sure if it was from the smoke or holding back tears.

Goose sat on his haunches as he looked between them.

Cam investigated the pot Skyler had brought from the cabin. Her mouth watered at the juicy-looking salmonberries. The red, orange, and yellow tints of the different berries brought a nice pop of color. It was a nice change from the blueberries that Skyler had found yesterday. "Where did you find these?" Cam popped a berry in her mouth, enjoying the flavor burst and liquid tickling her tongue.

"Oh!" Skyler said, perking up a little from their close encounter. "I found a patch a little way into the woods." She pointed to the right.

The proud look Skyler was giving her should have curtailed her response, but snarky Cam was firmly in the pilot's seat, it seemed, and she couldn't seem to stop the response. "Good for you." She stared pointedly at her leg and grimaced inwardly at the hurt expression that flickered across Skyler's face. Goose huffed once, almost in displeasure.

Skyler stomped to her backpack, pulling her med container out and taking her AEDs. Her hands were shaking, and Cam's anger melted away into the pine needle floor.

"I'm sorry," Cam said to her legs. "I'm having a hard time being so useless right now, and it's not fair to take it out on you." She paused, and was grateful that Skyler allowed her the time to gather her thoughts. When they were growing up, Skyler had always been good at instinctively knowing when to pause and let her think without pushing or overstepping, which was a surprising trait for a child. "Thank you for finding us food. I'm sorry." Cam's voice softened as she repeated her apology, feeling terrible for lashing out again when Skyler was just helping out.

Skyler looked back at the beach before shaking her head. "It's fine. It's been a stressful couple of days. Should we head to the cabin soon?" She looked over to Cam before placing more green branches on the fire. The smokestack billowed from the burning branches.

"I'm not sure if we should leave the beach right now," Cam said to Skyler's back.

"Why?" She turned from the fire to face her. It didn't appear like she was angry, more so curious. "I'm not leaving you here if that's what you're thinking."

It had been, and not for the first time Cam wondered how Skyler could so easily read her mind. She picked up a pinecone and started tossing it from one hand to another. "Well, okay, you caught me, it did cross my mind—but hold on," she said quickly when she saw Skyler about to interrupt. "There was a helicopter, and if we heard it once, we might hear another one soon. I'm not sure we should be playing house in a cabin in the woods right now."

Jesus, why can't I talk without putting my foot in my mouth? Cam thought, going over the words she'd just said before sighing. "That came out wrong. I just mean I'd feel better being closer to the beach right now. Maybe give it a little more time."

Skyler tilted her head from side to side, as if listening to debates of competing voices. That was another thing Cam liked about Skyler: Whereas Cam tended to react then regret, Skyler always took the time to reflect, and when she talked, people tended to listen because it was always well thought out.

"Okay, one more night." She held up a finger. "But remember; there's a nice place with a campfire, a pot to cook in, and most importantly, a bed that is off the floor. We can get the fire started, and we'll have the flare. Playing house doesn't sound like the worst thing." The last part was mumbled, but Cam still caught it.

Cam couldn't help it—she laughed, her first genuine laugh in a long time. Her body shook from the exertion as her stomach cramped from unused muscles. Once she started, she couldn't stop. Goose took this inopportune time to start cleaning his fur which set off another round of giggles as she heard his tongue licking. Her laughter started Skyler off, and they passed their giggles off to one another, unable to stop. Finally, Goose got fed up with their laughter, and he wandered around, sniffing the area.

"Okay, okay, I yield." Cam gasped, trying to calm the giggles that were bubbling up again. "Thank you, Skyler. It's a good plan." Cam's side hurt from laughing so much.

"Well, I guess I should grab some more berries since most of them fell out when I dropped the pot." Skyler stood up and swiped the dirt off her backside, ready to hunt and gather again for them.

"We should also try and find a water source. The water bottles are running low, and I mean, we may get rescued soon—the helicopter is a good sign—but you never know." Cam looked around as if she could magically find the source, just to be useful, but internally rolled her eyes. She'd been staring at the same scenery for a few days, and nothing had changed. "If you see any chocolate lilies, grab some. They usually grow around the water. You have to dig up their roots, but the bulbs are edible." If Cam couldn't provide physical help, she could at least try and impart some knowledge about edible food around here.

"Goose has been licking dew off of plants and has eaten a lot of berries, so at least he's self-sufficient, but yeah, a water source would be good." Skyler nodded. "It's crazy to think we are surrounded by water but could still go thirsty."

Cam smiled as she looked around. "That's why he wasn't eating any of my Lärabar. Been filling up on berries, huh boy?" Goose popped his head up near a bush, a leaf stuck on his muzzle.

"Okay, I'll see what I can forage. Goose, are you staying here, buddy?" At the mention of his name, he trotted over to where they were talking and sat between them, looking back and forth as if waiting for direction while Skyler went to her bag to root for the camera.

She placed it securely around her neck before turning and lifting it with a small smile.

"No, you go with Skyler. Protect her, okay?" Cam rubbed the top of Goose's head before snapping her fingers and pointing to Skyler. "Go with her." Goose snapped to attention and bounded to Skyler's side. "Good boy," Cam said softly, a half-smile tugging at her lips.

The two women shared a smile, almost like proud parents of their kid, before Cam watched Skyler disappear.

***

Skyler was sore and achy, but she held her smile. It had been nice to put Cam in her place and have a lighter moment. She hadn't seen Cam laugh like that in years, and her heart clenched at seeing some of the sparkle return to her eyes. When they were younger, she'd go out of her way to try and coax out that low chuckle.

Goose seemed to get his second wind, and his boundless energy was hard to watch when Skyler felt like collapsing. She wasn't used to all the walking, and yesterday's excursion was still pulling at her muscles. Her lips were chapped, and she felt like she had a layer of scum on her skin. The stings from grabby branches started to scream at her, but nothing compared to the no-see-ums that were out now.

The blood-sucking tiny beasts were swarming now that there was no rain and only a light breeze. With the afternoon turning to evening, Skyler had forgotten what a literal pain they were. She slapped her arms and tried not to breathe too deeply, or else she'd be getting protein in a vastly different way than how she'd want.

Reaching the beach again, her eyes scanned the area between where the beach ended and the trees started. There she found the chocolate lilies that Cam had mentioned. The thought of using her fingers like a claw caused a shudder to crawl up her spine, so she searched for a few sticks to help dig up the roots. She poked around the ground, then lifted, excited to see the white roots of the plant. Memories of sixth-grade science class of when they went on a trip to the beach to learn about flora and fauna around Sitka floated in her mind. She couldn't remember anything about reading or math, but the practical lessons of survival had stuck in her mind.

"Not that I would have lasted long without Cam," she said to Goose, who was marking a trail along the beach. The memories of the survival class had surfaced only after Cam provided the initial nudge.

Looking towards the water, something caught her eye. Near the shore, an eagle was circling above the water. Pushing the haul in her sweatshirt to the side, Skyler lifted her camera to watch and wait. Then, taking a few test pictures, she continued observing the smooth flight of the majestic bird.

Without warning, it dove before pulling up at the last second and splashed feet first into the ocean. Skyler's fingers were vibrating with the quick pace of photos she captured, and her breath left her when the eagle's wings propelled from the water holding a wriggling fish in its talons. The fish appeared bigger than the bird, but even seeing the powerful and sporadic wiggles as the fish fought, it wasn't enough for freedom from the predator's grip.

Throughout the whole interaction, Skyler took pictures, and when the bird was finally out of sight, she released the breath she'd held, not wanting to disturb the moment.

Goose's wet nose against her hand broke the reprieve, and Skyler startled at the motion. She looked down and smiled. "Let's get back to Cam, shall we?" Goose barked once in agreement as she gathered the sweatshirt with the bulbs. On the way back, she grabbed more berries, although thinking about eating them was causing her mouth to close. If she never ate another berry in her life, she'd be okay.

"And we've only been here three days. What will I do if we're here much longer? Huh, Goose? I could go for a juicy steak and eggs, mmm, and a milkshake." Skyler looked down at Goose, who was licking his lips. "You'd like that. Well, I'll get you a nice porterhouse steak, and we'll eat it together. How does that sound? Maybe we can get a garden burger for your mom, and…" Skyler trailed off in thought, her mind wandering to the nonexistent date night with Cam she'd just come up with.

"Dangerous thoughts, Goose. Very dangerous." She continued walking, shaking her head, trying to scatter her wishes to the wind.

When Skyler walked up to camp, Cam was leaning against her tree with her eyes closed. Skyler took the time to look at her face. With the tension smoothed out, she almost looked peaceful, making Skyler's heart squeeze painfully as her eyes trekked to Cam's lips.

If only, Skyler thought as she unconsciously brought her fingers to her own lips. She scrunched her nose when she got a taste of the dirt and salt that coated her fingers and quickly pulled them away before turning to tend to the fire.

"Hi." A voice floated to Skyler a while later. She was watching the flames dance along the wood, lost in thought, and tensed up when Cam spoke.

She turned with a small smile. "Afternoon. Are you hungry? These should be done soon."

102

Cam craned her neck behind her, catching a glimpse of the roasting bulbs. "Umm..." Her hand snaked to massage the back of her neck. "They might be a little bitter. I just want to warn you since we have to cook them like that." She pointed to the roasting bulbs. "They tend to have a creamier taste when boiled in water or fried in oil." Cam looked away before turning back to her. "But they smell good, and we won't last long with what we have. Thank you."

"Well shit," Skyler said, looking at the meal. She didn't know that, but at least Cam wasn't a jerk about it. If anything, she was rambling, probably nervous about her reaction. "Thanks for letting me know. It's still edible though, right?"

"Yes, for sure. I just wanted to prepare you." Cam shrugged, petting Goose.

"I mean, unless we want more berries, but even after a few days, my stomach is ready for something else. I might have to choke down some bitter roots." Skyler pulled the plants from the fire, handing a few to Cam before twisting one end of the stick into the ground, leaving the rest of the bulbs floating in the air on the other end. She placed more wood and moss on the fire, working up the smoke again.

"I'll take anything over the taste of berries right now," Cam said with a grin. "It's not bad. Thanks, Skyler."

Skyler nodded before opening her med bottles, then taking a sip of water and popping the pills in her mouth. "I'm a little nervous with how little meds I have left. If we're not rescued by tomorrow, I'll have run out." She was frowning at her medication, which was taunting her with its near emptiness.

Cam's smile faded into concern, and she started fidgeting with the pinecone.

"Smells good," Skyler said, looking to change the subject. Fretting wouldn't do them any good. She picked up one of the sticks. The root was slightly bitter, but her

103

tongue and stomach were happy for something other than berries. The starchy root provided a surprisingly full feeling.

She sat next to Cam as they watched the sun set through the tree line. The smoke for their signal was doing an okay job keeping the bugs at bay, but they were still a nuisance and the only thing that put a slight damper on the moment.

Skyler's gaze wandered over to Cam's profile as they watched the changing colors in the sky. The light radiated off her cheeks, and she couldn't hold back a click of her tongue as she whispered, "Beautiful," before quickly looking away. She reached into the bag and grabbed her camera, taking a few pictures of the sunset while wondering if she could pivot for a profile photo of the person next to her. Being stuck on an island was turning out to be sweet torture for her battered childhood heart, as memories of her final days in Sitka filtered through from the past.

"Were you able to take pictures today?" Cam's voice broke through Skyler's thoughts, and she blinked a few times to clear the small tear that had formed in the corner of her eye, hidden in the dusk.

"Oh, yeah, I think there might be a good one from when I was at the beach. Want to see?" Skyler looked over, holding her camera close to her heart.

"Yes, please," Cam said, patting the ground next to her.

Skyler settled near Cam's side before stiffening when she remembered that she hadn't had a shower in a few days. It didn't matter as much for Cam, but Skyler had been traipsing along the forest, working up multiple layers of sweat. She was about to put her head on Cam's shoulder, but self-consciousness won out, and she leaned further away.

Cam reached across her back and pulled Skyler into her body. Skyler's slight smile was a secret in the dark as she fired up the camera. The smile turned radiant when she heard Cam gasp and sit up to get a better look at the camera.

Having not seen the pictures herself, Skyler was curious how they'd turned out but waited until Cam's head moved, giving her better access to the viewer. "These are amazing, Skyler."

Her thumb was moving through the photos, and Skyler had to agree. They were pretty good. The camera caught the glistening water drops falling off the fish and bird, along with the different angles of the wings as the bird lifted to fly, curled in, then majestically spread. Each image provided a new and powerful angle of the predator and prey.

"You could sell these." Cam's awed voice broke through Skyler's critical concentration as she tried to find fault in any of the images.

"Maybe." Skyler shrugged. She wasn't about to get her hopes up.

"Maybe? Are you kidding me? These are inspiring." Cam was a little breathless, and it was distracting Skyler. "You have talent."

"Eh, that one was luck. I was at the right place at the right time, and the light worked out." Skyler could feel the blush start on her neck.

"Isn't that what life is? A series of pictures and memories, where individually you might not see how they fit into your journey until the passage of time shows the overall picture of your life." Cam turned slightly, tipping the camera back into Skyler's hands but never letting go of her eyes.

Skyler swallowed, not sure if they were still talking about the photos. Goose barked once, breaking the fragile connection. "We should try and get some sleep," Skyler said quietly, looking at the ground. She had seen a lifetime of memories reflected in Cam's eyes and was sure the same pictures were playing in her own.

After going through the nighttime ritual they had established—relieving themselves, then helping Cam into the sleeping bag—Skyler settled next to her. She was trying to keep some space between them to protect her heart from the inevitable ache when they were rescued and went back to their separate lives.

Skyler stared at the twinkling stars filtering through the trees along the black canvas above her head when they settled for the night. Without the city lights, the stars seemed more condensed. The deep, even breathing from Cam provided an extra layer of comfort.

Sleep for Skyler was elusive. In Portland, her bedroom was near the fridge, so there was a humming sound, plus the road was near, and there were always sounds of cars driving by or drunk people shouting and stumbling home. Here, the quiet was thick, and the pure silence was almost painful. Her brain strained to hear anything, any sound, yet there was nothing. She snapped her fingers just to make sure she could still hear and felt comforted when the sharp sound filtered through. She let her mind travel along the Sitka sky, bouncing from one star to another. She jumped slightly when a sleeping hand slipped into hers—*unconsciously*, she told her stuttering heart.

***

Micah sank to his knees, the stress of the day seeming to press into his shoulders, causing Lily's eyes to burn in sympathy. It had been a long day for both of them as they made countless calls, finally finding success in getting a rescue crew via helicopter to check out the area to see if they could find anything. Lily had seen Cam in action with the plane multiple times. She had flown, landed, been in hairy situations with a flight, and not once had Lily been scared. Cam knew what she was doing, and it was incomprehensible that she was missing. But, unfortunately,

106

they had just received word that there was no sign of the plane or passengers. Lily was trying to decide if that was a good thing or a bad thing. She felt like Schrödinger's cat at the moment, in limbo between both realities.

Lily rubbed her belly, soothing the discontent that was bubbling from her gut.

Micah's sobs snapped Lily out of her contemplative state. She fell on her knees to wrap her arms around his shaking shoulders.

"Micah, honey, look at me. They haven't found anything. No bodies, no plane so far, so there is no bad news right now. We're not giving up. I know Cam, and she will do anything in her power to survive and save Skyler. There is no way she's not alive. This baby needs their aunt, and we are going to find them."

"I'm going to have to help with the search party. Would you mind if I took the boat and camped for a few days? Their last ping was near their destination, and it's pretty far to trek back and forth every day." Micah's shoulders slumped, and his eyes held pain in their depths.

"I don't mind you taking the boat, of course, but I do mind that you think I'm not joining you. Cam's like a sister to me too, Micah. Two sets of eyes are better than one, plus we can help each other drive the boat." Lily shook her head. "God, almost a decade of marriage, and you still don't know me well enough to know I'm coming with you whether you like it or not."

Micah looked at her belly, then up to her face. She knew he didn't want to put her in any danger, but damn if she was going to be left behind.

"Don't you even, Micah. People have been going camping while pregnant since the beginning of time. I know my limitations and know I can handle it." Lily put her hands on her hips, her chin jutting out.

"I'm sorry, of course, you can decide. It's just—I'm worried, mostly for my sister and Skyler, but if something

107

happened to either of you…" He put his hand on her belly. "I don't know what I'd do." The tears that had been on the edge slipped down his cheek as his glasses fogged up.

"We'll be alright. They are okay. They are strong. Cam knows her shit out there. But come on, we've got some packing to do."

Lily's tight hug carried Micah forward towards the next step.

The calm Lily felt would have scared her, but instead it assured her she was ready. Ready to find her family and bring them home. Nana Winnie hadn't only helped the Porter siblings, she had helped Lily as well. After the last attempt at a child had failed, Winnie's arms were the first ones Lily had sought out. She could still feel the comfort and smells of Winnie's house when it had felt like her heart was ripping in two. Winnie had held her until the well of tears dried, then made a batch of cookies. There was no way Lily would sit by and do nothing as Winnie's family was stuck somewhere. They were alive. She felt it in her bones.

A knock on the door brought them both out of their grief. Lily kissed the side of Micah's head as she pulled herself off the floor. When she opened the door, she was blown away by the number of people standing on their porch.

"We're here to help. What do you need from us?" Hank Reeves asked, motioning behind him.

"Come in, come in." Lily waved the group of gruff Alaskans through her door. These were people who had boats, planes, and diving equipment—people whom they had helped with their engines, fishing gears, and anything in between.

The bat signal had gone up unknowingly, and the small fishing town had answered.

Chapter Nine

Day 4

The cold was piercing Cam as she waited for Skyler to get back. She was gnawing on her upper lip, knowing it was going to chap further, but was unable to stop. Worry for Skyler mixed with guilt at being incapacitated was churning her gut. As the days progressed, she was looking increasingly dead on her feet. She had to give it up to Skyler, though; with everything she had to take care of, she was doing a fabulous job of getting things done, and somehow usually with a smile.

Cam gave a rundown of a few plants that would work for food, but the sting in her parched lips told her they would have to find a source of water, and quickly, since the last of the water bottles were going to be used up today. She'd given Skyler the majority of the water since she was the one hiking all over the island.

Skyler had gone to the beach to work on the SOS sign again, and they debated making three fires, which was another signal that indicated they needed help. Ultimately, they decided to hold off on the extra fires to save matches, plus they were having a hard time keeping their own campfire going. It was killed off by strong winds and needed a lot of wood stockpiled to keep it lit. Cam was scooting her butt along the ground, using her hands to propel herself over the forest floor. She had a bunch of bushy branches on her lap that kept tickling her mouth. She couldn't wait until she could bend her leg again.

At least the movement helped ward off the chill. With the temperatures ranging from thirty degrees Fahrenheit at night to fifty-five or sixty during the day, it was imperative to keep the blood flowing to stay warm.

To feel useful, she started the day weaving together some branches she had gathered around her, hence the branches in her lap. The mossy bed had been a success, but now she was working on crafting walls to help insulate them at night. Her dad had taught her how to create a survival shelter using different materials. She sent a thanks to him while her fingers weaved branches together for the shelter.

If they were going to have a hard time keeping the fire going, they'd need a way to preserve heat, which meant getting some rough walls up. The thought warmed her, and she started scooting towards an area that had sturdy-looking branches. Of course, if worse came to worst, they could always head to the cabin, but they were more likely to hear rescuers while on the beach.

"Hey, what are you doing?" Skyler's voice popped out from the trees, and Cam looked behind her, guilty at being caught moving around but also glad to see she was okay. "You promised you'd take it easy." Skyler walked up and squatted next to her.

Goose, who was never one to sit by and be left out, put his nose in Cam's ear while whacking Skyler in the head with his wagging tail. Cam heard Skyler giggle then yelp as she fell over, landing on her butt.

Over Goose's body, she saw Skyler's wide eyes, and they both laughed at the same time.

"Goose, you goof, get out of here." Cam scratched behind his ears before sitting up and pushing him away.

"You said you'd take it easy," Skyler accused as she stood up.

"I was going to start on the walls for our shelter. But, unfortunately, there isn't much else I can do to help around here." Cam looked at her leg, then back at Skyler.

"That's not true. It was your idea to use the branches for the toothbrushes, you said to look for chocolate lilies, and you were the one that created the nice bed. If I wasn't constantly thinking about the bugs that could be crawling in the moss, it would have been an extremely relaxing sleep." When Skyler finished her rant, there was a delightful blush creeping up her cheeks.

Cam shrugged, trying to deflect the attention. "What's in the bucket?" She pointed to a beach-combing treasure Skyler had found yesterday, just a run-of-the-mill white bucket that had washed up on shore. It had a few holes in the bottom but was great for berry picking or chocolate lily roots.

Skyler looked at the bucket as if forgetting it was there and needing a reminder. "The tide is pretty low, and I found some clams. Do you think they will be safe to eat? Oh shoot, I forgot you are plant-based." Skyler looked back down at the clams near her feet.

"Did the water smell like ammonia?" Cam asked, pulling the bucket closer to her for inspection.

"Ammonia? No. Just the normal seaweed and salt smell." Skyler wrinkled her nose. "Why?" She crouched down, watching what Cam was doing in the bucket.

"Okay, they should be safe from red tide," Cam said, grabbing a clam and inspecting the non-hinged side, tapping on the top of the shell and observing the object closing quickly. She nodded and put it aside. As she continued, she occasionally had to push Goose's nose out of the way.

"What are you doing?" Skyler asked, bringing her head in closer.

"Checking to make sure they are alive." She pulled two clams out and held them towards Skyler. "See how this one is closed, and this one is slightly open here?" She pointed to the slit where the clams would open. "The ones that are already closed are most likely dead." She tossed the closed one and picked up another one, holding the two open clams in her hands before tapping the top. "See how this one shut quickly? It's alive, but this one hasn't moved, so it's most likely dead as well."

"Fascinating," Skyler breathed out, watching Cam work the bucket of clams. "I can finish them up," she offered, although her wrinkled nose and frown indicated it wasn't something she particularly wanted to do.

Even though Skyler must have had to dig for the clams, her hands seemed relatively clean. Cam had to hold in a grin. "I don't mind helping out, but I don't want any. I still have a few things to eat." Cam shrugged, grabbing another handful of clams.

"Well, I appreciate it. I saw the bubbles in the sand, and I remember Nana Winnie taking us out for a clam dig. She gave us shovels then, but today I had to get a few sticks so I wouldn't get my hands dirty." Skyler held out her palms. "I can't stand the thought of germs and dirt, and the fact that I haven't showered in four days is making me itch."

Cam just shrugged in her 'it's no big deal' movement and went back to working on the clams but stilled when she felt a warm hand wrap around her bicep.

"I mean it. Thank you, Cam." Skyler's eye contact was piercing into Cam, and she started looking for an exit ramp, not wanting to face the traffic of her mind yet.

She cleared her throat. "It's nothing. Honestly, it's the least I can do. So, what other things can't you stand or are afraid of?" Cam asked, trying to lighten the mood.

"Are we talking irrational or rational?" Skyler pulled at the branches Cam was gathering for the sides of the shelter.

"Both, I'm definitely curious about both," Cam said with a decisive head nod.

"Now you can't laugh. Promise you won't laugh?" She looked at Cam, waiting for the cross-heart sign over her chest before taking a deep breath. "Irrational, okay. I'm terrified of black holes. Now before you say anything" — Skyler held up a hand— "I realize the likelihood of me coming across one is not going to happen, but those bastards are terrifying." She looked up and shook her head, holding a leaf over her mouth. "You promised you weren't going to laugh."

Cam was turning red, pressing her lips together to keep from making a sound, but it was a failed mission. Skyler snorted her permission to carry on, which was all Cam needed to burst out a full-bellied chuckle. "Black holes? That's the most random thing." She got herself under control before continuing. "Although if you are going to have an irrational fear, it's pretty smart for it to be that one. We don't know much about them, and they have the power to snuff out light." She looked out towards the ocean. "Damn, now I'm nervous about those things."

"Yes!" Skyler pumped her fist. "I've converted someone else to team fuck black holes, FBH club if you will."

Cam looked at Skyler, willing her to hear what she had just said. Instead, she was going to give herself a hernia, holding in this much laughter. She could see the moment Skyler figured out what she had actually said because if she had held up a cooked lobster to Skyler's face, they would have been sporting the same color.

"I—uh," Skyler sputtered. "Well, that's not exactly what I meant. That's what I get for just speaking without talking things through in my brain first."

Once Cam stopped shaking from laughing, she finally asked, "So what's the rational fear?" Subconsciously she slid closer, not wanting to miss what Skyler said.

"Bugs," Skyler said with a smile. "I can't stand them. They bite, have way too many eyes and legs, and a lot of them are poisonous. Now, if that isn't a rational fear, then I don't know what is," Skyler added, tying the last of the branches together. They were a little looser than Cam would have done, but it looked like the lesson from the night before had stuck.

"You know, you could try some exposure therapy," Cam said, throwing the last of the dead clams in a pile and putting the good ones back in the bucket. Cam set a mental reminder to get the dead clams far from camp, not wanting wandering wildlife rooting around so close to them.

"What kind of exposure therapy? If you think I'm going to put my hand in a vat of bugs, à la Fear Factor, you've got another thing coming." Skyler rubbed her arms while Cam chuckled.

"No, nothing like that. Take pictures. I'm sure you can find some crawlers around here. I bet if you see them in a different element and maybe observe them a little, you'll find they aren't so bad." Cam smiled as Skyler took in what she was saying.

"Seems to track. I'll try and do that. If nothing else, I'll get some good pictures." Skyler stood up and stretched her back.

"I used to be afraid of the open ocean, not so much in the boat or plane, but if I swam, I'd flail, imagining all types of things nipping at my toes. So I started slowly, staying on the beach and going out a little more each time. Exposure therapy won't work for everything but might help settle a little of your fears." Cam wiped her hands together, getting the gritty sand off them.

The sun was setting, and Cam was struck by the easy companionship they had. Maybe the years growing up with Skyler allowed for a certain ease that she didn't feel around many people. But Cam didn't want to get too close or start finding comfort in Skyler's presence. After they were rescued, Cam would still live in Sitka, and Skyler would return to her life in Portland. But if Cam's burning cheeks were any indication, she hadn't utilized the smiling muscles in a long while.

Sighing, she settled back to her tree, and both women seemed lost in their thoughts.

***

Laughing with Cam was easy. It lowered the tension Skyler was feeling from running out of AEDs. However, laughing with Cam was also a little torturous. She had always had a thing for her laugh, and hearing the low chuckle was doing things to her stomach.

"How's your leg doing?" Skyler asked as she dug the bundle of clams out of the fire coals. Cam had said they would be good wrapped in seaweed. She took a stick to look inside the wrapping, and the clams were opening, but not far enough. She tucked the corners and put the food back among the coals.

"It's stiff, but I think I'll try moving it around a little tomorrow," Cam replied through a mouthful of dandelions and berries.

Skyler watched Cam from the side of her eye as she poked the fire. The smoke had permeated her clothes. She was pretty sure five washings weren't going to be enough to get the smell out.

"As long as you take it easy. I'll find you a walking stick." Skyler turned to the sunset before pulling out her camera. "I'm going to take a few pictures on the beach. Want me to grab more chocolate lily roots?"

Cam nodded once. "That would be great, thank you." She looked up and met Skyler's eyes. "I'll make it up to you sometime, you having to do all this work." Cam's eyes looked away as they gravitated towards her 'rabbit food,' as Nana Winnie had so lovingly put it.

115

Skyler cocked her head, knowing in her heart she would have happily done even more. Helping Cam wasn't a hardship; it was a pleasure. "I'm happy to help and glad I haven't killed us yet with the foraged food."

"Your clams should only take about ten minutes. I'll watch them. Go have fun. I hope you get some good pictures." Cam smiled, and to Skyler's delight, it reached her eyes. Her fingers ached to take a picture and capture the majestic beauty. "Oh, while you're out, could you try and find some water? Grab the bottles there. I messed up. I thought for sure we'd be rescued by now, but it's imperative to find water now." Cam winced.

Smiling, Skyler grabbed a few water bottles before heading to the beach with her camera. She'd see if there was a river or source somewhere nearby.

"Take Goose with you!" Cam called, and Skyler's heart sped up at the concern threaded through her voice.

"See you soon." Skyler waved and started walking the now worn path to the beach.

The SOS sign was holding steady. A silent pride filled her lungs and set her shoulder straighter at having used the seaweed lines to show how far up she should make the sign without it being ruined by high tide. However, she had a feeling it should probably be more prominent. From her view, it was large but still might be hard to see from planes flying overhead.

She took a few pictures of the sunset, not finding them as brilliant without Cam near, so with a sigh, she called Goose over to see if she could find some water.

Squatting down, she picked a few more roots for Cam before leaving the beach and walking through a path she hadn't explored yet. Skyler moved a branch to the side and almost screamed when she came face to face with a spider in a web. She let go of the branch and let out an "Oomph" when it hit her in the face. Goose bounded to her side and was shaking with excitement at the fun new sequence of events.

Centering herself with a few deep breaths, Skyler moved the branch again, and she held up the camera. Then, finding the correct angle and light, she took a few pictures of the beast in its home. If Skyler thought of it like that, the bug wasn't as nasty. She got some excellent shots with dew hanging off the delicate thread and the spider working on its web.

Cam was right, Skyler thought as she walked a small path. *Just a little exposure therapy and I'm seeing the little freaks in a new light. Probably best not to let her know she was right, though. She might get a big head.* Skyler smiled. If there was anyone who didn't have that problem, it was Cam.

Goose's bark pulled her out of her thoughts. She looked around to where he was but didn't see him. A little to her left, she heard a splash and more barks. Picking up the pace, she followed the sound and whooped when she saw Goose in a little river. His bobbing head was visible near a fallen tree, where its branches were spread out in the water. It looked like he was trying to grab a branch and was swimming back to shore with it. However, it was still stuck to the tree, so he wasn't getting anywhere.

"Nice find, Goose!" Skyler called.

The water looked refreshing, but she was debating the risk of taking a dip. She had a mild form of epilepsy, so there was a slight risk of getting in the water, but her itching skin and incessant need to get at least a little clean won out as she took off her shoes and wiggled out of her pants before placing the camera on the little nest of clothing she created.

The calm river was calling to her. This was the longest she'd ever gone without a shower, and now that a bath was near, she could feel the film of grime on her skin. Skyler's parched mouth watered at the sight of the cold-looking water, but she knew it should go through the purifier first. No way was she going to drink germ-infested water, even if it looked better than a burger at this point.

There didn't appear to be a wind, but on her bare skin, she could feel the slight breeze rustle through her tiny hairs. Goose had given up on the branch and was now swimming to shore, presumably to escort Skyler into the water.

Walking to the side of the riverbank, she sank her toes into the cold mud. Getting this close to the water, she couldn't hold out any longer. Skyler rushed into the river. It shocked her system and covered her body in goosebumps. After the initial jolt, it was the most refreshing thing she'd felt since the last Portland heatwave where she bought popsicles for the first time in her adult life.

Skyler scrubbed at her skin before ducking under briefly. Very briefly. Feeling cleanish for the first time since they landed, Skyler got out when she couldn't handle the cold anymore. After redressing and filling up the water bottles, she asked Goose to find Cam and get them back to camp.

Goose took his job seriously, and in no time, the trees started looking familiar, and the smell of the campfire called her home. "I come bearing water," Skyler said, holding up the bottles.

Cam turned at the sound of her voice. The smile she gave Skyler took her breath away. One of the hardest things about crashing on an island with your crush was trying not to make things weird by staring too long. Skyler allowed herself short bursts that she sometimes failed at, like right now.

"Impressive. I made dinner." Cam waved her hand in front of the steamed seaweed that held Skyler's clams. "Well, you did most of the work. I pulled the seaweed from the fire." Cam chuckled, and Skyler's stomach swooped again. That damn laugh got her every time.

Skyler had busied herself by getting a pot boiling on the fire and putting the chocolate lily roots in the water. As she was cooking, she said to Cam, "Well, that's the hardest part and the one that I would have failed miserably at. I'd be sporting a burn the size of Texas if I'd tried to grab them." She winked and grabbed the water filtration out of one of the bags before settling near the fire. "How does this work?" Skyler turned the device over, trying to get a handle on which part went where.

"Grab the almost empty bottle over there." Cam pointed to the object, and Skyler leaned over to grab it. "Careful." Cam brushed Skyler's hair out of the way as it hung precariously close to the open flame.

"Thanks," Skyler murmured, feeling off-balance from the touch. She grabbed the bottle and tried to hand everything to Cam.

"No." Cam gently pushed the objects back to her. "You need to learn how to do it. I wouldn't be doing you any favors by doing it for you." She smiled and patted the area near her. "Okay, so you see this piece with the tube? Put it in one of the bottles that has the water, but you can also put it directly in the water source. Now screw this bottom piece to the bottle you want to fill. There you go. Yup, it will click into place. Now take this lever here and start pumping."

Skyler thought she understood the mechanics of it but was having difficulty concentrating with Cam's fingers brushing against her wrist or the top of her hand. Her mind went into overdrive, wondering if the touches meant anything or if she only wanted them to mean something. She glanced to her side but didn't see any sign that Cam was thinking anything other than just friends using the contraption. Skyler had to hold in a sigh of unrequited love.

The water started getting sucked from one bottle to the next. There was a certain level of excitement at learning something new. After a few more pumps, the water was sufficiently filtered. They took turns taking long pulls from the bottle. The water was so cold that Skyler's teeth hurt.

She had never had anything so fresh. She could practically taste the history flowing from the source.

"Want to try your clams?" Cam asked, wiping her mouth.

"Sure, let me get your pot off the fire so we can eat together." Skyler grabbed a few sticks to lift the pot before carefully settling it near Cam's other side.

Cam produced a few utensils she made from wood. "See? I wasn't completely useless today." She handed Skyler a stick that looked like it could pass for a fork while she clamped usable chopsticks together.

"Nice work," Skyler said, holding the carving to the light of the fire for a better look.

"Thanks. Here, get under here. You're shivering." Cam pulled the sleeping bag open a little.

"Thank you," Skyler replied, cozying up in the bag while munching on the steamed meat of the clams. She felt warmer knowing that Cam seemed to care about her comfort. "Mmm, pretty darn good. I could go for some butter and garlic, but not bad with what we had." Every so often, she would toss meat from the clam to Goose, who usually caught it mid-air with an excited tail wag.

"Smells good." Cam lifted her nose in the air as her nostrils waved before she wrapped her lips around the stick and pulled a root with her teeth.

Skyler cleared her throat, finding it suddenly dry. "We never talked about your fears, Cam. So what keeps you up at night?" She was just trying to find a topic, anything to get her mind off Cam's lips.

Cam looked in the fire as if seeking answers in the flames. Skyler waited, knowing she would talk when she was ready. Finally, Cam spoke up. "People leaving."

Skyler blinked a few times, processing the whispered words. She had a feeling there was more, even though a thousand questions and platitudes were bursting from her gut.

"When my parents died, I used to sneak into Micah's room and sleep on the floor. I know I was older and should have handled things better, but I was terrified something would happen to him. Then…" She paused, looking at Skyler. "His best friend left."

The words were like a gut punch from a previously unknown hurt. It was a confession of a past they shared, but had never talked about.

"I liked having you around, helping chase Micah's darkness from under his eyes. I could have sworn we were going to have a Callaghan/Porter wedding in the future." They both chuckled while Skyler thought, *I wish, although wrong Porter.* "Then you left, and well, I don't really let people close because they tend to leave."

Skyler watched as Cam massaged the back of her neck. It looked like she'd opened up more than she had wanted. "I'm sorry you had to go through that, Cam." She reached over and squeezed her arm. She felt Cam shrug when their shoulders rubbed together.

"Did your book get ruined in the swim?" Cam asked.

Skyler allowed the abrupt subject change and crawled from the warmth to grab the book. It was warped but readable. "Want me to read a chapter before we lose the light?" Skyler asked with a smile.

Cam just nodded and snuggled under the covers.

Skyler started the story, noticing about halfway through the prologue that Cam's breathing had evened out. She slowed down, then stopped, putting the book aside for a moment and watching the peaceful look on her friend's face. Unable to help herself, she brushed her lips against the soft hairs of Cam's cheek and was rewarded with an unconscious smile from the sleeping form.

***

Micah was exhausted. Mentally, physically, and emotionally, he was tapped out. The hubbub of his house had died down somewhat, but there were still stragglers trying to be helpful. Every time he was close to breaking down, someone new entered the room. This wasn't bad, but he felt like a dishrag, needing to be rung out.

Lily, as always, was an anchor in the storm, and he wasn't sure how he got so lucky to have landed such an incredible human. She had navigated Micah to their bedroom, where he was currently lying on their bed trying to get a nap in, but his brain wouldn't turn off.

The coast guard had found the area of the last ping but hadn't located anything. Lily and Micah had been stuck at home base, fielding calls and coming up with a game plan with the volunteers. Micah hated feeling useless, and this was the epitome of the feeling. Somewhere near his side, his phone chirped. He chose to ignore it and curled up in a ball, wanting his older sister and best friend. He groaned when the phone started ringing again.

Looking at the display, he sat up. "Hello?" He answered right away this time, but his voice was timid.

"Oh, thank God you never changed your number."

The voice on the other end grounded him in a way that a thousand town folks hadn't, and in a way that only Lily had been able to provide thus far.

"Maggie," Micah whispered, as if the ghost from his past would evaporate.

"I know something is going on, Micah. Please, I can't get a hold of Skyler. I just—please tell me what's going on."

The voice was both salt in a wound and a salve. Micah clung to his phone like a life vest, feeling for the first time that someone else could make decisions, make calls, rally people. If anyone could, it was Skyler's mom, Maggie.

Micah started pacing the room while wiping his hands on his pants. His gut churned in guilt at not having called her.

"I'm so sorry, Maggie. It's been so busy here, and it completely slipped my mind to call you." Micah closed his eyes, feeling horrible for the oversight but wanting to be strong for her.

Micah had to hold the phone away from his ear while Maggie vented her frustration at being left out of the loop. After they both calmed down, Micah settled back on the bed and relayed what they knew so far, trying to be as objective as possible. The thing he was holding onto was hope, and he conveyed that as well as he could to Maggie.

For the longest time, Maggie had been like a mother to him, and he hadn't been prepared for the void the Callaghan crew had left when they'd moved away.

"Maggie, we'll find them," was all he could say.

"I'm coming home, Micah. Fuck! I knew it." Maggie never cursed. If Micah weren't in such a pit, he would have laughed at the absurdity of Maggie dropping the F-bomb.

There was talking on the other end, Maggie having a conversation with someone else, before coming back on and letting him know she and her sister Abby would be in the next day. They finalized the plan, and Micah promised he would be at the airport to pick them up. By the time they hung up, all Micah had taken in was that someone other than his wife, who was pregnant and needing to rest, was going to help carry the torch of hope. The town folks had helped provide resources, but nobody but family understood what they were feeling, and it was nice to know someone else was coming who would be able to share in their burden. With that, he curled onto his side. For the first time in a while, Micah slept.

Chapter Ten

Day 5

Something woke Cam from the warmth of a dream. Wondering what caused the sudden wakefulness, she stiffened when she heard Goose's deep growl. Again. Goose wasn't one for false alarms, usually greeting any potential danger with a lick to the hand or a wiggled welcome. Cam strained, trying to hear anything, and jumped when she heard the snap of a tree branch. She couldn't tell how far away it was. It was becoming hard to hear over her pounding heart. A feeling of gratefulness for Skyler washed over her because she had remembered to bring the shells of her dinner back to the beach. Hopefully it was far enough away.

Goose's growls lowered, then stopped. His head nuzzled back on her hip. The dark night around them had never felt so exposing. She patted Goose's head, rewarding him for a job exceptionally well done. Then, matching up with Skyler's rhythmic breathing, she was finally lulled back to sleep.

Cam's neck was stiff, her arm was asleep, and she was pretty sure she had dirt in places that would take several showers to get fully clean. Yet, even with all of that going on, she felt content as she transferred from sleep to waking. The night's terror was now just a memory. Still half asleep, Cam tightened her arm around the warm sleeping body next to her as she burrowed her face into the back of Skyler's neck. If she were any more awake, she would have pulled away, but her sleepy state was apparently cuddly.

She inhaled deeply, capturing the sensations of having someone she was so comfortable with being so close. The morning dew around them filled her lungs with fresh air. In her sleep, Skyler wiggled closer. A slight moan escaped Cam when Skyler pulled her hands closer and tucked them between her breasts. It felt terrific holding Skyler, and the comfort of her warm body and tight grip provided a cocoon of safety that allowed her to fall back to sleep.

A bit later, the sun now beating onto Cam's closed eyelids, there was no gradual wake-up. Cam was cold, damp, and alone. Sitting up, she saw Skyler staring into the fire.

"Morning." Cam's voice cracked with disuse. "How did you sleep?" She sat up and stretched. Her head was clearer, and her knee didn't feel as stiff. The extra time Skyler allowed for her to heal had done wonders, and they had to be close to being rescued by this point, right? She looked back at Skyler, who still hadn't answered her. "Skyler, are you okay?"

Skyler turned, her eyes red-rimmed and defeated. After five days, Skyler's sunny disposition had finally broken. Seeing the look brought pressure to Cam's chest that she tried to rub away.

"I'm fine." Skyler's voice was clear but devoid of any emotion.

"In my experience, when a woman says she is fine, the opposite is usually true." Cam tried to lighten her voice into teasing, but it only seemed to bring Skyler's shoulders up near her ears as she grabbed her legs.

"Maybe I'm the exception to the rule then," Skyler said, looking back at the fire.

Cam watched as Skyler stared into nothing. Her leg throbbed, but she wanted to crawl over and squeeze her until the haunted look disappeared from Skyler's eyes.

"Let's build this fire up, then maybe go check out that cabin you found?" Cam's voice was soft, and she warmed inside when a small smile found its way to Skyler's lips, pleased that she was able to put it there. After last night's scare, four walls and a door were looking mighty nice, plus they hadn't heard anything since the sound of the helicopter.

"Shouldn't we stay on the beach? We've got a nice setup here, and it's probably better to stay near the water, right?"

Cam looked up towards the tops of the trees, then out to the ocean. "I think it's going to get stormy soon, and it will be slow, getting me there with this bum leg. Plus, it's safer to have shelter. Something was roaming around last night. Goose's growls woke me up." She felt horrible for the strenuous hike they were about to endure because of her leg, but she tried to shake it off, knowing there wasn't much either of them could do about it.

"What? What kind of something was roaming around?" Skyler looked around wildly.

"I'm not sure, but I don't want to stick around to find out." Cam sat up fully and stretched.

They made short order of packing up the campsite, and after a small discussion, it was decided that the boat would stay on the beach. Skyler went off to pick more chocolate lily roots to bring with them to the cabin, and Cam sat on a log trying to mentally prepare for the pain the hike surely would bring.

When Skyler came back to collect her from her thinking log, Cam couldn't help but smile at the sight. Goose looked up at Skyler with such adoration that she briefly wondered how he would handle the separation when they got rescued.

She slammed the door on her thoughts of how *she* would handle it. No good could come by going down that path.

"I found you a walking stick, but Goose wanted to be the one to bring it to you." Skyler whistled, which brought him bounding down the trail. The stick was whacking against the bushes, but his eyes shined with pride as he dropped the walking stick at Cam's feet.

"Good boy." Skyler rubbed his head and bent down to pick up the stick, presenting it to Cam in both her hands with her palms up. "For you."

The previous haunted look had dissipated with the sunrise. Cam could only laugh and thank Skyler when she grabbed Cam under the arms to help her off the log. An embarrassing squeak of pain left Cam's lungs, and she felt Skyler's hands tighten around her waist before letting go once she saw Cam was steady. Skyler turned around too quickly, but Cam could have sworn she saw a wink.

Cam took two bags and slung them over her shoulders while Skyler carried the last one, along with most of Cam's weight. It was slow going and hard work. Both of their faces were covered in sweat within a few minutes. Since Skyler had to practically carry her, Cam could feel Skyler's arms shaking with each step.

The walking stick helped some since it was sturdy with a good length. Cam pointed out fresh bear scat. It was too close to their campsite to be comfortable, and she knew they were making the right decision to head to the cabin. However, seeing the scat put a hitch in their step. Ten minutes in, and they were both panting, and Goose was left wondering why there was such slow progress.

The three sticks were providing an excellent brace. Cam was glad that she could move around a little more because relying on Skyler to relieve herself had quickly become her least favorite pastime on the island.

"Is it weird that we haven't heard more airplanes or even seen any boats?" Skyler asked, breaking the monotony of the hike.

"Yes." Cam's voice was steady, but her hand shook slightly, the only outward sign that she was worried. She wasn't about to wrap Skyler in the ball of anxiety that had weaved its way through her body for five days. "By now, the wreckage could've been found. We were pretty close to where we intended to spread the ashes. I'm just not sure how long we drifted before we beached because I don't recognize any of these island clusters."

Skyler turned to face her. "I feel bad for not getting us to the island you pointed out." Her eyes skittered away. "What an inconveniently brutal time to have my first seizure in years happen at that moment." Skyler's eyes lowered to the ground.

"Hey, Skyler, look at me please, and hear me when I say it's not your fault."

"But, if I hadn't—"

"No. Don't," Cam interrupted before she could go on. "I'll repeat, it's not your fault. If anything, I owe you an apology. I've been going over the issue in the air in my mind, and I'm not sure what happened. But I'm the pilot, and I put you in danger. For that, I'll have a hard time forgiving myself. But you don't need to say sorry." Cam looked into Skyler's eyes and only looked away when she saw that Skyler was starting to believe her. "Good. Now, I think there is a cabin that has our name on it." Cam felt good when Skyler chuckled. She'd always enjoyed listening to her and Micah try and one-up each other before falling into a fit of giggles. She could hear that sound all day.

On their way down a large hill, Skyler stumbled. Cam tried to keep her upright, but she tore her hand from Cam's grip as she tried to find a more solid object to grab. Cam's fingers dug into a shrub as she wobbled off balance, then she rammed the walking stick into the ground. She held on for dear life, balancing on one leg on a slope. "Are you okay?" Cam called down, scared when she saw Skyler hadn't moved.

"Yeah, just got intimately introduced to a grabby branch." Skyler started working her way back to where Cam was perched, rubbing an area on the side of her hip. "The cabin isn't far, and this is the hardest part. It might be easier if you ease onto your butt, and I'll help you scoot down. I just had a flash of you tumbling down this hill, and it's giving me heart palpitations."

Weaving her fingers through Skyler's and trusting completely that Skyler had her, Cam gently lowered to the ground. It was a slower process down the hill but infinitely safer as they worked in tandem, scooting along the forest floor. Cam wouldn't be surprised if she would be picking pine needles out of her underwear for a month.

They finally reached the bottom of the hill and resumed walking. On the way, Skyler grabbed the pot out of one of the bags and started filling it with berries as they walked to the cabin. Well, Skyler walked, dragged, and picked, while Cam hopped and leaned on Skyler and a stick.

"Just a little further," Skyler puffed out, sweat gathering on her brow.

"You did a great job with marking the trail." Cam pointed to the ground as they passed another bundle of sticks that were peppered throughout the trail.

"It was hard keeping Goose away from them but thank you." Skyler chuckled. "Almost there."

Goose had run ahead and was waiting on the porch when they finally stumbled to the cabin. It wasn't much to look at, but with the glow of the sun peeking through the trees, all Cam could see was a beacon of hope.

***

129

For the second time, Skyler's eyes fell on the cabin. She helped maneuver Cam up the steps and opened the door with a flourish. "Welcome to our humble abode." She couldn't help but smile as Cam took in the tiny cabin.

"It must be an illegal hunting cabin," Cam said, looking around.

"Hmm, didn't think of that. I guess there aren't any forest service signs." Skyler helped maneuver Cam to the raised bunk attached to the side of one of the walls. "Let's get you off your leg."

She sat Cam down before unpacking their measly supplies. When everything had a place, Skyler grabbed the pot filled with berries, and Cam gave her a sheepish look as a blush dusted her nose before she dug into the food with a flourish. The dirt from her hands and the berries gave her pause, although Cam didn't seem to have the same hangup.

"Thank you." Cam's soft voice made Skyler turn as she was setting out the stuff from their packs.

"For what?" Skyler asked, holding a sweatshirt near her chest.

"For getting me down here, for helping out. The list goes on, Skyler." Cam handed her the pot and started working at unwrapping her leg.

Skyler looked down at her hands, cringing at the dirt tucked under her nails. She usually kept her nails below the fingertips, but now they peeked over the tops, trapping dirt, grime, and whatever else. Trying to keep her skin from crawling, she debated if she should reach in the pot or not. Finally, her stomach decided for her with a loud gurgle. She popped a few berries that held a balance of tart and sweet in her mouth as she concentrated on the texture. The burst of flavor on her tongue sent her reaching for more.

"It's not a big deal. It wasn't like I was going to leave you to the bears." Skyler turned back to the packs. She patted Goose's head on her way over to the bags. "Here, I think you should take these. It was a hard walk on your

130

knee, and you'll be in screaming pain soon if you're not already." She handed over the pain meds. "We have a few more tablets, but hopefully we'll either be rescued or after a few more day's rest, you'll be okay. I hope we didn't do further damage to your knee."

Skyler had known all of Cam's facial expressions at one point in their lives, but the look of pure gratefulness that radiated from Cam's eyes was almost powerful enough to blow Skyler backward.

Cam just swallowed and took the pills with a shaking upper lip. "Thank you."

"You should try and get some rest." Skyler brought out the sleeping bag and unrolled it onto the dirty-looking mattress. "I'm going to try and find some water and maybe start a fire. There is a pit close." Skyler helped Cam get under the sleeping bag and brushed the hair from her face. She moved over to her backpack, taking out her camera and a sweatshirt. The camera she put around her neck while she rolled up the sweatshirt to put under Cam's head for a pillow.

Cam's eyes were already closed. She jumped lightly when Skyler put the bundle under her head. Cam burrowed deeper and inhaled the sweatshirt, which brought a smile to Skyler's face. The bruise from the bump on her head was fading, and Skyler swept her fingers over the area.

Before Skyler turned to leave, she felt fingers grab her wrist to stop her retreat. "Please take Goose and the flare gun with you?" The concern beaming from Cam's eyes was too intense for Skyler, and she looked away first. "I could go for a shower," Cam mumbled, as she snuggled deeper.

Skyler nodded and smiled, and although the eye contact was no longer giving her heart palpitations, she was still finding it hard to step away from Cam's touch. She didn't have to decide since Cam's fingers slid away, leaving a path of cold longing in her heart. Skyler thought that twelve years would have been enough time to get over Cam, but her pounding heart indicated nothing of the sort.

She'd had her hands all over Cam's body today. At the time, she was working towards a goal of getting them to the cabin safely, and didn't dwell on the fact. Now, though, her memories were under the autopsy knife, dissecting every touch and conversation.

Calling Goose to her side, Skyler stepped out of the cabin for a much-needed breather. She found a small path through a few bushes, careful of the camera hanging from her neck. She made her way up the slight slope, and her thigh muscles were screaming. Skyler had done more walking in the past few days than she had in years around Portland.

Her mind turned to that morning, when she'd woken up feeling safe. Cam's arms apparently fit her frame like a perfect puzzle piece. Without thinking, she had grabbed her hand and pulled her closer. When she finally woke up enough to realize what happened, she froze, certain that Cam would be able to feel her pounding heart or flushed skin. She hadn't meant to release the moan that morning, but it was proof her feelings were right on the surface. Cam had never indicated any passion for or want of Skyler, so she was stuck with the unrequited crush on her best friend's sister. It was hurting more than the crash.

A sigh escaped her lips, making her wonder, if no one was around to hear it, did it even happen? The thought made her smile.

As she walked, her mind turned to the end of Cam's senior year, when Skyler had finally gotten the courage to tell her how she felt. Cam had opened her locker. Skyler knew the note was on top of the papers lying in the locker. Cam had gathered the papers and flung them in the trash. Someone then threw an open can of soda, soaking her note. It was an appropriate end to the way she was feeling, a soggy heart. Skyler had stared at the carnage she witnessed.

Of the multiple scenarios she had gone over in her mind, none had come close to that one.

It had come as a relief when her mom had said they were moving to Portland over the summer. Skyler was ready to run as far away from Cam as possible, away from her perfect hair and slightly acned face, from her aloof attitude and her beautiful laugh. Those feelings had washed over Skyler this morning and left her cold, needing to rebuild the brick wall where it came to Camryn Porter. Plus, to hear Cam's biggest fear was people leaving—well, that wasn't something to take lightly. It wasn't only her own heart she needed to protect.

Goose came bounding to her, and the stench hit her nose, pulling her from the past. His hair was matted, and there was a smug look on his face, just daring her to say something. She had to hold in a gag. Goose's face morphed into hurt when she sent him further up the path.

The problem with walking along the same line as the smell was that she couldn't get out of the stinky path. Skyler tried holding her breath, but that only made the hike harder. It wasn't long before she peered through a break in the bushes, gasping at the sight.

Shimmering in the sun was a waterfall falling into a cove of water. Goose's head was already floating in the water, lapping up the water and cooling off from the slight summer heat that had come upon them. Skyler had forgotten that Southeast Alaska was like a roulette of weather, never knowing which number it would land on: rain, sun, or hurricane-force winds.

She bounded to the pool, pulling the camera from her neck as she went. The light was perfect for a few candid pictures of Goose in the water. He had an expressive face, and right now, it was like he was smiling for the camera. Water dripped from his snout as he paddled through the water.

The rippling surface called to Skyler, who wanted more than anything to jump into the refreshing surface. She hadn't had a seizure since the crash, but this pool was different from the river. Putting her camera down, she squatted down to the water's edge and cupped her hands on the glistening surface. Then, sliding out of her sneakers, pants, and shirt, she jumped into the water, gasping, then almost choking as the cold hit her sensitive skin. She stayed near the edge, hoping she'd have enough time to get out if she felt a seizure develop.

Goose paddled near her, making sure she was okay. The wet dog, combined with whatever smell had permeated his fur, almost choked her again. She looked around for what she could use to help clean out the smell.

Lemons, which are a natural deodorizer, do not grow in Alaska. But looking around, she saw a bush of salmonberries. Skyler wasn't sure if they had enough citric acid to do the trick or not but was willing to give the berries a chance to neutralize some of the stench. So, grabbing the edge of the nature-made pool, Skyler hauled herself out and padded over to the bush. Goose followed, curious to see where she was going.

Crouching down, Skyler crushed and rubbed berries in Goose's fur. She longed for her yellow rubber gloves and vowed never to take cleaning products for granted again. The muscles in her arms were tiring since she kept having to turn Goose's head back around as he tried to lick off the concoction. The berries were staining his wet fur. Goose tolerated the massage, even putting his paw on her hand when she finished. Together they scampered back to the pool of water, and Skyler helped rinse off the pulp. The smell dissipated, not going away entirely, but enough to be able to handle being within a few hundred feet of Goose.

Skyler shivered when she completed the task, feeling accomplished at having found another source of water. She filled the empty water bottles and thought about cleaning their limited clothing. Maybe just rubbing it in the water would help wash the crusty clothes. She loaded her sweatshirt with more berries along with some chocolate lilies that peppered the sides of the bottom of the waterfall. Her stomach grumbled at the sight of the path leading her back home.

The dip had been refreshing in more ways than one. Skyler hoped she could leave her feelings for Cam in the water, shaking her off like Goose had when he got out of the cove.

"Honey, I'm home," Skyler joked as she eased the door open, her arms filled with the bounty of the hike.

She didn't get a response, and when she looked over, Cam was where she'd left her. The silent cabin filled with the soft snores of the sleeping form. In the dim light, she could just make out Cam's face where sleep had smoothed the worry from between her eyes. She gripped the doorframe tighter as she took in her face. So much for leaving feelings at the waterfall.

Skyler put the berries down and grabbed the pot, then went back outside to start a fire. There weren't many matches, and she cursed when it took two to start the fire after the first flame petered out and died on arrival. Finally, the kindling took, and she had a nice flame with warmth licking her chilled limbs.

The no-see-ums were out with a vengeance, and the smoke from the fire only slightly deterred the tiny bloodsucking creatures. Skyler tried to stay busy and moving, which seemed to help with the bugs. As the water for the chocolate lily roots started boiling, Skyler was startled when the cabin door opened, and Cam stood staring at her from the doorway.

"Dinner's almost ready." Skyler pointed to the bulbs boiling. "And there should be more berries." She nodded her head to the cabin.

"Why does Goose smell like death and berries?" Cam's voice carried down to the fire as she leaned against the doorframe.

"He got into something. He's a dog." Skyler rolled her eyes before going back to work on dinner.

"I'm sorry, I was a little disoriented when I woke up," Cam said, rubbing the back of her neck. "Thanks for dinner."

"Sure, it's no problem." Skyler accepted the apology with a smile. "You need to stay off your leg, though, so let's get you back in the cabin."

Cam turned her body slightly to let Skyler into the cabin, causing their arms to brush. Skyler tried to suppress a shiver but couldn't do anything about the goosebumps that had erupted along her arm.

"There. Now stay off it and I'll bring you some food."

Back outside, Skyler pulled the pot off the fire then tried to keep from getting burned as the hot pot swung in front of her.

"Goose, Goose, what am I going to do with you?"

Cam was talking to Goose when Skyler walked in with dinner. The stick utensils Cam made had varying levels of success depending on the consistency of the root. Some were mushier than others causing a few laughs as they wore more of their meal than they had the night before.

Goose didn't seem interested in the offerings, instead content to rest his head on Skyler's foot. *He must've found some dinner when rolling in death*, Skyler thought.

"Thank you for this," Cam said near the end of their meal. "Was it raining when I took a nap?"

Skyler looked towards the ceiling, trying to figure out what she meant before she felt Cam run her fingers through her still-damp hair. She was torn between leaning into the touch and jumping across the cabin for some distance.

"Oh! No, I found a waterfall. It's not far and would be easier to get to than the cabin was. Maybe I'll take you tomorrow. I got a couple of good shots of Goose. Want to see?"

Cam smiled with a nod.

Skyler hopped up to grab her camera, allowing her heart rate to return to its normal, albeit slightly erratic pace. Settling back next to Cam, she tried to keep a little distance, but Cam wiggled her way closer.

"Skyler, this is amazing. Look at the detail!" She pulled the camera closer to her eyes to get a better view. The picture showed Goose mid-leap into the water, the flying dog hovering over the surface of the water.

"Thanks." Skyler yawned. "I'm beat, going to turn in a little early."

Skyler settled in the bed, leaving enough room for Cam when she was ready to crawl into the sleeping bag. Another day down. They had to be closer to rescue by now, right?

***

Lily leaned against Micah as they waited in the crowded airport. She was dead on her feet, and her whole body felt swollen, from the tips of her toes to her hair. Yes, her hair somehow felt like it was swelling. People kept coming up to them, saying they were sorry for their loss, in reference to Cam, and the next person to do that was going to get a punch to the throat. There was nothing to be sorry about— yet—and until there was, well, people just needed to keep on walking.

The glare she gave Mrs. Adams was enough for her to change course, giving them a wide berth. She felt the deep breathing of Micah along her back and wondered how anyone could fall asleep standing up. It was a true gift. Lily felt her eyes slowly close.

People started walking through the gate, and the hubbub gently pulled Lily back to alertness. She stood straighter, patting Micah's stomach. "Come on, sweetie, people are coming off the plane now."

Micah blinked in confusion before he reached up, taking off his glasses and rubbing his face. "Oh, shit. They are right there. Must have gotten first class. Fancy." Micah hurried to put his glasses back on, but they hung crooked on his face and almost fell off when he bent down to kiss Lily on the cheek.

"Micah, it's so good to see you again. Look at what a fine man you've grown up to be." Maggie pulled him into a hug, but Lily was blinking between the two women.

She knew Maggie was bringing her twin sister but hadn't realized they were identical twins. She couldn't tell them apart, except they seemed to have vastly different wardrobe styles. Holding her hand to the twin, she said, "Hi, I'm Lily, Micah's wife. I hate that we are meeting under these circumstances, but it is nice to meet you all the same." The grip was firm and warm, but Lily's eyes widened when she felt a slight tug, then strong arms wrapped around her shoulders in a comforting hug. It was dizzying how completely at ease she was with these virtual strangers.

"Lily, I'm Abby, Maggie's better half." She gave a crooked smile when they parted.

"Abs, you can't say that. It implies we're married, and that's just wrong." Maggie had pulled away from Micah, and the two switched greetings. "Lily, I'm glad to meet you officially. Skyler has only amazing things to say about you."

Lily blushed, feeling a slight tinge of embarrassment. When she had first learned of Skyler and Micah's relationship, she hadn't been aware of a hot lava of jealousy that flowed through her blood. One night, Lily was surprised to find Micah talking to his mysterious friend in Portland at one in the morning. Clearing things up later, she learned Micah had confessed his love for Lily and asked his best friend for some advice. Once Lily cooled down, she saw the positive effect Skyler had on Micah. Of course, it didn't hurt that Skyler wasn't ever interested in him, and from the moment the air was cleared, Skyler had been a big part of their lives, and Lily felt lucky for it.

"Do you have any bags?" Lily asked as she pulled herself from the past. Each person discreetly wiped their eyes.

"No, we barely had time to lodge the cats before rushing to the airport. I might have six pairs of pants and no underwear for all I know," Abby said, holding up her carry-on.

They shared a laugh. It felt good to have people who knew what they were all going through, kindred souls bound together in the emergency. Lily felt a sense of peace settle along her shoulders, knowing she and Micah wouldn't have to carry the burden of hope alone.

Chapter Eleven

Day 6

Cam was nude, stretched out in the pool under the waterfall. Even though she hadn't been sweating and working as hard as Skyler, that didn't mean after six days she didn't feel gross and in need of a good scrub. The waterfall was refreshing, and sleeping indoors had helped her knee heal some.

Looking down at her skin, she gasped at the large bruises that crossed along her chest from the harness, a painted reminder of the unfortunate events with the plane. For the umpteenth time, she thought back to the landing, finally concluding there wasn't much else she could have done. They were alive, had a water source and a limited food selection, though the food itself was in abundance. They sure weren't going to get scurvy anytime soon, but what she wouldn't do for a nice portobello burger. Her mouth filled with saliva just thinking of the hearty food. "Mmm, onions," she mumbled as she let the waterfall cascade over her head.

There was something cleansing about bathing in a pool that held a waterfall. The water wasn't stagnant, the falls kept most bugs away, and there was a panoramic view of breathtaking mountains. The weather today was slightly warmer and Cam soon found herself floating towards the middle of the pool and smiled at the serene feeling. If they were going to land in the ocean and get blown to this island, well, it wasn't the worst place to be stuck or with the worst company.

Her mind turned to Skyler. Cam felt herself getting closer to her, and the thought made her heart skip, although not in a bad way. It was more like it was unchartered territory, and her heart didn't know how to act, torn between wanting to give her flowers and running away to protect herself from future pain. But where could she run to on an island? And was that really what she wanted? No, if she was frank, what she wanted was to run into Skyler's arms and never let go. To protect and be protected. She slammed the door on her heart. "She doesn't even live here, doofus. Don't, just don't," she murmured to the empty area around her.

She opened her eyes, and any thoughts about Skyler tumbled into the pool when her eyes landed on three deer grazing not six feet from where she was. One of them looked at her with its ears tilted forward before crossing her off as non-threatening and continued eating.

Goose's bark pulled a groan as Cam saw him shoot from behind and bound towards the lovely creatures. "Goose, no, stop!" Skyler shouted from behind her.

Cam turned around before sinking further into the area, trying to cover as much as possible with the water.

"Sorry about that. Did you see those deer? I'm so glad I had my camera." Skyler's face lit up the dusk air around them. "Crap, I'm sorry." Skyler's ponytail whipped across her face as she quickly turned.

"It's okay. I was just finishing up." Cam debated the best course of action. Her knee had enjoyed the buoyancy of the water, but it was still a little sore. She could probably handle the change, but it would go a lot faster with Skyler.

"Actually, could you help me?" Cam asked, swimming to the edge.

"Umm, are you sure? Umm, what do you need?" She backed up a step and started looking around but kept her eyes away from the water. "Need your clothes?" She pointed to the pile, and Cam could see the profile of her face trying to work out a few emotions, although she wouldn't even guess what they were.

"Yeah, if you could hand me that pile, then maybe hold my arms or hip while I try and get them wrangled on." Cam gulped. She hadn't thought through this request, and the thought of Skyler's fingers playing along her hip was making her feel like there was a plane doing loops in her stomach.

"Sure, yes, I think that will be acceptable. I mean, no problem." Skyler bent down to pick up a piece of clothing and yelped when she saw it was Cam's underwear.

Cam had gotten out of the water and was now leaning on one leg, waiting for Skyler to hand over the first piece of clothes. She chuckled, watching Skyler struggle with the cloth. "Sorry, you're going to have to touch my underwear."

Skyler's eyes were wide, and Cam could have sworn she heard a squeak come out of Skyler. With shaking hands, Skyler turned with the bundle. She handed the pile to Cam, who took the top piece off and held the corners of the underwear open with her thumbs. "Thank you. Okay, I'm going to lean on you and bend my good leg to get the bad leg in first. Then I'll need you to steady me while I work on getting the other leg in, alright?" Cam's perfect game plan was quickly ruined when she got the shock of her life as Goose's nose nuzzled near her groin.

Between a half yell, half-laugh, she started falling over, taking Skyler with her. Cam could feel Skyler's shoulder shake up and down in barely controlled giggles. This set off

Cam as they lay tangled in limbs with Goose putting his nose in places that he shouldn't be exploring.

"Goose, go sniff some bushes or something," Cam said through laughter as they helped each other up off the ground.

Skyler bent at the waist and started howling while clenching her side. "You. Did. Not. Just. Say. That," she managed to wheeze out through each breath.

Cam thought back to what she said and put her hands up to her face. "There is no coming back from that. Skyler, hand me my pants." Cam's face and side were aching in extended use of muscles she usually didn't use.

Skyler gasped when she saw the bruises marking her body. "Shit, Cam, these look bad!" Her hand went out to reach for her bare skin, but halfway there it seemed she changed course and instead put her hand on her shoulder to help steady her.

"I'm sure you have similar ones. Have you not checked out your bumps and bruises yet?" Cam managed to get her pants on without further incident and moved on to her shirt. Skyler had stepped back now that most of the danger had passed.

"Haven't looked yet. It hurts to move my neck down, so I haven't seen this." Skyler motioned to her whole body.

"Well, we can check your pains when we get back to the cabin." They fell into step, arm in arm, on the way back to the cabin and a companionable silence fell around them.

Later, they had eaten and checked on any aches and pains back in the room. Skyler had matching bruises along her chest from the seat harness, along with some scrapes and scratches from when she fell into some devil's club exploring with Goose earlier that day. There was a large scratch along her back that Cam wanted to keep an eye on and maybe get some ointment placed on the angry line.

"Can I ask you a question?" Skyler asked. They were sitting around the campfire they had going in the front yard as dusk turned to dark around them.

"Sure," Cam said, leaning back on the stump she was sitting on, stretching out her toes. Her socks from the dip were drying off near the fire.

Skyler didn't answer right away.

"Skyler, you can ask me anything. What's up?" Cam didn't have Skyler's ability to wait a person out. She wanted to help, but to do that, she needed to know the problem.

"Do you remember the year you graduated, the last day?" Skyler was looking at the twinkling stars above their heads. She always looked for the Big Dipper, then Orion's Belt. Cam wasn't sure why or how she knew that, but something about those stars called to Skyler.

"Yes, I remember that day. Pretty vividly, in fact." Cam was looking into the fire, thoughts of the past dancing in the light.

"Why didn't you say anything about the note? I mean, I knew it was a long shot." Skyler stopped talking for a second, and Cam froze, knowing they were on the precipice of something. Her brows furrowed in memory. "But to just throw it away and pretend it didn't happen. Well... It hurt, I guess." Skyler briefly looked at her, their eyes meeting over the fire.

"What note?" Cam asked in a whisper. "I had gotten a few rejection letters from colleges that I opened up in school, and they were on top of my books. I just grabbed the whole pile and tossed it." Cam could clearly remember that day because it was the last time she saw Skyler before she moved to Portland over the summer.

"You didn't see my note?" A tiny dimple formed when Skyler smiled. "Wait, you're telling me you didn't see my note!" Skyler shot up from her stump and started pacing.

"No, but I'm dying to know what was in it now." Cam's mind went wild with possibilities.

Skyler stilled her pacing and turned, shrugging once. "Well, that makes me feel a lot better." She chuckled.

"Skyler, you've got to tell me. What did the note say?"

"It's nothing. Just—" Skyler started picking at a thread on the bottom of her hoodie. "It was just a little note explaining my feelings. That I—" Skyler started coughing and Goose ran over to check on her. "Was crushing hard on you." She said the last part in a blur of one long word, and it took a second to pick out what had been said.

"Wait. You're telling me that you left a note in my locker letting me know of a crush in high school, and you saw me throw away a bunch of papers, probably thinking I had just rejected you. Is that right?"

"Yes." Skyler nodded once. "That sums up the situation succinctly. I didn't know we were moving to Portland yet, but to be honest, my young, bruised heart was excited about the move when my mom told me."

Cam needed a minute as her mind blew. Skyler Callaghan had a crush on her? Oh dear, that was a lot to process. Cam hadn't come to terms with her sexuality until much later, but things could have clicked into place a lot sooner if she had seen that note. Damn colleges ruining everything. Her mind shook its fist at the universe.

As always, Skyler gave time for Cam to process. "Well, that's new news to me. I wish I'd seen it." Then, finally, Cam confessed to the flames. "Might have changed the outcome of a few things." Cam looked back at the vast darkness and sighed, thinking of what could have been.

***

Skyler stared at Cam, wishing for her to elaborate but also knowing it wouldn't have changed the situation. If anything, it would have made going to Portland harder.

145

Instead, she found herself smiling into the night, and for the first time, a weight seemed to have lifted. Her teenage heart needed to hear that Cam had never seen the note and hadn't rejected her.

"How do you like Portland?" Cam's question broke their internal musings.

"It's a cool place. Lots of things to do outside, I mean, you know how that is." Skyler smiled, looking back up at the stars. "But what I like most is getting to know Aunt Abby and having a close relationship with my mom."

"Oh yeah, Abby. Nana Winnie told me a little bit about her. What's she like?" Cam asked while she whittled on a branch, little wood shavings littered the area around her.

Skyler chuckled. "She's a little indescribable unless you meet her. You know my mom. I mean, they look alike, but that's about it. She made a lot of money in the stock market. Like, she is a wiz at investing, it's nuts when she's in the zone, but her getting to the zone can be like raking leaves in a windstorm. When she finally focuses, she barely stops to eat. Other than that, she terrorizes her cat and rearranges everything all the time. Like once, mom walked in, and the house was color-coded, so no matter the item, anything red went in the kitchen, green in the living room, and white items went into the bathroom. Her cat didn't like that because she kept trying to keep her cat corralled in the bathroom."

Cam's laugh filled the night air. "She sounds like a character. I would love to meet her."

"Maybe someday." Skyler had a soft smile, thinking of what would happen once they got rescued.

"How did she and your mom find each other? They were separated at birth, right?" Cam put the stick away and leaned in to hear the story.

"Oh, it's crazy. So, Nana Winnie's best friend Janice was flying to Portland for some conference, and the person sitting next to her on the plane found out she was from

Sitka, and the person got excited, saying that her sister's family was from there. Well, it turned out the passenger was Abby's adopted sister, and they'd just found out about Maggie. Well, let me tell you the shock on Janice's face when all the pieces came about. As soon as they landed, you can bet your butt that Janice was calling Nana Winnie. Janice and the passenger exchanged numbers, and the rest is history. Mom went up to Portland to meet Abby in a bar. This guy who had been bugging Abby for months came up to Maggie and slapped her on the butt. Mom slammed his head into the bar counter, and that's how they found out they were identical. Abby thought she was having an out-of-body experience watching her."

"Wow, that's a miracle. I can't believe they didn't know, and then how they found out. Just think if one of those things didn't line up perfectly, they might never have met." Cam's voice was filled with awe.

"Life is like that, though, right? Just a series of missed chances and overlapping connections that you don't know about until the picture is filled out."

"Yeah, I suppose there is truth to that." Skyler could see Cam nodding in the firelight.

"So, any SO's back home?" Cam asked as she put more wood on the fire.

"SO's?" Skyler questioned with a head tilt.

"Significant other. I'm not positive how you identify now. I'm assuming it's on the queer spectrum, though." Cam grabbed the back of her neck in a clear sign of discomfort.

"Oh! SO. Ha, I wonder why I've never heard of that one. I like it, though. No one right now. I had a girlfriend a few years ago, but it turned out to be more of a hassle than it was worth. Plus, I work a lot trying to get my photography business off the ground. Umm, how about you?"

"There was a summer fling," Cam stated, but didn't elaborate.

147

"Oh? Want to tell me about it?" Skyler asked, plucking a berry from the pot they had near, needing to do something with her hands.

"She was pretty aggressive in her pursuit, but I knew she was only here for the summer. Her dad hired me to take him and his buddy flying around, then they would dissolve into a vat of alcohol at the P-Bar. She was stuck as the designated driver, and I took her to a few places, showing her the sights while she waited on the call to pick them up. By the third night, I couldn't stop the increasingly suggestive remarks and leaned into what was happening. It was my first time with someone, and I didn't find it particularly, umm, life-changing."

Skyler wanted to strangle the person who had made Cam uncomfortable as thoughts of her own clumsy first time filtered through her memory. "So that's it? One summer fling?" Skyler asked when Cam didn't continue.

"There was one other woman, but she studied at the university and left about a year later. She couldn't handle the small-town island life. So…I learned my lesson of not getting attached after that."

Skyler could hear the pain in Cam's voice and wanted to wrap her up in warmth and love and never let go. She cleared her throat. "It sounds like you cared for her."

"Later, I tried to connect with someone. You know there is a small but mighty queer force in Sitka, but most people just wanted to hook up, and I can't if I don't feel anything for them. So, I have given up even trying. There is probably something broken in me." It was too dark to see Cam's facial features at this point, but Skyler's heart went out to her.

"Don't say that," Skyler said fiercely. "There is nothing broken about you, Cam. You're the strongest person I know. You've been through so much, and look at what you've accomplished. You're caring, kind, and one of the most beautiful people, inside and out." Skyler was breathing heavily. When she was passionate about something, she tended to forget to breathe until she said her piece.

"Well..." Cam's voice was thick with emotion. "Thank you."

"Don't forget it, and we won't have a problem." Skyler teased out a chuckle from Cam. "Have you ever thought you might be demisexual?"

"I'm still barely at terms with being a lesbian, but honestly have never heard of the term. What is it?" Cam's voice was soft as they talked over the fire.

"I'm not an expert on it, but I think it has to do with not finding someone sexually attractive until there is a deeper level of feelings established."

Skyler could tell Cam's hamster wheel was turning in her mind, going over what she had said and probably applying different situations to the information. Eventually, Cam whispered, "Huh, well, that might explain some things."

Goose's head was resting on Skyler's leg before he looked up and out towards the forest. A low growl started in his body. Skyler whipped around and strained to see what was out in the darkened woods.

"And that's probably our cue to head into the cabin, huh." Cam stood with some finagling before wiping her hands on her pants.

Cam waited while Skyler picked up some things and added more branches that would cause a lot of smoke. They hadn't given up hope that a plane or boat might be near and see the signal. Looking down, she noticed their hands were entwined and wondered when that happened. Cam was getting around better, and somehow, they had graduated from full-body support to a light handhold. Skyler's teeth were the only thing visible in the darkness, and they were grinning fully.

***

Micah was driving the boat while trying to keep his eyes open. He knew they were going to have to anchor off soon, but there were endless corners. He kept convincing himself that just around *this* corner would be the magic spot where he would see Cam's jumping body waving at them from the beach. Just around *this* corner, he would be able to put a smile on Maggie's face, knowing they had rescued her daughter and his best friend. But each corner became a taunt, another dream broken.

Earlier today, after spotting the sunken aircraft from the sky, the search and rescue diving team dove to see what they could find. While it had brought a moment of elation when they said there weren't any bodies in the plane, things quickly crashed to reality when there was also no sign of them on the surrounding islands. The team was concentrating on Davison Bay, circling each island for any sign of life. Anything.

He stiffened when a hand was placed on his shoulder. Lily usually wrapped her whole arm around his hip, so without looking, he knew it was either Abby or Maggie.

"You look dead on your feet, Micah. We're not going to be any use to anyone if we run into a rock or you fall asleep at the wheel. Let's get to shore and set up camp for now." Maggie's voice was calm and low. After almost a full day getting to know both sisters, he knew Abby was more likely to hit him over the head to get him to sleep. She was a hoot to talk to, but subtle wasn't in her knowledge base.

He found himself lulled into almost following the instructions before shaking his head. "No, you can sleep, but I can go a little longer."

"Micah Sandwich Porter, you listen here." A new voice floated to him.

"Sandwich? That's not my middle name." Micah looked in Abby's direction, then flicked his eyes to Lily, who was slumped over a cooler, her chin resting on her sternum in sleep.

"I don't give a rat's ass what your middle name is, boy. You've got a wife to think about and a baby. Now we want to find them as much as you, but what good will we be if you sink this boat? What good will it be if we're fish food, huh? Now get us to an island because there is a hotdog with my name on it. We'll set up the tents but head out first thing in the morning. Got it?"

This time Micah didn't argue and turned the boat to a strip of land that looked okay to set up camp.

Chapter Twelve

Day 7

"Hey Skyler, did you get any pictures of the deer yesterday?" Cam asked after a lull.

They were both in their minds, processing the previous night's conversation, but Cam was going crazy in the silence of the cabin. The hike to the waterfall had twinged her knee again, and Skyler was making her rest. However, it was hard. The teasing taste of freedom was causing the extra caution to taste a little bitter, and she needed a distraction. Never one for sitting, the recovery was starting to grate on her nerves. She went to stand just to stretch her legs a little.

"Camryn Porter, you're still recovering. You've got a huge limp, and sweat is pouring from your forehead. Now sit down and rest." Skyler grabbed the camera and sat down next to Cam. "Here are some pictures. I've been working on taking photos of bugs like you suggested. It's helped a little." Cam could feel the shrug.

She looked at the pictures, seeing they all had great light and fantastic clarity. The way the photos picked up the movement of the subjects almost seemed like they were about to burst from the screen. Skyler captured the moments perfectly. Scrolling through the photos, she stopped on one from yesterday. It was her—well, her back—silhouetted against the waterfall, snow capped mountains flowing in the background. It would have been gorgeous if it wasn't such a violation.

"What is this, Skyler? What would make you think it's okay to take a picture of me naked? What's wrong with you?"

The words left her mouth, and it was almost like watching them journey in slow-motion. She wanted to reach out and swallow them back up, but instead, she watched them hit Skyler in the face, leaving her red from the verbal attack. She closed her eyes and wished for the last three seconds not to have occurred. She knew Skyler wouldn't have intentionally violated her trust. Her reaction was a combo of being cooped up and having a surge of vulnerability. Opening her eyes with an apology on her tongue, all she saw was Skyler's back already walking through the door.

Looking down at Goose, she patted his head. "Well, buddy, this is a class on how not to handle things properly. Are you taking notes?" Goose just looked up at her and licked his lips, which broke a smile on Cam's face for the first time that morning.

They had been at each other's throats all morning, probably a combination of cabin fever, anxiety, and a building of tension between them that Cam wasn't sure she was ready to act on or explore. Cam was also choked with guilt. It was her fault they were there, and she was stuck with her leg.

She got up, despite her leg, and paced the length of the cabin, berating herself endlessly. Her outburst wasn't directed at Skyler, specifically. Even the picture, if she thought about it for more than thirty seconds, was a complete overreaction. It was tasteful with a silhouette of her body in the waterfall with the deer grazing near. There

153

was no indication that the woman was her or that she was naked.

After all that Skyler had done, she was invaluable and seemed to be placed in Cam's path to show what it was like to rely on someone, to feel comfortable with someone, and let someone behind her walls. There was an ease to their relationship. Skyler was placing little touches on her arm or brushing Cam's hair from her neck. It felt natural to let Skyler in, but the guilt, and the fact that Skyler was stuck on the island without a choice, was eating at Cam and probably why she had pushed Skyler away today.

"What am I going to do, Goose?" She sat on the bench with her elbows on the table, cradling her chin in the cup of her hands. The only answer was a slight woof from Goose as he put his head on her lap.

***

Skyler had held back from slamming the door, but just barely. The tears were about to fall, and she didn't want to show Cam that type of weakness. It wasn't even the worst thing Cam could have said, but it hurt that she thought Skyler would do something like that. The picture was beautiful, but she had focused on the deer, not realizing Cam was in the shot. It seemed more than anything that they just needed a breather before one of them said something truly horrid.

Skyler had started walking down the path towards the waterfall before veering left, not having a destination in mind. Skyler wandered aimlessly, taking a few pictures of different trees, a bug she found on a leaf, and a squirrel that seemed to be following her.

Getting lost in her pictures was something Skyler had done before. However, it was always on paths she knew. Thoughts of their argument simmered in the background, not important enough to go over since she was chalking it up to cabin fever.

The first drop made her look up and blink. More followed, and a few raindrops pooled into her closed eyes before she craned her neck in every direction. Skyler's heart stuttered when she didn't see anything recognizable. The rain started coming down harder, and she stumbled along the wet ground, slipping a few times and grabbing a tree to catch her breath.

There was a little meadow that had forget-me-nots peppered throughout the ground. Skyler would have enjoyed the tiny blue flowers more if she had known where the field was in relation to the cabin. Skyler wracked her brain to see if she remembered the meadow on her way through but came up short.

The rain had soaked through her shirt, and instead of going further, she found an overturned tree to nuzzle up against for a second. She tried not to think of the bugs that must be crawling in the dirt. Pulling her legs to her chest and tucking her chin to the top of her legs, she waited.

"Wish Goose was here," she mumbled as the thick rain droplets fell around her.

***

Cam looked at the wooden walls, the dirty wooden floor, the bed she'd shared with Skyler the past few nights, trying to find meaning in the place around her. Without a clock of any sort, it was hard to know exactly how much time had passed, but the bright clouds that were hiding the sun showed it had been a few hours at least. A click of raindrops along the roof woke Cam from her melancholy.

"Let's get food ready. A peace offering is the best we can do right now. Right, boy? Next lesson, when you are the one to mess up, be sure to be the one to fix it." She looked down at Goose, who had tilted his head and looked directly at her.

The drag of her busted leg along with the click of the walking stick echoed in the cabin as Cam walked to the front door. She shivered when she opened it, not realizing the weather had turned and was now more of a downpour. Looking around the camp, she didn't see any sign of Skyler, and the first pang of worry hit her gut.

The fire they had kept stocked for almost a day now was out with a sizzle. Only a taunting wisp of smoke indicated anything had been burning there. Goose sniffed different areas of the ground, not finding anything of interest, and returned to her side as if waiting for the command to go in search of their friend. Goose's wise eyes searched hers, wondering when she would get her butt in gear. A whine started in his belly, and Cam's worry churned into fear for Skyler's safety. Skyler, who probably stomped in the woods, trying to cool off. Skyler, who hadn't taken Goose. Skyler.

"Come on, boy," Cam called, grabbing her stick and an extra sweatshirt that she tucked under her arm. The answering bark was all she heard before he tore down the path to the right, towards the waterfall.

Cam was soaked by the time she got to the waterfall. The rain was coming down in fat drops, and besides the fresh scent of pine the woods were giving out, there were no other redeeming qualities of the shower. Thoughts traversed back to Skyler, and Cam willed Goose to find her. Darkness descended upon them, and Cam didn't know when the tears had started streaking down her face. Her voice was raw from screaming Skyler's name, and visions of Skyler's body, half-eaten by a bear, or with a broken neck at the bottom of a ravine, started flooding her brain, almost causing a misstep which twinged her leg again. She sank to the ground, shaking as air became increasingly harder to come by.

Goose's nose stuck near her face, but even that wasn't enough to pull her out. What finally got her moving again was the thought of Skyler needing her, lost and alone. That thought, above all else, got Cam moving again down the path.

***

The cold was starting to seep in. When Skyler was walking, she hadn't noticed the temperature as much, but now that she had stopped, it was all she could focus on. There was relative protection from the overturned tree providing shelter on at least three sides, but her shirt was soaked, and the tree didn't give back any warmth. Skyler was fighting between getting up and moving again with the potential of getting further lost or staying in the relative protection of the tree while slowly leaching any warmth she had available. Decisions decisions.

She lifted her head and tilted her ears towards a sound and waited. No, it hadn't been her imagination. She heard the bark of Goose before she saw his bounding body run up to her. She unfurled her body and flung her arms around the wet neck of her companion.

Not sure how long she held him, her ears pricked up again when she heard the yell of her name. She and Goose looked at each other, then back toward the source. Nervousness prickled her skin at the panic she heard echoing along the forest walls.

"Goose! Skyler! Goose, where are you?" The yell was getting further away, and Skyler scrambled up and started running towards the sound.

Goose shot past her, and she lost his wiggling butt in the trees. Skyler continued walking to where she had last seen Goose disappear before she saw his tongue sticking out of his mouth and wagging tail when he caught sight of her again.

Laying eyes on Skyler, Goose turned around and disappeared one last time before returning with the one person who sped up Skyler's heart. She felt her face stretch in a grin at seeing Cam's worried face clear when their eyes met. Skyler didn't mind being soaked, lost, and cold in the woods. When she looked at Cam's face, she felt at home and safe.

Goose barked once before running full tilt at her. She vaguely felt a tingle in her arms but thought that was because of the cold. She barely had enough time to process anything when her whole body went rigid as a seizure took hold of her, then it all went blank.

***

Cam's elation turned to panic when she saw Skyler drop. Goose was already at Skyler's side, wiggling under her body to protect her head, and she sent up a promise to Nana that Goose would get the biggest steak of his life when they were rescued.

The bum leg was making walking terrible but seeing Skyler on the ground tensed up in a seizure made her hustle a little faster than she usually would have. It felt like the distance was teasing her, seemingly just out of reach. Finally, when she got to her destination, she had to battle gravity to try and get to the ground without bending her leg.

Cam could hear Goose's vibrating whines through the rain, and it looked like he was looking at her for direction, urging her to act. She pulled out the sweatshirt she carried and gently placed it under Skyler's head while Goose moved from under her before sitting next to them, watching. Cam gently turned Skyler to her side, sending a silent 'thanks' to the first aid class she took in high school. Her stomach heaved when she saw a sharp stump near Skyler's neck and shuddered to think what would have happened if she had slumped a few inches to the left when the seizure occurred.

Cam's pulse was pounding as she held her hand in front of the stump in case Skyler hit it as she helplessly watched Skyler's seizure. There was something distressing about witnessing the violent spasms wracking Skyler's body, and a sob burst out of Cam from the depth of her belly. Her heart broke, knowing there wasn't anything more she could do.

The spasms were starting to recede a little, and Cam gently stroked Skyler's hand, letting her know she was near. Skyler's curled fingers felt stiff in hers, but she was finally able to breathe a sigh of relief when the spasms slowed and then stopped. Goose came closer before settling near her shoulder with a paw resting on her side. Every once in a while, he would lean in and lick her face.

"Good boy, Goose," Cam said, squeezing Skyler's fingers, glad to feel a slight warmth return to them. She rubbed her palm up and down Skyler's arm, noticing the dew that had collected there.

They stayed as they were for a while, Cam alternating rubbing Skyler's arm and Goose licking her face. Skyler's body had slumped against the ground, and if Cam's memory was accurate, she should just be here for Skyler and let her wake up in her own time.

Fluttering eyelids were the first change, and Cam gripped Skyler's hand tighter. Seeing eyelid movements was needed to release the grip that had taken on Cam's heart. The next thing was an acknowledgement squeeze from Skyler's fingers, and Cam almost gasped in relief.

Cam noticed Skyler's eyes were clouded in confusion, but there was a hidden depth that she'd never noticed before. The emotions radiating from Skyler's eyes almost took her breath away. The rain was still falling, and the ground was quickly turning to mud. Being able to relax into other senses, now that she wasn't focused on Skyler one hundred percent, she noticed the earth starting to cake her pants and the sour smell of skunk cabbage floating around them.

"Hi." Skyler's wobbly voice was music to Cam's ears, the sound sharpening her focus back to her grey-green eyes. They looked slightly unfocused and were staring at something over Cam's shoulder. "You found me." Skyler's eyes then turned on her, and if Cam weren't already sitting down, she would have been blown over by the force of the look.

"I'll always find you," Cam said, holding her hand gently before bringing it to her lips.

One side of Skyler's lip curled up but quickly rearranged back to neutral, and Cam wondered how long she had been hiding little quirks like that. Now that she was looking, it was all she could see. A magnifying glass on their relationship. Who knew the in-depth talk the night before and then a stupid fight would cause such self-reflection that she'd notice each micro-movement?

Skyler's fingers gripped into Goose's fur to steady herself. Cam's arm slid around her waist to help her sit up, and they sat there huddled in a group. Cam gave Skyler a moment to acclimate to the new surroundings. Skyler was unsteady on her feet, but with Goose and Cam, the teamwork allowed for Skyler to inch up first, then she helped Cam.

Cam tried to keep all the weight off Skyler, knowing how weak and exhausted she must have felt, and vowed to make the trip back to the cabin as painless as possible. Unfortunately, this meant taking a lot of weight on her bad leg. A few steps in, Cam wasn't sure if it was tears falling or rain.

"Do you know where the cabin is?" Skyler asked, breaking the concentration of pain Cam was feeling.

"We weren't walking that long, probably another fifteen minutes." Cam's answer was through clenched teeth. The pain was nearly unbearable, but Skyler's arm around her waist was a nice distraction.

Goose's head popped back on the trail, his tail wagging before he turned and trotted back towards the cabin.

"I like Goose. He's well trained," Skyler said, and Cam suspected it was to try and provide a respite from their huffing breaths and painful steps.

"Nana Winnie gave him to me." Cam spoke in a near whisper. "She said, 'one day you will look around, and this puppy will have saved you in more ways than one.' I think she was right," Cam finished, unable to look at Skyler.

"She was something special, wasn't she?" Cam could feel Skyler turn slightly to smile at her, and she wasn't about to miss it.

"I wish I'd grabbed the eagle," Cam confessed, smiling sadly at Skyler before continuing down the path. "Don't get me wrong, I'm glad I grabbed the bag that had the radio for whatever that has done us so far, but I didn't even think of the eagle." Cam limped a few paces before continuing. "It was the last thing she carved and gave to me." She shook her head, trying to rid herself of the flood of emotions.

"I still have a bear she carved me. I can see how that would be a hard one to lose."

The stillness overtook them as the cabin came into view. Cam held in a sigh of relief even as a pang of longing stabbed at her chest when she slipped Skyler into the bed.

"Rest now," Cam whispered as she brushed Skyler's hair away from her face along with stating a silent vow to ensure Skyler was taken care of. Skyler had done her part, and now it was Cam's turn to step up and provide. Even if it was just to see a small smile on Skyler's face—that could be her little secret.

***

Lily was laughing at something Abby was saying, and Micah looked on with a soft expression. It was nice to see the light radiating from his wife since it had been another day of disappointment, and their spirits were starting to get low. They had worked their way through the islands in Davison Bay. There were helicopters, floatplanes, and boats in the area, all full of volunteers to help in the search and rescue, but they had all come up with nothing.

The crackle of the radio startled him out of his thoughts. "Come in, Micah, this is Hank, over."

Micah grabbed his radio. "Roger that, Hank, this is Micah, over."

"Turn to channel 78, over," the pilot said through the radio.

"Roger that, over," Micah said before switching to the indicated channel.

"Can we meet on Kinky in an hour? Over," Hank said as soon as Micah switched to the indicated channel.

Micah looked around, seeing they were near the island. "Affirmative, Hank. We are near, so whenever you're ready. We'll be on the Southwest side of the island, does that work for you? Over."

"Roger. See you then. Over and out."

The distinctive static lessened as Micah started making his way to the indicated island.

"Do you think they found something?" Maggie's voice made him grip the wheel tighter in surprise.

"Maggie, you scared the piss out of me," Micah said with a chuckle.

"It's a mom trait. I'm sure Lily will pick it right up—if she hasn't already." Maggie flicked her head to where her twin and Lily were talking dramatically with their hands.

Micah laughed harder as he remembered all the times Lily had scared him with her silent walk. He swore she had taken years off his life in fright and idly wondered if that was the real reason women outlasted men, besides being far more level headed.

"What do you think they want?" Maggie asked, motioning to the radio.

Micah was trying not to think about what they had to say. It could be nothing good, especially if they were calling on Hank to deliver any messages. Everyone knew he was the kindest, gentlest soul.

"I'm not sure, but I think we have to prepare for not liking the answer." Micah looked at the floor of his boat. He was doing his damnedest to stay positive, but every moment was pulling his heart deeper into the sea.

"That's what I thought." Maggie's strained voice cracked.

"We're not giving up. Even if the rescue team is pulled, we're not giving up." Micah's eyes were bright with unshed tears, and he saw Maggie's pained but determined smile and nod before she ducked out of the cabin.

Chapter Thirteen

Day 8

Cam was lying in the cabin with Skyler curled up next to her. She was playing with her hair and reflecting on the previous day. Never had she had such high emotions running through her veins. It was as if she'd been zapped. The sun filtered through the crack between the doorframe while Goose's nails scraped along the wooden floor as he chased rabbits in his dreams. This was the closest to content Cam had come in a long time.

Skyler snuggled closer before blinking, stretching, then rubbing her nose in the crook of Cam's neck, causing Cam to shiver as her breath caressed the tiny hairs. Cam felt her temperature rise and her heartbeat pick up as she pulled Skyler against her body. A protective surge flowed through her, especially seeing how wiped out Skyler was yesterday after all that had happened.

Once Skyler had recovered a little from her seizure, they had talked. Cam apologized profusely while Skyler explained she wasn't mad, just needed some time alone, but got turned around. The stress of being lost, not having any more meds, and the weather caused a perfect storm of emotions which most likely brought on the seizure. Cam would have given anything to have prevented it.

"Hi." Skyler's muffled voice came from her shoulder.

"Hey, did you sleep okay? Is there anything I can do?" Cam asked while putting pressure on Skyler's lower back. She didn't usually like people touching or hugging her, but she was having a hard time coming up with a reason to protest the closeness.

Skyler shivered under the blankets. "I miss greasy burgers. If you can conjure one up and have it delivered with fries and a Sprite, that would be fantastic." She looked up and winked.

Chuckling, Cam responded, "I miss coffee. I thought my headache was due to the hard landing a few days after, but it might have been caffeine withdrawal."

Cam could feel Skyler's shoulders move up and down in laughter before she heard her say, "You did start drinking coffee unusually early. I was shocked to round the corner to the kitchen and see you making a cup of java. You were only, like, fifteen. Not even wanting it sweetened or creamy."

"Micah hated the stuff, but what he hated even more was that I was one-upping him," Cam chuckled at the memory. "I had to set down the rules that he was younger and couldn't drink it."

"He was secretly glad for the rule." Skyler whispered the confession near her ear. Cam had to hold back a moan.

"It's not a Sprite, but let me make you some tea. Hold on." Cam untangled herself from Skyler's arm. The grunt of disapproval, to her surprise, had bubbled from her own mouth, but she needed a moment to gather her wits.

"Goose, come up here." Cam patted the place she had vacated, and Goose smoothly complied, glad for the comfy mattress and warm body over the wooden floor.

Cam slipped out, shaking her head at almost placing a kiss on Skyler's head.

The weather was still rainy, and Cam sidled up next to a spruce tree, picking a few small twigs with care to avoid losing the needles clinging to the branch. Her knee was still stiff, and she limped back to the fire pit, taking a moment to look around and, for the first time, observing the strategic placement of the pit. There was a natural clearing, but an overhang of tall trees provided a canvas of cover to protect a fire. Whoever had built this place was thoughtful of the land, and she nodded her approval.

Setting the spruce needles on top of the stump, she started the water and waited for it to boil. Leaning against a tree, Cam thought about their situation. It wasn't dire yet, but would they have to think of the winter months? She knew Micah wouldn't give up hope, but he was expecting a child soon. She thought of the land and the abundance it would provide if only they had the tools.

Cam's eyes fell to a branch, thinking of the spear, bow, and arrow possibilities. Maybe she could fasten a pole together for fishing. She would do what was needed to take care of Skyler. At the thought of her friend, a smile spread across her face. Skyler was worming her way into her heart, and she didn't know how she felt about it.

Right now, it didn't matter. Cam had a job to do. Cam grabbed the sticks they used to take the pot off the fire and put it on the ground near her. Thinking things through, she held off putting the needles in. They didn't have any honey, and the sticks, while nutritious, provided a bitter taste. Gathering the branches and putting them in the pouch of her hoodie, she walked with the pot back to the cabin.

After placing the pot on the table, she contemplated what to do with her companion. Goose had lifted his head briefly but set it back down when he determined there was no danger. It seemed like he wiggled under Skyler's arm and stuck his tongue out at her. She even put a bowl of berries down to see if he would move, but so far, he'd been self-sufficient in the food and water department. Skyler and Goose were two peas in a pod, and Cam wondered how Goose would handle Skyler leaving.

166

For a long time, she had tried not to think about the future. After losing her parents, she was in survival mode, only able to make decisions that would affect the current day. Get Micah through school, become mom, sister, confidant, friend, and disciplinarian. It was a lot to take on and not something she would have changed, except she forgot to live. She had been in this stasis gel for so long, and now she was looking at Skyler, trying to envision a future together. The thought both terrified and excited her, but she wasn't sure which one would win out.

"How long was I out?" Skyler's sleepy voice jerked her out of her existential crisis.

"About a half hour. How are you feeling?" Cam came over and placed her hand on Skyler's forehead. She was a little worried that Skyler was still cold, even after they had changed into dry clothes. She felt a little clammy but not overly warm, which loosened a clamp on Cam's chest.

"A little better, but still tired." Skyler rubbed her eyes.

"I have some tea here." Cam motioned behind her towards the table. "Do you want it a little mild, or do you want stronger but potentially bitter?"

Skyler blinked rapidly, processing the question. "I don't mind a stronger taste. I can pretend it's a large cup of Sprite." She winked over Goose's ear.

"I thought you might feel that way." Cam chuckled as she walked back to the table, pulling out the branches and dumping them into the still steaming water.

Cam busied herself by wiping the counters and folding clothes while Skyler fell back asleep. Once the tea seeped, she pulled a Nalgene out and poured the hot water into the container, trying hard to keep the sticks and needles out of the bottle.

Walking over, Cam scooted Goose's tail out of the way and placed a hand on Skyler's side. "Skyler, wake up. Can you drink this?" Skyler sat up while Goose huffed his displeasure at being displaced before settling back on the ground.

Skyler sniffed the tea before taking a tentative sip. She rolled it around her mouth, swishing like the wine folks do, before swallowing with a smile. "It's not soda, but dang, it's refreshing. Thank you."

She tipped the cup to Cam with a smile, and even if Cam consumed the entire bottle, she doubted it would have warmed her insides like an unguarded Skyler grin.

***

Skyler hid her smile over the lid of the bottle she was holding. Cam was looking at her like she would hang the moon, and Skyler relished in the attention.

Something had changed in their relationship, but Skyler wasn't ready to reflect on what those changes were. She would look to Cam for direction on their new dynamics. For the longest time, she'd averted her eyes from the oldest Porter in fear that she would read the feelings on her face, but now she looked, studied, and observed the light and twinkle in Cam's eyes.

Not ready to hold a mirror up to her emotions, she looked down towards Goose. "Thanks for the hot beverage. It's helped to warm me up some," Skyler said as a small moan escaped when she took another sip.

"Glad you like it." Cam looked around the cabin. "Is there anything else I can help with?"

"Could you read to me?" Skyler asked with a small smile.

Up until then, she had done all the reading, but they had plenty of light, and she was sure more than anything that Cam's low tones would be soothing.

They settled with Skyler sitting up cross-legged on the bed and Cam leaning against the wall a little behind her.

Cam cleared her throat and began reading where they last left off.

Cam's voice flowed over Skyler as she listened. She could almost quote the book at this point but loved the new inflections that Cam provided. Still sitting up, imagining the characters' trials on the Oregon Trail, she almost didn't notice the soothing motion on her back. Cam gently scratched along her back and Skyler's body melted into a puddle of comfort.

Scratching her back was something Nana Winnie had done when she was sick. One time, she couldn't hold her head up and felt herself placed in Nana Winnie's lap, where she entered another dimension of comfort and support as her nana gently scratched her back. She had to go in later and get her tonsils removed, but the only thing she remembered of the ordeal was how safe and loved she'd felt.

Not wanting to call any attention to the movement, Skyler was in suspension, unwilling to move an inch. It wasn't until she heard the book crash to the floor that she figured out Cam had fallen asleep. Wiggling down the sleeping bag, she fell asleep on Cam's shoulder.

A light movement on Skyler's head peacefully woke her from the nap. Cam was playing with her hair, and Skyler could feel the vibration from her faint humming where her head rested in the crook of her arm. "What are you humming?" Skyler's voice was husky from sleep.

"It's a lullaby my mother used to sing to us when we were young." Cam's reply was soft as she continued playing with Skyler's hair.

"It's beautiful," Skyler mumbled, closing her eyes again.

"Skyler…" Cam started but kept silent for a while longer until Skyler's head bobbed up and down with the motion of Cam's deep breath. "I'm sorry about the picture. I looked at it again, and I'm not sure why I got so upset. But, honestly, if I wasn't so embarrassed, knowing it was me—well, the photo is amazing."

"I wasn't thinking, Cam. I just saw the deer at first, but when I saw the shot, I had to take it. I didn't think about what you might have felt like not being able to give consent. I'm going to delete it." Skyler had propped herself up on her elbow as tears stung her eyes, threatening to fall. She sat up and scooted near the end of the bed but had to sit still for a second as a dizzy spell overtook her, and she gripped the sides with white knuckles, trying to ground herself.

She wasn't even sure why she was on the verge of crying. Maybe it was close to that time of the month, or perhaps she still had a lot of things to process.

"No, no, shhh." Cam pulled her closer. "Don't worry. I calmed down like thirty seconds after you left. The picture is great, and I don't want you to delete it." Skyler didn't move, so Cam sat up and gently pulled her back to lay down next to her. "Rest up and take it easy, please. For me." Cam looked into her eyes, and Skyler was pretty sure mirrored glimmers were reflecting back.

"Okay." Skyler lay her head on the balled-up sweatshirt.

"I'm going to see if I can find something for you to eat," Cam said, and Skyler could feel the warmth beside her dim. Sleep was near, but she could have sworn she felt a dusting of a kiss placed on her forehead, and with it, a smile formed.

***

Cam called for Goose and tiptoed out of the cabin. She had to call twice because Goose seemed reluctant to leave his charge.

"She'll be okay, Goose, come on," Cam whispered as she held the door open and waited for Goose to throw one more look before shaking his tail out of the cabin.

The nap had rested Cam, and even her leg was feeling better. Deciding to check back at the camp on the beach, she soon found herself sweating as she made her way through the woods. In one hand, she still had the walking stick they'd found and used it generously, but the walk through the damp woods was invigorating. "Goose, what am I going to do about Skyler, huh?" Cam wondered aloud while tenderly stepping over a branch.

The sticks Skyler had placed to mark the trail were holding up nicely, and soon Cam's mind wandered as she sang to warn off the bears while hiking through the woods.

Knowing Skyler's life was back in Portland was the only thing holding Cam back from grabbing the collar of her shirt and pushing her against the cabin door for a kiss. Her mind enjoyed the movie for a second before she shook her head.

Just thinking about the kiss had increased her heart rate and flushed her cheeks.

Goose had run ahead and was now walking back with a stick that was larger than the trail and was currently trying to figure out why he was stuck. First, he stepped backward to free himself, then walked forward again only to get stuck at the same spot. Cam smiled and traded a smaller stick for the gigantic one, although Goose kept looking back at it with his head tilted.

They arrived at the beach, and Cam laughed when she saw the SOS sign Skyler had made. It was a bit small, especially for the pilots in the air, and crooked, but in all actuality, the sign had held up remarkably well and was along the beach line that rarely got touched by the tide.

Cam spent the next few moments enlarging the sign and thinking over the past few days. If she was honest with herself, she was starting to develop feelings. The test came to its unfortunate conclusion when she pictured Skyler leaving through security at the Sitka airport, and just the thought almost brought a sob.

Taking a break, she sat down on the edge of the raft still tied to a tree on the beach. She found comfort in Goose's fur. He always had a sixth sense about things. Even the way he handled Skyler's seizure was stunning to see. "Well, buddy, I think I can acknowledge some feelings, but do I use these days to get closer to her, knowing she has to leave? Or do I try to distance myself to protect my heart, and we will be destined for near misses each decade?"

All she got was a paw on her thigh, but it was grounding. She thought about what would have happened if she'd seen the letter all those years ago. Would she have stayed in closer contact with Skyler? Or had she used Nana Winnie as a surrogate Skyler all along, clinging to the one person who was close?

Sighing, Cam started digging for some clams as a surprise for Skyler. She tested them before putting the live ones in her sweatshirt. The last order of business was finding some seaweed, remembering the smile Skyler had with the first bite of the salty treats. She might not eat animals, but that didn't mean Cam couldn't do something nice for Skyler.

Back at the cabin, Cam felt good being able to provide dinner for the first time. While she worked on the food, her mind wandered past an imaginary kiss, playing out all types of possibilities in the remote cabin. "Goose, I'm in trouble," she mumbled as she gathered their meal before opening the door to the cabin with the tasty, cooked treats.

***

Lily, Abby, and Maggie were huddled near a fire watching Micah freak out on poor Hank. Lily, for her part, was entirely on Micah's side but did find herself feeling a pang of sympathy for the mild-mannered pilot.

"I wasn't sure he had it in him." Abby broke the silence of the three.

It seemed she was trying to distract them from the words ping-ponging back and forth: "Giving up…haven't found anything," and the worst one that had caused all of them to gasp: "Presumed dead."

That was the one that got Micah worked up and in an uproar. Hank had told them yesterday when they met on Kinky that they were giving it one more day, but for some reason, today he was throwing heavy words around. Lily had seen many sides of her gentle husband, and shaking with rage was not one of them.

"Lily, dear, do you want some tea?" Maggie offered the boiling water that was resting on the campfire.

Lily was unconsciously rubbing her belly, and she smiled gratefully at Maggie while holding out her cup. She regarded Maggie while she poured the tea. "Why aren't you more upset?" Lily looked between the mild-mannered woman and her red-faced husband. The only external stress she saw on Maggie was in her eyes, and she was wondering what deep reserves she had to present so calmly throughout this tense trip.

Maggie tilted her head as she contemplated the answer. "I know they are okay. I'm worried sick for Skyler because I'm not sure how many AEDs she had left, but I know in here she's okay." She held her hand to her heart and a surge of love flowed from Lily. Maggie and Abby had become their rocks, and without knowing it, they were already a big part of their life.

"Hank, what if it was your sister, huh? What the fuck would you do?" Micah's booming voice broke their moment as Lily watched Micah take off his glasses to wipe his eyes.

All three women got up to walk towards Hank and Micah. Lily knew when Micah threw out cuss words, it was almost too late. She needed to defuse the situation or a family feud lasting centuries would start, right now, where their children would hate Hank's children, and nobody would know why after a few decades.

"Hank," Lily started, placing a hand on Micah's arm and squeezing. She let go when she felt Micah's body deflate. "We understand you've got things to do as well, and they may have called off the search, but that doesn't mean we are going to stop. They didn't find any bodies in the plane, which means until we have proof otherwise, we will stay out here, at least for a few more days." Micah's head snapped to her in a glare, but she held up her hands to stop him from going off again. "We have to get more supplies, but not yet." Lily's voice was soft.

"We'd appreciate it if you didn't say things like presumed dead," Maggie added tightly. "We're not giving up because I know they are still alive, but we understand that you have other obligations."

"Mags, would it help if I offered a missing person reward?" Abby asked in Maggie's shadow. She had been so quiet that Lily forgot she was there.

Maggie thought for a second as she turned to her sister. "That's a kind thought, Abs, but let's keep that as an option later, okay?"

"You know I'm good for it," Abby said, shrugging as she looked Hank up and down. "Speaking of good, they breed them sturdy up in Alaska."

The group chuckled, and Lily was pretty sure this was the only time she'd seen Hank blush, which was a feat because of his bushy beard. It wasn't until a second later that she turned to Abby with newfound respect. The offhand comment had broken the tense spell that was around everyone, and when she met Abby's eyes, she could have sworn she saw a discreet wink with a slight smirk.

Lily gave an acknowledging nod, thinking she found a secret that not many people got to see. Maggie and Abby, at times, seemed opposite. Abby was brash, loud, and hilarious, while Maggie was more subdued and thoughtful,

174

but there was a depth to them both that brought out the best in the other when they were together.

They had all gotten close over the week, and she was sure going to miss the motherly presence and hilarious stories. Turning back to Micah, she saw he and Hank were mumbling something through a hug. They patted each other on the back, and when they parted, both turned around and brought their hands to the corner of their eyes.

"Okay, he's going to keep in touch and come out when he can," Micah said, pulling Lily close as she snuggled into his side.

"Let's set up camp and call it a night. We'll hit the water early and focus on the distant islands of Davison Bay." Maggie pulled out the map they were using to mark the areas they'd covered.

Having a game plan for the next day allowed the group to relax into a comfortable silence, each lost in thought of what the future might hold.

Lily hated thinking about it, but what if? What if they hadn't made it? She rubbed her belly, trying to sooth her turning gut as silent tears fell on bleak possibilities.

Chapter Fourteen

Day 9

Skyler was looking around the cabin, wondering if the walls had gotten smaller. Cam had done everything in her power to keep her relaxed to help decrease the chance of a seizure. She massaged and rubbed her back, hummed, and sang as she made some more utensils out of wood. They now had a workable spoon, plates, and she was currently working on a bowl. The project had given Cam something to do. However, it made Skyler wonder how long they would be stuck there.

She ran her hand over her arm, then sat up and dangled her legs over the edge of the bed. "I'm going to do some laundry in the waterfall, maybe scrub off some of this dirt." Skyler held out her elbow that was caked with dirt from where she'd fallen when she was lost.

Cam looked up with wide eyes. "I don't think it's a good idea for you to be swimming or to be around water."

Skyler looked back at her but held in a snippy retort when she saw Cam was gnawing on her lip in a nervous gesture. "I don't usually have seizures. In fact, I've only had seven total, including the two recently, and they were all brought on by stressful situations. You've done a great job relaxing me, so I think it will be okay, but do you want to come with me?" She slipped on her shoes and started gathering the crusty clothes they'd been cycling through the days, wrinkling her nose at the smell wafting from the pile.

There was only so much they could clean off. Skyler missed things like a washer and dryer, not realizing the massive part the objects played in her life. A picture of her running up to the appliances and hugging them flickered through her mind, bringing a smile. Cam looked at her with soft eyes, and Skyler blushed at being caught almost acting out the play in her mind.

"Yeah, I'll go with you." Cam winced while putting the knife away.

"What happened?" Skyler asked, pointing to Cam's thumb that she had tucked under her hand.

She put the clothes on the table and pulled Cam's hand to her lap. Tisking at the sight of an angry cut, she looked up at Cam. "What happened?" she repeated, pulling the first aid pack to her. It looked clean, but she didn't want it to get infected.

"I couldn't stand my fingernails that long and tried cutting them with the knife. It was working until the blade slipped on this finger. Could have been worse." Cam pulled her hand back, seeing what Skyler was trying to do. "It's fine. We need to save the supplies. What if you need that Band-Aid at some point? See, it stopped bleeding." She brought her fingers to her face and studied the cut before looking at Skyler and shrugging. "It's fine," she said, bringing her non-injured finger across her body to rest on Skyler's leg and squeezing lightly.

Skyler failed at not melting a little at the gesture. Since their talk, Cam had started touching her a little more. She wasn't sure if it was because of the seizure and wanting to help keep her calm or the fact she might be a little more comfortable with her. Either way, Skyler was soaking up the attention like a cat in front of a sunny window.

"Let's go to the waterfall," Cam said, squeezing her leg one more time.

Skyler stood and helped Cam up. It appeared she was getting around better. They both called for Goose. Skyler grabbed the clothes again, and Cam picked up the water bottles and water filter.

"What's the first thing you're going to do when we're rescued?" Cam asked as they walked.

"Shower," Skyler said without thinking. "Refill my meds, and then I'm going to eat all types of foods: Burgers, burritos, pizza, with a Sprite and a beer. Finally, I'll probably enter a food coma and sleep for three days."

Cam's delicious laugh rang out through the woods, scaring a few birds that took flight. It was a sound Skyler could hear every day and not get tired of the melody. "What about you?" she asked when Cam's laughter died down.

"Shower, definitely, while having music blasting, I miss listening to songs. After that, I'd say do laundry, but let's face it, these clothes are getting burned." She picked at the pile in Skyler's hands, then waved her hand in front of her nose, causing a round of laughter to shake from Skyler.

"I'll come to that bonfire and happily dance on the ashes of these fallen clothes," Skyler said as they made it to the waterfall.

It seemed they both were chewing on the inside of their cheeks, looking at each other then away. Skyler's tongue peeked out the side of her mouth in thought. *Should they strip? Would that be weird?* Goose kind of forced the issue when he jumped between them and splashed both of them, breaking the awkwardness.

Turning their backs on each other, Skyler started pulling off her current clothes and adding them to the pile. She wouldn't have any dry clothes, but they had a fire to come back to, and the idea of the clothes getting cleaned was too good to pass up.

They turned around simultaneously, and Skyler's voice caught at seeing Cam in full light. She still had a sports bra and boy shorts on, but it was only the second time she had witnessed such a display of skin, and she was pretty sure her brain was short-circuiting.

Cam grinned, looking at her up and down, not in a leering way, but a way that appreciated what she saw. Skyler noticed a slight blush darkening her cheeks. Skyler put her arm over her stomach, and immediately she felt a light touch on her arm, pulling the block away.

"You're perfect," Cam whispered as she intertwined their fingers and turned to the water. "On three."

Skyler smiled at the playful tone, even though her breathing hadn't settled back to its baseline yet. She took the countdown to try and get her beating heart wrangled back into its corral. By the time Cam got to three, her heart had gotten the message, and they jumped.

Feeling her fingers being gripped tightly, Skyler gasped when the cold water hit her body. As her head dunked below the water, Skyler thought, not for the first time that day, of the wonders of things they took for granted, such as warm showers.

When her head breached the surface of the water, Skyler wiped her face to get the droplets cleared. She was trying to let go of Cam's hand, but she wasn't releasing her grip. She briefly wondered if it was because Cam was overprotective of her because of the seizures, or she just didn't want to be apart from Skyler, but she found she didn't care. Either way, she was happy to be swimming with Cam.

Skyler's eyes fell to Goose, who was paddling nearby, chasing a pinecone that had fallen. She was about to turn and point it out when she felt a tug on her arm.

"Come on, I want to show you something," Cam said as she propelled herself to the waterfall. When they got to the powerful stream, she turned to look at Skyler. "Do you trust me?" she asked, and Skyler could only nod her answer. "I won't let go; I promise." She held up their joined hands out of the water.

For the second time in ten minutes, freezing water hit her head, and she started swimming. For a moment, she had a split second of panic. Maybe she was doing it wrong, but the reassuring grip of Cam's hand in hers calmed her fears, and a hand soon gripped her arm and pulled her up. There was a natural ledge made of stone behind the waterfall, and Cam was already perched on the edge while helping guide Skyler to the seat.

Everything was muted behind the cave, leaving them feeling even more isolated from society. Skyler stuck out her hand and let the stream fall through her hands. Cam watched her as she explored this new area.

"It's too bad the only way to get here is having to go through the water. I'd love to take a few pictures of this area." Skyler adored how untouched it felt.

Cam put her hand on Skyler's leg, rubbing her thumb back and forth on her skin. Skyler hadn't realized she could create more goosebumps, but here they were. Her body was on a precipice, ready to tip into Cam's orbit. If she had thought about it for any length of time, she had been leaning at the finish line, just waiting for Cam to get to where she was since they were teens.

Skyler's shy smile met Cam's nervous one as she leaned in and put her arm around Cam's waist to pull her closer. As a rule, she had tried not to touch Cam often. It was hard on her heart, and she knew Cam didn't like touch all that much, but with the increased comfort Cam was showing, Skyler decided to take another plunge.

She leaned in. "It's okay if you kiss me, you know," she whispered into Cam's ear. "But if you're not ready, that's okay too." Skyler was happy to see the shiver run through Cam's shoulders.

Skyler tried to lean back upright, but Cam stopped her progress with a hand to her shoulder. Cam leaned in closer, and with the most delicate of touches, their lips met. She couldn't be sure, but it seemed for Cam, it was like a test, a dip with her toe to see if the water was acceptable. For Skyler, it was a promise, a placeholder, a split in the road that would take her on a new path. One she had wanted to be on all along.

Her eyes widened when Cam leaned in again, grabbing her head and bringing them closer. Skyler opened her mouth eagerly when she felt Cam's tongue caress her lips in a passionate inquiry to which Skyler was more than willing to answer. After a few more seconds, they broke apart but stayed near, breathing in each other's air and looking into each other's eyes.

The waterfall pounded around them, but the most considerable thump was coming from Skyler's heart. She wanted to go back in time and sit down with her fourteen-year-old self and explain that kissing Cam was better than anything she could have imagined. As she sat there staring into Cam's eyes, she knew this would be a memory she'd go back to for years to come. It was picture-perfect.

Skyler leaned in, eager for another kiss, her mouth parted slightly in anticipation. Cam's tongue slid tentatively over her lips, and Skyler couldn't hold back her moan. She wrapped her arms around Cam's shoulders and pulled her closer. Cam moved one hand from her hair to Skyler's hip and squeezed lightly as their tongues explored. Skyler was squirming on the rocks, unconsciously seeking out friction as she tried not to dwell on Cam's hand that was playing over the sensitive part of her hip.

Just as Skyler was plotting out the course to swing her leg to settle in Cam's lap, Cam pulled away. Her lips were swollen, and the waterfall drowned out their collective heaving breaths.

Skyler was about to lean in again. She was pretty sure she'd never get enough kisses to satisfy her when she heard Cam say, "I'm sorry, Skyler."

Cam slid back into the water, and a stunned Skyler was left looking back at the empty space, wondering what had just happened.

***

Cam swam to the side and tried to get her body under control while shaking her head at what she had just done. After trying hard not to fall for her brother's best friend, that's what she indeed ended up doing. It didn't matter though; Skyler lived in Portland. But that kiss. Cam had never whimpered in her life, but at the edge of a waterfall, in the middle of an emergency, she found herself mewling. She was torn between her head and her heart.

Goose wasn't any help because his ears perked up, and he started swimming towards the falls, which could only mean one thing. She cursed and couldn't believe she'd left Skyler. Kicking powerfully off the edge, she met Skyler in a few strokes, mentally berating herself for her selfishness. Skyler's safety was more important than an awkward encounter, although part of her was scared to be facing Skyler so soon. She wasn't looking forward to seeing the possibility of her devastated face full of anger and disappointment. Cam straightened, ready for anything.

When she turned to face her fate, her eyebrows entered her hairline because before her wasn't the angry, devastated, disappointed person she had been expecting. No, instead there was a playful and almost laughing Skyler, which didn't connect with what she was expecting.

"Alright, so it's going to be like that," Skyler said, swimming up to her. "I kind of had a feeling you would run, and that's okay. I'll wait until you are ready."

Skyler's understanding completely baffled her. In all her interactions with women, they always got mad when she got overwhelmed and had to take a time out. This calm, relaxed and thoughtful interaction wasn't something she'd come across before. She sat there in the water, blinking rapidly at Skyler, not sure what to say. Skyler had grabbed the clothes and was rubbing them together in the water.

"So, how do you like Lily? I know her as my best friend's wife, but just curious, what are your thoughts as the sister-in-law?" Skyler asked, breaking the tension.

Cam's shoulders released their rigidity, and she sent a grateful smile Skyler's way before grabbing another piece of clothing to help clean. If Cam thought it was possible, she would have sworn Skyler was a mind reader. She never understood how Skyler would just know what she needed or how much time in a thought process Cam required.

"She's delightful—a spirited welder who threw traditional gender roles out the window. Micah's heart honestly didn't have a chance. She came up to Sitka, following her girlfriend up here. After a few months, the girlfriend wanted to go back to Arizona, but Lily was finally home. It was quite the breakup in the bar." Cam chuckled at the memory. Feisty was the best word that came to mind for Lily back then. Cam grabbed the edge of the pool and extended her arms, twisting out of the water.

"I don't think I ever heard the breakup in the bar story. What happened?" Skyler allowed Cam to help pull her out of the water. They sat side by side on the edge while Skyler started ringing out her hair.

Splashes of water rained down on them as Goose shook out his fur near their faces. "Goose, come on, buddy, do you have to shake right where we're sitting? There is a whole forest for you to shake off in," Cam scolded softly as they shielded themselves from the onslaught, laughing at the dog's antics.

Once they started dressing, Cam answered Skyler's question. "I was at the bar when I heard shouting. Lily was standing her ground with this woman towering over her. I was about to see if they needed any help when Lily's ex-girlfriend poured a drink over her head before storming out.

Lily was dripping with a bloody Mary on her white shirt, and she turned to me asking if I knew anyone who needed any welding done, and, well, I did. I Introduced her to my brother the next day, and the rest, as they say, is history." Cam grabbed a wet shirt and pulled it over her head while Skyler did the same. "They started as friends. Micah helped provide odd jobs at the shop and gave an ear when Lily needed to talk. One day she stomped into the shop and cornered him behind a boat we were working on and just went for it, grabbed and kissed him. She didn't know I was there helping out." They both chuckled softly. Cam shivered as a light breeze kicked up.

They started walking back to the cabin, hand in hand. Cam hadn't even realized she'd grabbed Skyler's hand until they were back at the cabin and she went to open the door, bringing Skyler's hand with her. Skyler kept light banter, and there was never an awkward moment of silence.

Cam turned to Skyler, then looked around the cabin. "Want to get the fire roaring and dry off these clothes?" They were both shivering, and Cam was sure if she cut her skin, it would just show her blood as a block of ice.

"Sounds good." Skyler turned around to build up the fire again. "But it's your turn to cut some wood," she called over her shoulder and left with a wink.

"Come on, Goose, let's get warm," Cam called, and went back to the pit.

Grabbing the rusty axe, she started cutting wood. It felt good to use her muscles again, finding the action relaxing. It was more challenging work with a bum tool but better than nothing. She cut a few sizes and gathered some more small sticks for kindling since the joke about having to use the paper from Skyler's book a few days ago hadn't gone over well. The entertainment value of reading it together was worth more than a few minutes of kindling to get the fire started anyway.

When Cam got back with a loaded arm of wood and a limp to her step, Skyler rushed over to help.

"I'm not a hundred percent sure I can eat rice again after this, or potatoes for that matter, and I love potatoes." Skyler pouted while poking the boiling roots and watching them dance around in the water.

"I think I'm good with berries as well," Cam remarked, plopping one in her mouth and grimacing as she choked it down. After days of the same food, it was getting harder to swallow. It seemed they both needed a bit of variety in the foods they ate. Who knew?

"Why do you think we haven't seen anybody come through here yet?" Skyler asked, her eyes falling to the flare they always kept near but hadn't had a reason to use yet.

Cam started moving her lip back and forth, trying to come up with the mental map of where they might be. She wasn't coming up with anything concrete, and she hated to conjecture. "I don't know, I would have expected something by at least day three, and there was nothing. So I can speculate that we either drifted farther from the landing spot than I thought, or we drifted out of the main strip in Davison Bay. So maybe a combo of those, plus we're definitely in a dead zone since the radio isn't working."

Skyler nodded along. "Do you think we'll have to row back? I mean, we have the raft, and we can stay near the shores, hopping out for provisions. It would suck, but maybe we could do it?"

Cam laughed. "No, we aren't anywhere near that dire yet. I mean, maybe in a little bit, but it would take us a long time to get to Sitka. Plus, we want to stay in one area. Hopefully, it's close-ish to the landing spot. There is more likely a chance of rescue that way." Cam pulled her hands close to the fire to warm them up. The sun was setting, making her combination of wet clothes and no heat from the sun a dual-threat to her warmth.

"Why do you say landing? You've said that a few times. Cam, we crashed, like full-on kaboom in the water." Skyler was grinning to take the sting out.

"At the time, it felt like more of a fender bender until the plane sank. But I hate the word crash. Landed hard is more up my alley." Cam smirked, trying to hide a blush. She knew it sounded a little ridiculous, but crash, no matter how true it was, was a bruise to her small ego.

Skyler looked up at the sky, shaking her head. She was mumbling something under her breath, and Cam couldn't quite make it out but picked up 'fender bender' before Skyler started laughing.

"Want to come snuggle with me?" Cam asked, patting the ground near her.

She cringed a little inside at the mixed signals she was sending. One minute she was kissing Skyler, the next running away, then asking if she wanted to get close again. If Cam were to look at her actions under a slow-motion replay camera with a sports announcer, the conclusion would be that she was blind not to see the course right in front of her. But instead of a linebacker sneaking up on the quarterback, she was just a woman scared of her feelings for another woman. A woman who most likely would get on a plane back to Portland when they were rescued.

Cam startled when she felt a warm body curl up next to her. Goose had followed Skyler over as well and laid his head in her lap. Unconsciously she threw an arm around Skyler to pull her closer, while her other hand fell to Goose's body. There was an echo of sighs as all three of them released held breaths.

"I'll always want to snuggle with you, Cam," Skyler said from Cam's shoulder. The dual smiles were hidden in the dusk.

They had moved to the cabin to sleep after laughing, talking, and finally getting to something that resembled warmth. Their nighttime ritual was the only time that there was a stumble. Skyler looked at the bed for a long time before glancing at Cam. Seeing Cam was watching her, their eyes held, and Cam got in first and held the sleeping bag open for Skyler to crawl in.

It had become second nature to throw her arm over Skyler. In the beginning, it was for the extra warmth, but now, it was turning into an action Cam was going to have a hard time going without. The only person she had felt a hundred percent comfortable with, both physically and emotionally, had left her after a year to go back to the lower forty-eight. Holding Skyler like this was both a revelation and a curse for her future self, but her current self was settling down to enjoy the benefits and comforts of a warm body.

They had drifted to sleep when Goose's growl woke them up at the same time. They shot up from their homemade pillow like synchronized swimmers. There was scraping on the porch, and they could feel the vibrations as something massive walked along the area, shaking the house and causing dust to shake loose from the walls.

Goose's growl became a bark-growl combo when the creature seemed to start rubbing along the framework of the cabin. "The Three Little Pigs" story flickered through Cam's mind, and she imagined the cabin tumbling to the ground like the straw house. Skyler tensed next to her and grabbed her arm.

They stayed motionless, waiting for the beast to walk away from the cabin. Goose's hairs raised, and he didn't let up his growl until the cabin was free from scrapes and movement for a good five minutes. Cam could feel Skyler shaking near her, and was worried about another seizure, so she pulled her to her side and started rubbing her back. Then, she called Goose up to snuggle near their legs. It was a tight fit, but something they both needed tonight.

Cam could feel Skyler's rapid and heavy pulse every time her hand grazed her neck, up her head, and then down her back. Soon the rapid beat settled as she snuggled further into Cam.

"Will you sing me something?" Skyler whispered, so quiet that Cam, six inches from Skyler's mouth, had barely heard.

"What do you want me to sing?" Cam asked, equally quiet. She smiled when she saw Skyler mimic Cam's movements on Goose.

"Anything," she said.

Cam started humming another tune from her childhood. It was about the trickster, Raven, and had been a favorite of hers and Micah's growing up.

Without warning, a stream of tears started falling silently down Cam's cheeks as she continued with the song. She usually didn't cry, especially when nothing brought it on, but she was crying for her parents, for Winnie, for her childhood cut short and a potential love that seemed impossible. She was crying for no reason other than she felt safe.

***

"Micah, everyone has been up and down Davison Bay. Don't you think if they were here, we would have found them by now?" Maggie's voice was harsher than Micah had ever heard. He looked around to the others before his eyes landed on Lily.

She was pale, but he knew she was putting on a brave face. His heart lurched for her and his baby. He reached out for her, silently asking if she was okay.

"Micah, are you even listening?" Maggie loudly asked again.

"Maggie, come on. We were following the plan we all came up with. So why are you getting on my case now?" he snapped back.

They both squared up to each other, glaring.

Lily stepped in between them and grabbed Micah's hand. "Micah, back off, okay. We've all had a hard time out here, but you need to step back before you say something you'll regret. Remember, Skyler is her daughter, and she has a point. We haven't found anything around here."

Micah sighed. He loved having a strong-minded wife, but it felt like everyone was ganging up on him right now.

"Now, you two talk and make up a plan. Lily, let's get you some tea," Abby said as she looped her arm through Lily's but not before Micah caught the disappointed look from Abby, loud and clear.

It deflated his sails as he and Maggie looked at each other warily. It had been a long and emotional week. Davison Bay seemed to have countless islands, and each island held multiple cracks and crevices tucked away, which made a thorough search frustratingly difficult.

They were running out of supplies and gas. They needed to head back soon to refuel, and if Micah had anything to do about it, Lily would be staying behind this time, but in his heart, he knew he had no control over it. Lily would do what Lily would do, and in this moment, it was the reminder of the strong personality he'd fallen in love with.

"I should have listened before jumping down your throat. I'm sorry." Micah swallowed, trying to get his emotions under control.

"I'm sorry, too," Maggie said, stepping up to him with her arms held out for a hug. "I should have communicated more clearly."

Micah stepped into the hug, and allowed himself to be held, much like his mother would have done. Maggie rubbed his back as they both let out frustrated tears.

When they parted, they looked at each other with clearer minds and hearts. "I get your point, Maggie. I really do." He looked up at the setting sun with sad eyes, not sure how much longer the tenuous hold of hope would last.

"I know we are running out of supplies. All I'm saying is everyone has looked up and down this way." She pointed to the map, completely marked up of points they had looked at, then followed her finger downwards and cut through a bay that led to a bigger straight. "The currents push this way. On our way home, let's just check out this route. It won't hurt any and gives us a new area to search." Maggie looked up with glassy eyes from lack of sleep and high emotions. "Please, Micah, can we just try?"

His mind didn't think they could have drifted that far out of the way, but his heart couldn't take Maggie's pleading eyes. And what was the worst thing that could happen? When he came out again, he'd follow the path originally drawn. His shoulders sank. "Okay, Mags, we'll do it your way on the way home." He nodded with a small smile.

Lily and Abby sauntered back with smiles. "Did we stay away long enough?" Abby asked as she leaned over the map.

Everyone laughed, breaking the somber mood. Micah might have had a waning grip on hope, but he couldn't have had better company to go through personal hell.

Chapter Fifteen

Day 10

Skyler woke up in a warm cocoon of limbs and hair.
Goose had wedged himself between the wall and her back,
and Cam's hair was draped near her mouth, where every
breath in was a dangerous game of a potential choking
hazard. She might have been boiling and spitting out hair
with every breath, but she woke with a smile.

Wanting to pull Cam closer but knowing her body
temperature wouldn't allow for such things, Skyler gently
extracted herself and went to sit by the fire. Cam was a
deep sleeper, she'd found out, and Skyler liked to take
pictures of the sunrise, then sit by the fire. Some of her best
thinking came at the crack of dawn.

Tiptoeing out of the cabin, she looked back once at the
sight, her heart swelling with what she saw. Cam had
wrapped her body around the only source of heat and was
now cuddling Goose, who didn't seem to mind one bit.
Skyler gently closed the cabin door behind her with her
camera around her neck and the flare gun tucked into her
hoodie.

Looking at the porch, she swallowed hard at the claw
scuff marks marring the wood. It appeared there was some
tuff of light brown, coarse hair poking out on the corner of

the cabin, and she almost hightailed it back to bed, ready to have Cam's strong arms wrapped around her again.

Since she didn't hear any movement in the woods, she shook off her worry. The night visitor was most likely a brown bear looking for food and sauntered off when it didn't locate any. Maybe if she made noise, it would stay away. She walked up to the dying campfire with renewed determination and threw some little sticks on the embers to get the fire started again.

Sitting on a stump near the pit, Skyler's mind turned to the future, more specifically, what her future looked like with Cam. She thought of Cam coming to Portland and quickly rejected the idea. Cam belonged in Alaska. She fit there. It would be almost cruel to take her away. Skyler looked around and imagined living in Sitka again. The main reason she had been glad to move away was her wounded heart. If the note scene had played out differently, would she have moved back at some point?

Skyler could do photography anywhere, and Alaska provided ample opportunity for photos. People in Sitka got married, had children, graduated, and they wanted those moments captured. Plus, if she had an in with a certain pilot, she could get some incredible remote shots.

Smiling to herself, she thought about what Portland held, and the only true answer she could come up with was it was the place she knew. It held the predictability of life's ruts. She knew what most of her days would look like, going from one photography appointment to the next, helping her mom at the library, or tearing a room apart looking for something Abby had misplaced. The third time that had happened, she had made a mental note to start the hunt in the freezer since that's somehow usually where the missing object ended up.

Her life was predictable, but it was lonely. She could bring Raven to Sitka. Yes, she would miss her mom and aunt, but that wasn't a reason to keep her life on pause, taking pictures of other people's happiness while she sacrificed her own.

Her heart picked up speed when she thought of walking into the grocery store hand in hand with Cam. She laughed at the thought of Goose learning quickly that Raven was a menace. A dog named Goose and a cat named Raven, how could that not be soulmate-level compatibility? Could she really move?

The answer appeared when Skyler looked up from the fire towards the house and saw Cam leaning against the doorway, her arms crossed along her body and a silly grin on her face. The smile grew when their eyes connected, and Skyler got her answer. Yes, absolutely yes. She could do anything with a smile like that waiting at the other end.

She stood up and brushed off her pants. Shyly, Skyler looked back to Cam and started walking back to the cabin, towards her future.

***

On her way out of the cabin, Cam had grabbed the sticks they were using for toothbrushes. She cut off the tips they had used last night to clean their teeth and frayed the ends of the new area of the soft branches. As Cam placed her stick and started rubbing gentle circles to clear off the gunk on her teeth, she opened the door and stepped into the dewy morning. Skyler's face, which seemed lost in thought, stopped Cam in her tracks. Leaning against the door, she just observed Skyler, wondering what she was thinking. A smile had developed on her face, making Cam think she had either come to a favorable conclusion, or maybe, she was thinking of her too.

When their eyes met, Cam knew they would have to talk about things. Skyler still lived in a place that wasn't Sitka, but looking into Skyler's understanding, kind face, a brick from Cam's wall fell. She watched as Skyler walked towards her. Neither said anything and when Skyler got close enough, Cam reached out for her hands. Her fingers were cold, and she wrapped them in her hands, pulling her closer.

Skyler, as always, was patiently waiting for her. Cam saw the understanding and vast amounts of patience swimming in her eyes along with, if she wasn't mistaken, love. The emotions caught in Cam's throat, and she looked down, giving herself a minute to gather her thoughts.

The feeling of an icicle tipping her chin back up startled her before she realized it was one of Skyler's freezing fingertips. "It's okay if you're not ready." Skyler's voice was strong, and it felt like it was echoing out in the silent morning.

The words broke the spell on Cam, and she grabbed Skyler's shoulders and twirled her around until her back was pressed against the wall of the cabin. She leaned in and kissed her, pressing her lips urgently against Skyler's. It was nothing like the waterfall. Instead, it was carnal, needy, and passionate. Their lips parted as their tongues reacquainted. Nothing was tentative, and Cam slid her hands from Skyler's shoulders down her arms to settle on her hips. She squeezed them before yanking them closer to her in a movement that frankly she didn't know she had in her.

A gentle moan escaped Skyler, and Cam felt the vibration in her lips, providing an extra layer of tingle throughout her body. Cam slid her leg between Skyler's, and she gasped when she felt Skyler grind into her. She could feel Skyler's heat radiating, which was spreading like wildfire on a direct path to Cam's core which caused Cam's body to vibrate with want. Skyler's hands were busy gently caressing up her body, causing a wake of goosebumps before Cam felt Skyler's fingers tangle in her hair.

Goose's bark from inside the cabin was the only thing that kept Cam from going any further in front of the singing morning birds. They broke apart, panting, Cam's forehead resting gently against Skyler's. Their eyes were searching, albeit in a small range being so close, but Cam could feel Skyler's smile wrinkle up her nose.

The dew of the morning provided a visual of their increased breath as they sat panting and sharing air back and forth.

It was Skyler who spoke first. "We should probably let him out. He must have to use the bathroom." Skyler flicked her head to the door when Cam didn't move.

"Right, yes." Cam nodded before tearing herself away and stepping aside to let Goose out.

"Did you know I have a cat?" Skyler asked. The question seemed random, but she was staring at Cam like the answer would provide the key to Atlantis.

"No, I don't think I knew that. What's its name? Is your mom watching over them?" Cam asked, watching Goose bound out of the cabin and inspect the claw marks on the porch she hadn't noticed before.

"His name is Raven. He is completely black, except for green eyes, and yes, mom and Aunt Abby are watching over him. Well, they should be. If they know I'm missing, I could see them coming up to help. They probably boarded him along with Abby's cat."

Skyler was rambling, and she wasn't much of a rambler. The thought amused Cam to no end, knowing she had a hand in melting Skyler's brain a bit. It didn't last long since her brain was in the same state. "Goose and Raven for a cat and dog, huh?" Cam reflected, her voice a tad wispy before clearing her throat and adding, "I've always wanted a cat."

The smile she got in return was better than her first flight.

***

195

Skyler patted Cam's stomach as she walked down the porch. "I have some roasted dandelions on the fire. Let me grab them, and we can eat in the cabin and figure out our day." Skyler gave Cam a peck on the cheek as she hopped down the stairs, knowing Cam needed a minute to gather her thoughts and adjust to the new parameters of their relationship. Skyler smiled at how well she knew Cam, like they had always been on the same wavelength.

Goose followed Cam inside the cabin after finishing his business. Cam shut the door to not let in the cold air, and Skyler set out to get the small breakfast she had cooked on the fire.

A snap of a branch made Skyler look up, thinking it was a deer. Instead, what greeted her made her blood run cold, the grip of panic running through her veins. A huge grizzly bear was standing up at the edge of the camp near their cabin, its nose quivering in the air. Her first thought was taking a few shots with her camera, but the bear was uncomfortably close, and her shaking hand made it impossible for her to capture a good photo.

Like a Rolodex, Skyler's mind filtered through thoughts of what to do when confronted with a grizzly as she tried to find the correct information. The fight or flight battle was raging while the freeze response was sitting in the driver's seat. On one level, she knew running wasn't a good option. But on the other hand, the bear was standing between her and the safety of the cabin.

Skyler wasn't sure how long she stood in a standoff with the bear, but Goose's deep guttural warning barks finally broke through the panic. He tore out of the cabin, and Cam's screams for Goose and Skyler were met on deaf ears of terror. The only reason Goose's bark had permeated through was because he was practically on top of her and was barking, growling, baring his teeth, and keeping himself between her and the bear.

The creature would have been majestic if it were farther away. It slammed down to all fours again, giving a mighty roar that Skyler swore caused her hair to ripple. The bear started striding towards her and Goose, huffing as it walked. Skyler's hand grazed the outline of her pocket, and without thought, she aimed at the bear and pulled the trigger.

***

Flames licked up the walls unnaturally fast, and Cam sat frozen, watching the area where she had felt such peace just that morning. She remained rooted to the spot near the door, not sure where to help. Goose was locked in a dance of wills, always keeping his body between Skyler and the giant beast. Thoughts of losing Goose and Skyler almost brought her to her knees as she tried to figure out how to be helpful and unglue herself from the frozen state she found herself in. Never one for inaction, she found it puzzling why her legs weren't jumping to help.

A second ball of flame hit the porch near her feet, and Cam dove out of the way, feeling a pull in her leg as she slammed against the wood. A shriek had her lifting up her head and looking around. What she saw had her scrambling to her feet again.

The second flare had grazed the bear, and it lashed out at Goose with a swipe before turning around and working its way back to the woods. The creature seemed to look back every couple of steps, and Cam mentally shooed them along.

A yell pierced her heart as she turned back to Goose and Skyler, and heat from the flames started to lick up her back. She turned to the cabin and saw a wall of fire, her heart sinking at the destruction of the one place they felt safe. There was no way to grab supplies. Stumbling down the steps, Cam tried to find the feeling she'd had just a few minutes ago. In shock, she stood and stared at how much could change in such a short time.

The daze Cam was in was broken when her eyes fell to Skyler, hunched over Goose. Her shoulders were shaking, and Cam rushed over, hoping that Skyler wasn't having a seizure. When she reached Skyler, she saw she was sobbing. Cam almost didn't want to take any more steps forward.

She forced herself to take four stiff steps and fell to Skyler's side when she heard Goose's whine. Skyler's hands were coated in blood as she pressed her hands to Goose's side. Cam looked at Skyler's tear-streaked face and found the calm she needed in an emergency. It helped that when she placed her hand on Goose's side, it moved up and down with his breaths.

"Good boy, you are such a good boy. You are getting so many steaks and sticks. You're not even going to know what to do with them all." Skyler's voice repeated the mantra over and over as she pressed into his side.

As the cabin went up in flames, all Cam focused on was Goose and Skyler. She looked into the wild eyes of Skyler and settled herself before speaking. "Skyler, go over to the fire, and get it as hot as you can. Use the wood that we've been using for spruce tea. It's soft wood and will burn a little hotter. Make sure it's dry as well. Once it's hot, take this knife, and stick it in the flames. You want it hot, but not white or red." Cam held the knife out and waited until Skyler looked her in the eyes before letting go of the blade. "We have to cauterize the wound. We have to stop the bleeding. Do you understand?" Cam asked and received a tentative nod.

Skyler gulped. "Why not the first aid kit?" Skyler asked, finally putting together the last piece of what they were about to do, her eyes wide in horror as she looked between Cam, the knife, and Goose, who was whimpering in their laps.

Cam gestured her thumb behind her. "I don't think we can get to it. Plus, it's probably a melted pile of nothing at this point."

Skyler looked to where Cam was pointing and yelled, scrambling to stand up. It seemed she had just noticed the flaming cabin, having been so focused on Goose. Luckily, Cam had a good hold on Goose at this point as she pulled him more firmly in her lap.

"Where's the water!" Skyler screamed, looking around.

"No! Skyler, there's no point. We're going to need the water bottle to clean the wound, plus what will a few ounces do to that inferno? The cabin is gone. Let's help Goose. Please?" Cam looked at Skyler, then down at Goose.

All the blood drained from Skyler's face as she looked between the fire and Goose. Goose lifted his head, trying to lick the wound, which shook her out of her inaction. With shaking legs, she walked towards the campfire with the knife in hand.

Cam was trying to think of different things they could use to stop the bleeding, but nothing that wouldn't take time was coming to mind. She was trying to keep Goose safe while cleaning his wound with some water. His breathing slowed, and he stopped trying to get at the cuts. The injuries weren't very deep, more like a warning swipe than anything, but the lack of medical supplies was freaking her out.

Skyler came back with the knife. It looked like the perfect temperature, although they would have to do the process a few times. Cam looked at Skyler, and a bundle of wrinkles appeared over her eyes as she tried to keep herself from sobbing. Taking a breath, she looked at Goose, whose blood was still flowing, and pressed the knife to his wound for a second. Goose yelped and nipped at her knuckles, but she quickly did the next track of lines down his side.

With each cauterization, the blood flow slowed. Skyler had put a stick near his head, but he was oddly quiet by the fourth track of claws, either resigning to his fate and waiting for the day he could exact his revenge or most likely wondering why he was such a bad boy that his pack leader was hurting him so much. Cam suspected the second reason when his eyes met hers with pure confusion and betrayal.

By the time they had finished, the cabin was completely engulfed. Cam sat rocking Goose in her lap with her back to the cabin, not wanting to watch the place she had felt more at home the past couple days than she often did in her own lonely trailer be destroyed.

Skyler stopped pacing and sat down next to her, gently pulling Goose's head into her lap. His eyes were closed as she rubbed his head. Cam massaged his back legs, careful not to touch the hurt, raw, red area on his side.

"Do you think he will be okay?" Skyler asked, her voice catching slightly on the difficult question.

Cam sighed, not able to stop the tears streaking down her cheeks. Skyler put an arm around her, and they both broke down in sobs at the unknown. "We'll have to keep the area clean since I'm worried about the wound getting infected. I might be able to make a salve from devil's root, but it might take a bit, and I don't have all the ingredients." Cam's shoulders slumped. "I don't know what to do."

Skyler looked at her, and instead of adding to her burden, she surprised Cam. "We'll figure it out together, one thing at a time." She leaned against Cam's shoulder, and with the day's early events already pressing down on them, they both closed their eyes.

Chapter Sixteen

Lily's stomach cramped as they made their way back to Sitka. They were getting low on gas and needed to gather more supplies. Lily had it in her head they would stay a day in town before heading back out, but her body was screaming another story.

"Lily? Are you okay?" Maggie's calm voice floated down to the bunk where Lily was in the fetal position, most likely emulating her unborn child.

"Grahhhh," was all Lily could get out, which she hoped meant, *something is wrong, I'm in a shit load of pain, nauseous, and I need help. Please and thank you.*

Maggie placed a cool rag on Lily's head and started rubbing her back. The rocking boat and Maggie's comfort lulled Lily to a tenuous place of rest. That was until her leg seized up, causing her to kick out with a whimper.

"Alright, you're going to be okay." Maggie's voice was soothing, and Lily found herself wondering if she would have the knack for soft mom voice. It was damn comforting.

A brown banana was partly opened and shoved in her hands. "This will help with the leg cramps and nausea. Go ahead and eat it." Maggie pushed the mushy fruit near Lily's mouth. She was too weak to protest and nibbled on the end.

Her stomach rolled, and her muscles breathed a sigh of relief as she finished the near rotten fruit. "Thank you," Lily managed and she handed the peel back to Maggie then felt a fresh cool cloth placed on her head.

Maggie's usually calm face was wrinkled in worry, and Lily's gut clenched at what it could mean. Without another word, Lily leaned back down and cradled her stomach in her arms before falling into a restless sleep.

***

Micah hadn't spent much time with Abby but found her to be a riot as he tried to teach her how to steer a boat. Unlike a car that stopped at a certain point, a boat wheel could spin three hundred and sixty degrees and Abby was trying to use all of them, making the boat turn in a circle. She also kept twisting her arms around, forgetting to let go of the wheel.

It was nice to laugh lightly and joke. Micah was looking for logs to dodge while pointing at different landmarks and tidbits to look out for when driving a boat when a column of smoke caught Micah's eye, and he squinted towards the sun. Without thinking, he grabbed the wheel and started turning it towards the smoke.

"What are you doing?" Abby swatted him on the knuckles and tried to grab the wheel again. "I won't ever learn if you do it for me," Abby said, holding tight.

Micah's teeth clenched and he tried to keep from taking over the wheel as he pointed out the smoke and a beach they were going to investigate.

Abby looked to where he was pointing and squealed before she took her hands off the wheel and started running out to the back of the boat. She leaned over the side and helped guide Micah to the beach. He started bouncing in anticipation when his eyes fell on a rough SOS sign, and it was Abby who pointed out the raft.

He wasn't sure who screamed to Maggie, but by the time they were near the beach, he could tell both he and Abby were vibrating with excitement. It had to be them. It just had to be.

Maggie's face appeared from below deck where he knew Lily was resting. Her expression gave him a slight pause. Maggie's face lit up when she looked around and saw the smoke and sign.

"Lily needs some tea, and I think someone should stay here with her," Maggie said as she ran fingers through her hair. Micah and Abby stopped fussing with a small raft on the boat's roof that would help carry them to shore and looked back at Maggie.

"I'll stay with her." Micah stepped away from the rope. He was close to running down to the small sleeping area.

"No, we don't know what we'll find or if they'll need help getting to the boat," Abby reasoned, her hands on her hips. "I'll stay with Lily. I've got a bum shoulder from my shot-putting days in college." Abby started walking and winding her shoulder. "Tea and washcloth?" she questioned as she passed Maggie, grabbing the rag that was hanging loose at her side.

"Yes, thanks Abs." Maggie pulled her in for a hug.

"Bring our girl home." Abby patted Maggie on the back before continuing down to Lily.

"Alright, let's go see what we'll find." Maggie passed Micah and squeezed his arm. "Lily is doing okay. She's in a little pain right now, but there isn't much you can do. She's resting. So let's go check out the beach."

Micah nodded, but quickly went down to kiss Lily on the cheek. Seeing her resting gave his heart a little peace, but she looked pale, and all he wanted was for her to be at the house, near a hospital, and resting fully.

Micah and Maggie paddled the orange raft to shore after anchoring off the boat as close to the beach as possible.

Their raft scraped along the rocky ground, and Micah hopped out before dragging it a little further up so Maggie wouldn't get her feet wet. He put out his hand to help her off the raft, looking in every direction. His heart was pounding out of his chest in nervous anticipation.

They decided to start their search for the cause of the massive column of smoke. As they looked around, Maggie was the one that found the trail. There was a bundle of sticks near a trail from the boat. Once they found them, it was easy to follow the trail to the smoky column. With each step, both dread and excitement bubbled up in his chest. They were so close, but what were they going to find?

An inferno met their eyes when they turned the corner, and they scanned the area. It looked like a cabin had caught on fire, and Micah's heart clenched at the doomsday possibilities. Maggie's screech brought him back to the task at hand in time to see her running to an area near a fire pit.

There he saw two huddled figures with something in their lap. Tears started streaming down his face as he started running after Maggie, who had stopped in front of them, looking down. When Micah got to the group, he grabbed Maggie's arm, feeling woozy from the blood that coated their clothes and hands.

Skyler was leaning against Cam's shoulder, and their eyes were closed. Goose lay on both their laps, and Micah's heart lurched when he saw Goose's fur coated in blood. Micah let out a breath when he saw Goose's tail start to thump.

Micah and Maggie both fell to their knees at the same time. Micah grabbed Cam's shoulder while Maggie went for Skyler's, and they shook them gently. Goose's head was now partly lifted, and it looked like he was trying to get to Micah, but he started whining when he moved.

***

When Cam opened her eyes, she blinked a few times in confusion. Micah and Maggie were squatting in front of them. She felt Skyler's head lift off her shoulder as shouts rang out. It took a second to register what was happening. Her brother's concerned face was right in front of her, and his smile illuminated his features when her eyes focused on his.

"Cam, oh my God, it's good to see you." Micah was a little too close to her face for her liking, and she tried leaning back a little while she reached out to make sure he was real.

Looking over, she watched Skyler's reunion with her mom. Skyler leaned over into Maggie's arms, and they both held on, rocking and murmuring indecipherable words. They were careful of Goose, who was still lying across Skyler and Cam's laps, but it looked like neither of them were going to let go anytime soon.

Goose was wiggling, and Cam maneuvered him down on the ground before struggling to stand. Micah held her arm as she stood. Standing face to face with her brother was surreal, and she was grateful he hadn't gone in for a hug. When Cam hugged people, she had to be the initiator. The one exception to the rule was currently laughing at something Maggie said. Micah was vibrating with excitement and tears. She took a step forward and wrapped her arms around his shoulders.

She felt his arms tentatively embrace around her, keeping the pressure light, and as soon as she stepped away, he dropped his arms.

Skyler and Maggie turned to them, and Skyler jumped up and squeezed Micah with a grin. Maggie waited to see if Cam would be okay with a hug, not moving until Cam stepped in and folded her arms around Maggie for a brief but meaningful embrace. It warmed her that Maggie remembered that piece from her childhood and had allowed

Cam the decision. There were a lot of emotions to process, and Cam found herself wanting to wrap her arm around Skyler's waist and pull her close.

"How did you find us?" Cam asked, looking around as if trying to find a clue to their story and sudden appearance.

"We saw the smoke, then found the bundled sticks. Brilliant, sis." Micah went to high five, but Cam was shaking her head and pointing to Skyler.

"It was all her." Cam hitched her thumb towards Skyler. "The sticks on the trail, and I guess the fire is your doing as well. I had a bum leg for the first couple of days and have just barely started to gain more mobility." Cam hip-checked Skyler, who pulled her close when she went to step away again.

Skyler chuckled. "Yeah, that worked out well. Umm, do you have a plane, or boat, or something? Maybe we can catch up as we walk back to the beach?" Skyler squeezed Cam's side.

The little action helped Cam calm down from her anxious feelings about the new changes that were upon them. "Will you help carry Goose?" She looked to Micah, who was already bending down to pick him up.

"What happened?" Maggie asked, speaking up for the first time. She was frowning slightly as concern marred her face.

Cam hadn't spent much time with Maggie, but her presence was calming, and she must be alright, having raised a kickass daughter like Skyler practically by herself. With Goose secured in Micah's arms, the small group started making their way back to the beach. Cam took one last look behind her at the cabin and the place that had provided safety for a few days.

With a final nod, she followed them out towards freedom.

***

Skyler fell in step behind her mom as they caught up on the events of the past ten days. She gasped when she heard the number, not having paid attention to how long they had been stuck on the island. Skyler retold the bear story and how Goose had protected her, possibly saving her life by jumping between it and her while taking the swipe. Her voice was shaking as she told the story, feeling the effects of the adrenalin again. By the time she recounted scaring away the bear with the flare and the cabin fire, Skyler's heart was racing and her palms were sweaty.

Looking behind her a few times, she was worried about Cam's silence, but then again, Cam tended to go into her head when she was processing things. She'd always been that way, and it was almost comforting in its familiarity. Walking up the hill, she stopped every so often to help provide support, knowing Cam's leg was still healing.

Her mom provided an update on what had happened, and Skyler was surprised to hear that Aunt Abby was also there. Maggie assured her that Raven was safe with a co-worker from the library. After telling them what had happened, almost everyone at the library had offered to take the animals for them as long as they needed while Maggie and Abby went to help look for her.

Skyler smiled at hearing Abby's antics, and Micah even provided a few breathless quips as he struggled with Goose, but he wouldn't take up any of their offers to take him. She grabbed the camera hanging from her neck and took a few pictures of the hike back and of her mom, Micah, and Cam, wanting to capture the moment of relief.

Reaching the beach, Micah pointed to the SOS sign, giving a few pointers on how it could be better. Skyler laughed when she made eye contact with Cam as they both slightly rolled their eyes with a smile. Skyler saw the boat anchored and whooped at the sight.

Maggie asked about the small life raft and if they should bring it with them. Skyler saw Cam slap her forehead and turn back towards the raft. Then she asked her mom to help Micah with Goose while she went to help Cam, knowing she would struggle with her leg.

In a moment of silence, Skyler slid near Cam's side and pulled her to a stop. "Hold on. I want to check in. Are you okay?" Skyler asked, searching Cam's eyes for any sign of potential lies that might come out of Cam's mouth.

"I'm just processing all this. I'm ecstatic, but also just wondering what will happen when we get back." Cam smiled, but it didn't reach her eyes.

"Well, we already know what we are going to do. Food and shower, but not necessarily in that order." The corner of Skyler's eyes crinkled in a smile, then she sighed when Cam leaned in and placed a delicate kiss on her lips. When they parted, Skyler added, "Teeth brushing. I want to clean my teeth of their sweaters. I'm adding that to the list," before leaning in for another kiss.

The tension she had felt radiating off Cam during the hike seemed to melt away as they parted. "I can handle this." Skyler pointed to the raft. "How about you start walking to the boat, and most likely, I'll still beat you." She grinned, then laughed when Cam swatted her butt.

Skyler walked to the raft, undoing the knot around the tree. She took a moment with her hands on her hips, taking in the sights, not sure she'd ever be back to this mystery island but grateful for what it had provided while they were there. Then, with a final nod, she gathered the boat and started walking towards the group, laughing when she saw Abby on the bow of the boat, flapping both her arms in a full windmill wave.

***

Cam had to hold herself back from kissing the side of Micah's boat as they rowed up to it, dragging the second raft behind them. Micah got in the boat first, and he and who she could only assume was the infamous Aunt Abby helped them into the boat. Doing a double-take when Maggie and Abby were side by side, she broke out in a sweat trying to remember which one was which. Maggie was softer spoken, but that only helped when one of them was speaking. Their clothing styles were different, but she couldn't remember what Maggie was wearing. She felt a sheen of sweat start on her forehead.

Skyler slipped behind her with her arm on her shoulder and her mouth near her ear. Cam melted into her body and listened to her words.

"Aunt Abby has slightly more gray hair, a more pronounced bump on her nose, and speaks at a louder volume. Mom is a little rounder, has a darker red tint to her hair, and usually has some sort of glasses, either hanging from her shirt, on her head, or sitting precariously near the edge of her nose." Cam then felt a gentle kiss on her neck before she felt Skyler busy herself with securing the rafts.

Cam felt calmer knowing how to tell the twins apart and loved how Skyler could sense her anxiety and what it was about and quietly explain without making a big deal. She shook her head with a secret smile just for Skyler. Feeling more confident, Cam went up to Abby and held out her hand. "Abby, I'm Camryn, or Cam. I've heard a lot about you, and it's nice to meet you."

Abby looked at her hand, then up at Cam. "Cam, I'm so happy to meet you. Thank you for taking care of Skyler." She wrapped her fingers around Cam's in an impressive handshake. "I'm a hugger. Would you mind if I hugged you?"

Taken a little aback, Cam had to smile at the question. In her experience, most huggers didn't give her the option, and she found herself leaning in for a quick hug.

"I've got to check on Lily. Cam, would you mind driving the boat for a little bit?" Micah said once they got underway.

"Lily's here? Is she okay?" Cam looked around.

"She had some pain this morning and has been resting," Maggie pointed to the area Cam knew held a small sleeping alcove.

She itched to say hi but knew Micah would need to reassure himself that Lily and the baby were okay, so she switched with her brother, telling him to tell Lily hi for her.

"Wait, I'm not sure where we are." Cam tilted her head.

"Oh, right." Micah pulled out the map and pointed to where they were. "This is your island, and we're right here." He moved his finger to the area, and Cam studied where they had landed as Micah left to check on Lily.

"Wow, we drifted far!" Cam looked up to Skyler. "This is where we landed." She pointed to the area, keeping her other hand on where they were.

"This is where the rescue's search focused on." Maggie marked a few islands near the landing site.

"It's lucky you came this way, and the cabin caught fire when it did," Skyler remarked as she patted Goose's head. He was resting on a bench, seemingly content listening to everyone's soothing sounds.

"How about you put some kick in the step and get this party home," Abby said, swinging her hips in a jerky dance move, hip checking Maggie and causing her to stumble. "Sorry, Mags, these hips have a mind of their own right now." Abby jumped around the cabin before stopping and pointing to the wheel. "Can I drive? Micah was showing me how."

Cam got the confirmation nod from Maggie that Abby was telling the truth and switched spots with her. She gave Abby a few tips, but for the most part let her have at it, only providing a few correction tips and telling her the way to go now that she knew where they were.

Every so often, she would look around and catch Skyler's eye. When that happened, she always got a wink in return that made her blush. Skyler would then turn and continue her conversation with Maggie.

Chapter Seventeen

Skyler felt her eyes struggling to stay open as the weight of Goose's head on her lap provided a security blanket. The lull of the boat was rocking her to sleep and the craziness of the day was bearing down on her. There was a bag of chips open on the table in front of them, and she was having a hard time staying away from the salty snack, even as it shredded her dry tongue. Micah had a few other snacks, but Skyler was ready for a full meal with plates, utensils, and an ice cold beer. The thought of it made her stomach clench.

Not wanting to fall asleep and miss anything, she carefully laid Goose's head down on the bench and stood to check on Lily. Micah hadn't been back up, and she wanted to see if she was okay. On her way down to the sleeping nook, she felt Cam's eyes on her back, and when she turned, she wasn't disappointed in the quick snap up to her eyes and the deep shade of red coating her cheeks.

With an extra sway to her step, she ducked her head and stepped below. Her eyes adjusted to the dim lighting, and she saw Micah curled around Lily as they both took a nap. Micah's glasses were skewed on his face as if he hadn't meant to fall asleep. Seeing them at peace, her heart ached for the same thing with Cam, and she wondered, not for the first time, what they were going to do.

Walking back to the cabin, she stopped when she heard Abby's voice. "You know that girl has been in love with you since she was a teen, right?"

Skyler's heart stopped, and she closed her eyes. That wasn't a confession that her wacky aunt should tell. Yes, Cam knew about the letter now, but there was a massive difference between crushes from the past and current heart-aching love. Those words needed to be whispered right before a kiss or shouted from the mountaintops after a hike. Leaning against the stairway wall, waiting for her heart to settle back down, she yelped when a hand was placed on her wrist.

"Hey, it's just me," Micah said, grinning.

"How's Lily?" Skyler nodded to where she had just come from, hoping he hadn't heard what Abby had said.

"She's good, sad she missed all the fun but will be up in a second." Micah looked up at Skyler with a smile. "How are you doing? It's good to have you back."

Skyler started walking back up the stairs. "I'm okay. I'll need to talk to my neurologist as soon as possible." She took out her phone and checked to see if it magically started working again, but alas, all she saw was her rat's nest of hair reflected in the black screen. "It's been a trip, and I'm ready to sleep for a week, but it could have been so much worse. I was lucky Cam was able to give me a rundown on the local plants that were okay to eat." She stepped inside the cabin and everyone turned to her, but she only had eyes for Cam.

Cam looked a little shaken, but her eyes were bright, and a small smile was trembling at the corner of her lip.

"How's Lily doing?" Cam practically had to yell to be heard over the hum of the engine and the splashing water. She looked away from Skyler towards her brother.

"Good, how's Abby doing driving the boat?" Micah asked as he settled behind the driver's seat.

"I'll have you know, I'm a natural and will soon be purchasing one of these beasts," Abby stated, patting the wheel and turning in the seat.

Cam had to grab the wheel as Abby talked about horsepower, boat length, and the benefits of fiberglass versus aluminum. Skyler laughed at how much she had already learned, having no doubt that she would buy a boat soon. When Aunt Abby found something she liked, she sank her teeth into it with vigor.

Lily came up, holding her stomach. Maggie handed her a ready-made cup of ginger tea before Lily nodded her thanks. Taking a tentative sip, she looked back and forth between Skyler and Cam, her eyes holding a well of emotions.

"How are you feeling, Lily?" Skyler asked as she tried to make her way to where she was standing.

Micah took over for Cam in instructing Abby, which allowed Cam to make her way over to Lily.

Skyler wrapped her arms gently around Lily's shoulders, careful of the protruding belly. They had only been gone ten days, so it was fascinating to see the changes to Lily's body already. She stepped back to let Cam greet her as a new round of tears started going for the group.

"Damn, it's good to see you two." Lily looked between them, and Skyler felt she was looking for something, although she wasn't sure what.

"Thanks for coming to get us." Cam ruffled Lily's hair, then her eyes widened and she ran to the window.

Sitka was in the distance, and the sight made Skyler's heart soar. It wasn't unlike her flight in, but now held even more emotions. Cam and Skyler made their way to the back of the boat and stepped onto the deck to get the full view. Goose had gotten down from the bench with Maggie's help and was limping his way out to follow them.

Standing side by side as the wind whipped around them, Cam put her arm around Skyler and pulled her close. Goose was lying between them, not wanting to be left out. Skyler willed the boat to go faster so they could get him to the vet.

The quiet lap of the water and hum of the engine was all that enveloped their little group as they watched the shoreline. It was the first time they'd had to themselves since being rescued, and the affirmation and connection was a balm to Skyler's high emotions. She leaned into Cam's side and wrapped her hand around her waist, squeezing lightly when her fingers settled.

They didn't say anything, just watched as Sitka grew in their view. When they felt the boat slow down into the harbor, they turned at the same time, and Cam leaned down to place the lightest kiss on Skyler's cheek.

"What are we going to do?" Skyler asked, turning to face Cam fully.

"One thing at a time." Cam gave a one-shoulder shrug, echoing their mantra from the island.

Laughing, Skyler turned back to the town. There were people lined up at the docks, shouting with signs. Skyler forgot how fast news could travel in the town, and she grinned at the strangers celebrating Cam's safe return. She knew the Porter siblings were well-liked, but seeing the proof brought tears of happiness. If anyone deserved the love and respect, it was the woman in her arms. She knew she wouldn't have lasted ten minutes alone on the island.

***

Cam didn't want to let go of Skyler as they made their way to the dock where Micah kept his boat. The reception of people lining the harbor brought a burst of anxiety. There was a peacefulness from the island that Cam was craving at this moment to have it be just her, Skyler, and Goose.

215

The boat pulled up to the dock, and Skyler turned again to her, then looked down at Goose. "I have to get my meds."

Cam looked at her, then down at Goose. They were about to part since she needed to get Goose to the vet. The thought of being apart from Skyler was putting a hole in her chest, and she wasn't sure how she'd survive her going back to Portland, even if it was for a little bit.

"Want me to meet you at the vet?" Skyler asked after Cam hadn't said anything.

Cam shook her head. "I don't think we'll be there very long, and I don't want to miss you in case I'm not there when you're done since I don't have my phone. How about we reconvene back at Nana Winnie's house later today?" Cam wanted to pull her in a hug and never let go.

Skyler's head slumped slightly before she smiled and reached to her for a hug. "Okay, we'll talk later." She leaned down and kissed Goose on the top of his head, letting him know he did a great job and that she would see him soon. As she stood back up, she reached out and ran her fingers down Cam's arm, squeezing her hand before letting her hand drop.

The boat bumped into the slot as people started pouring from the cabin. Cam lost Skyler in the shuffle as they disembarked and split ways. Goose's breath was getting shallower. Someone had brought Cam's truck from the plane ramp. Micah had gotten on her case for leaving the keys in the truck, but this was one of the benefits to the practice.

Micah needed to take Lily to the hospital. The cramps had started up again, and they were worried there might be something wrong with the baby.

When Cam looked around again, she had lost Skyler in the crowd. Hank, one of her pilot buddies, was helping carry Goose to the truck since her leg was still hurt. When she settled in the truck, she felt a pang of loneliness. Abby and Maggie had gone to help Skyler get her refill. She looked at Goose, who was breathing hard. Hitting the gas to get Goose to the vet, definitely not to run away from her feelings, Cam left the harbor without looking back.

She gripped the wheel tightly, watching her knuckles turn white. Cam funneled her feelings of powerlessness through the tight clutch she had on the wheel and ground her teeth in frustration at the traffic clogging the parking lot. It was nice that people were glad they were safe, but she had to get Goose help. Nearly taking a few side mirrors with her on her way up a grassy hill and completely bypassing the line to get out, she hit the gas when the tires finally hit the paved material of the main street.

The vet was clear out at the other end of town, and Cam was soon growling in annoyance at the slow progress to get her dog help. There were only two stop lights, but she got stuck at them both, wasting precious time as Goose's breathing became increasingly labored. He had crawled across the front seat of the truck and now had his head lying on her thigh. Cam's fingers were scratching and petting his head when she finally pulled into the gravel driveway of the vet. Throwing her truck in park, she sighed in relief when a vet tech came out to meet her.

"Cam, oh my God, you're alright! We were so worried. Is it Goose?" Sandy peered into the truck, cooing lightly at Goose, who had picked his head up an inch off the seat. Cam's heart thudded in a double beat when she noticed he didn't have the energy for a tail wag.

"Yeah, he got swiped by a bear this morning. He was lucky, but we were stuck on the island. I cauterized the wound because there wasn't much else we could do, but he's gotten progressively worse. I hurt my leg and don't think I can carry him alone. Would you mind helping?" Cam's forehead wrinkled in worry.

Sandy jumped into action, scooping Goose up in her arms and walking swiftly into the building. There were shouts of excitement from the reception area. Cam waved but kept pace with Sandy, who was taking Goose to the back straight away.

"I'll get the vet to see him since this is an emergency. You can stay with him for now, but if he needs surgery, we'll need to clear the room," Sandy said before sweeping out of the room, most likely to grab Dr. Maxin.

"You'll be okay. You've got to be okay," Cam chanted over and over as she patted Goose's head.

Every once in a while, he would look around, whine once, then put his head down, almost like he was looking for something, or more likely, someone.

"Cam, it's great to see you. You've been the talk of the town," Dr. Maxin said, walking in and squatting in front of Goose. "Goose, you got into a scrape with a bear? Now that's a story to get you a few drinks at the bar. Women love scars, you know." Dr. Maxin laughed at his joke as he examined the cuts before standing up and talking again to Cam. "I'm going to need to clean these wounds up. We'll see how deep they go and hopefully rule out internal damage. You did great work with limited supplies but let me fix him up for you." He held out his hand, and Cam took it with tears in her eyes.

"Please do whatever you can. I can't lose him." She tried to hold back the emotions of the day, but the thought of losing Goose was too much to bear. She kissed the top of his head and told him to be a good boy.

"We'll have to keep him overnight, but he'll be in good hands. We'll call you when it's done." Dr. Maxin walked her to the door before turning to the tech and setting a few things up.

Cam walked in a daze over to the reception desk. "I don't have my phone anymore. Can you call my brother if there are any updates?"

"Sure." The young man typed in the computer and recited Micah's number to double-check. He clacked a few times before nodding once and looking back up from the computer. "We'll give you an update as soon as Goose is out of surgery. He's in good hands."

Not able to speak clearly without completely breaking down, she mouthed "thank you" on her way out the door.

***

Skyler was standing in line at the pharmacy with her mother and aunt flanking her sides. They were talking about something, but she was having a hard time following the conversation. Somehow in the hubbub of getting into town, she had lost Cam in the crowd. The ache of not being near her was growing by the second.

She loved her family, but right now she was missing the calm, silent presence she'd grown used to over the past ten days. If she weren't in such desperate need of her meds, she wouldn't have left Cam and Goose's side. She was anxious to know how he was doing.

"I need some cream or something for these bites," Skyler blurted out, scratching her bug bites as she walked up to the counter.

"I'll go grab some," Abby offered, hoofing it to the ointment aisle.

"Hi, I need to pick up my prescription." Skyler started rapidly tapping her fingers along the counter. There seemed to be too many people, and were they staring? Staring because she hadn't had a proper shower in days or because they knew she was someone who was lost on an island? She fiddled with the Calamine lotion that Abby had placed on the counter.

Thinking everyone is looking at you and judging? Your paranoia is showing. Skyler looked around while the pharmacist brought up her prescription. That type of thinking was definitely a product of growing up in a small town.

219

"Alright, here you go." The lady handed her the bag. "Have you taken these before?" the pharmacist asked as she rang up the meds.

"Yes, thank you," Skyler said before grunting as her mom pushed her out of the way.

"I'll pay for these and this ointment." Maggie handed the calamine lotion to the amused-looking pharmacist and tried to hand over her the credit card.

"Looks like it's already been taken care of." She handed them the receipt.

Both Maggie and Skyler looked at each other before Maggie caught Abby walking out of the store holding her smartwatch up in the air.

"Technology. I'm not sure I'll ever understand it." Maggie shook her head as she grabbed the bag.

"I'm with you. Give me a paperback with some tea, and I'll be content for hours, until I have to pee."

Maggie laughed and grabbed her daughter's arm. "I'm so glad you're okay."

Skyler patted her arm and slowed her steps to walk more comfortably with her mom. "I can't believe you're both here."

Maggie smiled at Abby, who was looking intently at each window they were passing by as she quickly pumped her arms up and down, muttering something about closing rings. "It was nice when that damn watch was dead, but Micah just *had* to find a charger." Then, looking up at Skyler, Maggie continued, "Of course we're here. You're my kid. We weren't going to sit in Portland waiting for news."

Skyler's mind froze on Portland. At the very least, she'd have to go back to grab her stuff. *But would Cam want to make a go of things? To date, and what if it didn't work? Would she try to stay in Sitka?* Suddenly, all she could think about was getting to Cam and talking things through.

"Abby's thinking about buying a place here," Maggie said, side-eyeing her daughter. "We talked it over with Lily and Micah one night and we want to help with the baby. At first we thought it was a joke when they brought it up, but Micah's eyes lit up at the thought, and Lily almost cried in relief when we said we'd think about it."

Skyler sputtered to a stop. "Wait. You'd stay part-time in Sitka?" Her mind was racing, and she was a bit jealous that her mom had no problem having life-changing talks with people.

"Well, nothing is official, but Abby has taken a liking here. I've always loved this town and was hoping to move back at some point when I was ready." Maggie looked around at the storefronts then nodded to a group of people walking by.

Skyler really looked at her mom. If she ignored the darkness under her eyes from sleepless nights and the worry and tension that had yet to dissipate, she could see it. She could see how her mom came alive back in the town that had provided the foundation of her adulthood.

"That's great, mom. I'm happy for you." She squeezed her arm and started walking down the street again.

"From where I'm standing, your heart is here as well. Don't let her go. I'll drop you off at the house. I know you are desperate for a shower, but then I'm going to the hospital to check on Lily."

Maggie had dropped her camera in her hand and started walking faster towards Abby. The camera was on, and the last picture was already queued up. It was of her and Cam on the back of the boat. Their arms were wrapped around each other, and Goose was at their feet. The picture had caught Skyler looking up at Cam, both with the softest expression on their faces. She wasn't sure what she saw on Cam's face, but something unknown and sweet was there. In hers, she knew that love was radiating out.

Holding the camera tight to her chest, a lone tear fell down her cheek as her heart fluttered. It was just going to work. Somehow, they would make it work.

Chapter Eighteen

Cam tossed and turned in her bed as she tried to get to sleep, growling at the lumpy cardboard it felt like she was lying on. She couldn't figure out why she was so uncomfortable. It seemed like a lifetime ago, but Cam couldn't believe she had been on the island just that morning and was now trying to fall asleep in her own bed.

On the island, they used sweatshirts and backpacks as pillows, and she could practically feel the splinters poking her in the back on that thin mattress. Turning again and putting a pillow between her legs to see if that helped, she almost screamed in frustration when sleep was still elusive.

She had checked in on Micah and Lily earlier that day. Lily was regulated to bedrest after it was found she had slight bleeding, and Micah flitted around her like a hummingbird, trying to guess her every whim before she had thought it into consciousness. Cam gave it three days before her brother would come crawling to her couch, having been kicked out by his wife for her needing some peace.

Goose's vet had called. He handled the surgery well, and she could pick him up tomorrow. Maybe that was the reason she couldn't sleep. She'd talked with Skyler briefly at the hospital when they checked on Lily. Eating their first full meal under the bright, unforgiving lights of the hospital cafeteria, Skyler had been falling asleep in her soup bowl, and Cam asked Maggie if she could take Skyler home. They'd made plans to meet up tomorrow, but the time was dragging by. Reflecting on her choice now, it seemed she was trying to determine if she could sleep alone. She now had her answer, and it was definitely no, no she could not.

Sighing one more time, she switched to her back and stared at the ceiling. One hand draped over her stomach, and she tried to pretend it was Skyler's arm holding her. Lost in thought, she didn't hear her bedroom door squeak open and screamed while scrambling out of the bed when a soft voice called out to her.

Flicking on the bedside table lamp, her heart both fluttered and slammed at the adrenaline pumping through her veins. Wide-eyed, Skyler was staring back, blinking, with her hands up. "Sorry, I'm sorry. I figured you heard me come in when I said your name, but you didn't respond, so I thought you might be asleep."

"You gave me a heart attack." Cam clenched her chest as she took deep breaths. "Is everything okay?"

"Well, you should probably lock your door if you don't want people sneaking in, but I'm fine. I couldn't sleep." Skyler looked down at her feet before looking back at her. "Did I wake you up?"

Cam took a second longer. She didn't like having Skyler in her house—not that she didn't want Skyler there, but for the first time, her trailer didn't seem worthy. She had never gotten around to building the house on the land she'd bought after her parents died, and she felt her cheeks flame at the thought of Skyler walking through the tiny hallway to get to the bedroom.

"Should I go?" Skyler asked, and Cam realized she hadn't said anything. Skyler had started walking towards the door.

"No, no, I'm sorry. I was in my head. Please." Cam brought the covers down and swept her hand over the area. "Please, stay. I can't" —she swallowed then looked into

Skyler's eyes— "sleep without you, it appears," she finished and watched Skyler's face light up.

Skyler hopped up on the bed and landed on her knees. "Oh, good." She grabbed the blanket and burrowed into the bed while Cam clicked off the light and got settled beside her.

With Cam on her back and Skyler's arm thrown over her chest, Cam felt the tug of sleep and knew she was in trouble, but for the first time, she found herself not caring. With matching smiles, they gently sank into sleep.

***

There was something soft rubbing up and down on Skyler's arm as she gradually woke up. It took a second for her brain to register what was happening, where she was, and most importantly, who she was with. Once she got to the who, an involuntary smile broke across her face, and the soft tickling on her arm stopped.

"Are you awake?" Cam whispered before continuing to run her fingertips across her forearm.

"Possibly," Skyler answered before squealing as probing fingers dug into her side in a tease.

Chuckling, they both settled back down, not ready to leave the bubble and meet the day.

"How's your knee?" Skyler asked after a bit, practically purring when Cam resumed caressing her arm.

"Better. I was able to get an appointment after we visited Lily in the hospital, being a town treasure and all that." She wiggled her eyebrows up and down. "Nothing is torn, it's just swollen, and they believe I may have stretched ligaments in my knee. I'll have to continue taking it easy. Did you get your meds?" Cam asked, sitting up slightly to reposition her arm that had fallen asleep.

"Yes, but I need to check in with my neurologist. What about Goose? Can we go see him today?" Skyler almost laughed at herself. She was basically going to insert herself into Cam's life and just not give her a choice. She could be very tenacious when she wanted to be.

"They said we can pick him up any time after two, which will give them time to observe him and make sure he's ready to go home."

Skyler felt herself close to nodding off as Cam continued stroking her arm, but Cam's low voice pulled her back to wakefulness. "When do you have to go back to Portland?" The query was asked in such a whisper Skyler wondered if she had only imagined the question, but Cam's inquisitive eyes were drilling into her, waiting for an answer.

"I don't know. There are still a few things I need to take care of here. Do you..." She started tracing the stitching of the black and red quilt as she tried to gather her thoughts. "Do you maybe want to go on a date? Brunch or something?" She switched tactics, opening the floor to the woman in her arms.

"Brunch?" Cam furrowed her brow as she sat up.

Skyler moved to the middle of the bed to sit cross-legged in front of Cam. "Will you go on a date with me today?"

Cam's eyes widened as the information finally sank in. *At least she's smiling*, Skyler thought as she braced herself for the possibility of rejection.

"A date?" Cam's nose wrinkled. "Aren't we way past dates? We just spent ten days on an island. That's practically marriage, isn't it?" Cam shrugged her shoulders with a smirk.

Skyler leaned over to lightly slap Cam's good knee. "Come on, Cam. I'm serious." She chuckled. "I want to know what a date would be like with you."

She left out the part that she'd been imagining a date with Camryn Porter since she was a teen. The thought of being on a real-life date made her skin tingle. Imagining holding the door, the ambiance and flirting—oh, and can't forget about the potential kiss—had her licking her lips in anticipation.

Cam's eyes were looking at something on the ceiling. Then she turned towards Skyler. "Well, I've always wanted to see what brunch was about. Let's start there. But first…" Cam bit her bottom lip and leaned towards her, and Skyler almost groaned. "I like having you in my bed."

The low timbre of Cam's voice caused Skyler's breath to hitch. It felt like she was back in the floatplane as her stomach swooped. Skyler sank back to the pillow as Cam rolled over on her side.

Cam closed the gap and placed a teasing nibble on Skyler's lower lip, encouraging Skyler to deepen the kiss.

Skyler ran her hands into Cam's hair, wanting to bring her body flush with her own. When Skyler moved to slip her leg between Cam's, her leg accidentally hit Cam's bad knee, which caused Cam to wince. She broke off the kiss and looked down in concern, pulling them from the moment.

"Shit Cam, I'm sorry." Skyler's hands moved above Cam's knee, wanting to provide comfort but not sure she should touch anything at the moment.

"I'm fine. Let's get some brunch. I wasn't joking. I need to know what this cult-like phenomenon is." Cam chuckled as she detangled herself from Skyler.

"Okay, but it might be overrated. It's pretty much just an excuse to eat either breakfast or lunch with booze," Skyler replied, laughing as Cam tried to put on shoes before pants.

"What are you doing? Goof." Skyler rifled through Cam's drawer to find a pair of sweatpants.

"Here." Skyler tossed the sweats to Cam, who just shrugged and put on the fabric over her shoes.

"I'm just really excited about this new dining experience." Cam held out her hand, and Skyler gladly took it.

"I'm a bit afraid you'll be super disappointed, but let's go."

Skyler's smile was brighter than the sun in Sitka that day. Of course, they still had a lot to talk about, but the first step was a date, right?

***

Skyler was right, brunch was way overrated, but it was nice to eat with her using plates and utensils that didn't give splinters. The game of footsie they were playing under the table didn't hurt either.

"How's Lily doing?" Skyler asked as she broke into her eggs benedict.

Cam poked at her tofu and veggie frittata, finding the aroma mouthwatering. "Good, although she might kill Micah. He's got no chill." She took a bite, letting the texture roll over her tongue. Not usually one for trying new things, she was surprised to find the dish acceptable.

Skyler took a sip of her bloody Mary. "No, he was never one for keeping calm in emergencies. Remember that one time you were swiped by a car on your bike, crashed into the pavement then you were almost hit by another car? After all that, you had to sit and console your brother for half an hour while your blood dripped into the gutter. Didn't you need like thirty stitches?"

Cam laughed. "Oh yeah, that was a fun afternoon. He wouldn't let me back on a bike for like three years. I had to sneak out of the house so he wouldn't catch me on one. I'm glad to hear he retold the story correctly, though, and didn't macho it up for his sake or anything."

"No, he wouldn't embellish a story to make himself look better. I think he wanted someone on his side to keep you away from bikes." Skyler snorted, which caused the balanced eggs on the fork near her mouth to tumble back to the plate. "I wish I was there when you said you wanted to fly a plane. He probably turned thirty shades of green, huh?"

Cam wrapped her hand around her mimosa. She didn't really like champagne or any sweet, sugary drinks for that matter, but Skyler said it was the most brunchy drink there was. "You've got that right." She took a sip and winced at the taste, wishing she had gone with Skyler's choice of a Bloody Mary.

"So, Cam." Skyler fidgeted with her napkin. "How is your first brunch experience?" she asked, looking down at the table.

Cam sensed she was working her way towards something but wasn't sure what it was yet. "I'm not sure I understand the big deal, but the food was good." She leaned back in the chair.

"Was the date okay for you?" Skyler asked, glancing once at Cam before her eyes skipped away.

"The company was great." Cam reached over and squeezed Skyler's hand as her heart sped up.

"Umm, okay. I have to ask. What do you want, Cam? I can take pictures anywhere. I don't have to sell Nana Winnie's house, or I can just rent it out, or sell it, I don't know. But the direction I go in depends on what you want. Because" —she took a deep breath— "I want to try this." She waved her hand between them.

Cam tried to calm her racing heart. She found a napkin that needed folding pronto and took to the task with gusto. She swallowed a few times. It felt like a rock was lodged in her throat, thoughts of paths past and present intertwining to land in this moment. She knew she had feelings for Skyler but hadn't had enough time to process them. It felt way too soon for life-changing decisions. Wasn't it?

"Skyler, umm, look," Cam started when she noticed Skyler shifting nervously in her seat, waiting for an answer. "It's just, um." Fantastic, now she can't find her words. "I don't know. Um. Skyler, these are huge life-changing decisions. Don't you think it's a little soon?"

Skyler just blinked. It looked as if she was trying to keep tears from falling, and Cam's spirit broke.

"I just think we need some time to process things. A lot has happened in a short amount of time. Our first kiss was just a handful of days ago." She sighed. Her words so far were a rambling mess, and what she was trying to say wasn't coming out right. She took a drink to clear her parched throat before continuing. "Without time to process everything, all I can say for certain is that I want you in my life. Definitely as friends, hopefully as more, but right now, can we see where life takes us?" Cam went to grab Skyler's hand, but she pulled away with a deflated look.

"Friends," Skyler whispered to her half-eaten eggs.

Cam could practically see the shutters closing on the woman sitting across from her. She tried to think of what she could have said differently, but it was all true. She needed time to process but hated seeing Skyler's shoulders slump. Brunch was quickly losing its appeal as the food turned to dust in her mouth.

"Are you okay?" Cam asked when she felt the silence seem to stretch for a year.

Skyler lifted her pointer finger and wiped the side of her eye. "Umm, yeah, I'm fine. I'm not hungry, do you want my stuffed tomatoes? I don't think there is any sauce or eggs on them." She pushed the plate over to Cam's side but still wouldn't look at her.

"Skyler, please. Look at me." Cam was worried she had just ruined their easy camaraderie.

Skyler looked at her, her eyes bright, and a small fake smile tight on her lips. "It's okay, Cam. I understand. I see I was pushing you towards U-hauling. I've had a lot more years to think about us, and hopefully, someday, we'll meet at the finish line." She slipped a card to the waiter passing by.

Cam tried to protest but just got a sad smile in return.

"I've always wanted to take you out." Skyler shrugged and grabbed her card back. "Shall we?" She stood but hesitated at the chair. "Can I go with you to see Goose one more time?"

Tripping, Cam looked back to Skyler. "One more time? What do you mean?"

She knew what it meant. Skyler would be going back to Portland, but Cam hadn't prepared for it yet. She wasn't ready.

"I'm going to try and get home soon. Most of the stuff I can do from Portland, and well, I think it's time to lick my wounds and head on home."

Cam swished her mouth back and forth as she reached for Skyler's lower back. It was unconscious, and she hadn't realized what she was doing until she felt Skyler's muscles bunch up from the contact. Slowly she pulled away, shaking her head at herself.

***

Skyler's nose was twitching from the antiseptic smell that still clung to Goose's fur as she buried her head near his neck. Tears of frustration, pain, and exhaustion overflowed from her body. She was sitting on Nana Winnie's floor while Cam went to check on Micah and Lily. They didn't want to overwhelm Lily, so they decided to trade off. Skyler got some much-needed Goose time while Cam brought over some supplies for Lily.

In her heart, Skyler knew Cam wasn't the type to jump without thinking of all the possibilities, but going back to Portland without some sort of plan was going to be like sleeping on glass shards. On the one hand, she wished there was a way to get Cam to see that they would be great together. But on the other, she knew that Cam wasn't the type of person to jump into something without reviewing everything and that she needed to back off to allow Cam to process. Walking away from something she had wanted for so long was almost unimaginable, but she knew, in the long run, it was the right thing to do.

A new round of tears started bubbling up. Goose was patiently waiting to lick his fur clean, but with the inflatable pillow around his head, he was going to have to wait a while. When she no longer held any tears in her body, she laid down on the floor, and Goose gently put his head on her belly. The pillow dug in a little, but it was nice to reacquaint with her buddy. There were increased vibrations from his tail thumping on the ground, but she placed her hand on his non-injured side to try and calm him down.

Opening her eyes, she shrieked when she saw Abby's upside-down face hanging over her, having not heard the creak of the door hinge.

"I told you that would scare her," Maggie said from the couch.

Skyler scrambled to sit up, displacing a grumbling Goose, who went over to the couch and laid at Maggie's feet with an indignant look thrown Skyler's way.

"What are you doing here?" Skyler rubbed her eyes, trying to lubricate her dry orbs.

"We were with Lily and Micah," Maggie started.

"That boy means well, but he is a smotherer. We have to run interference to make sure Micah isn't bugging Lily every thirty seconds," Abby finished.

"Cam came to visit, and we thought we'd leave them to catch up, and it gives us a chance to see how you are doing." Maggie patted the seat next to her, and Abby went to sit down before she got a glare from Maggie and went to sit in the chair across from them. Skyler slid into the seat next to her mom with a smile.

Maggie grabbed Skyler's hand. "What are your plans?"

"She went on a date with a tall drink of water if the gossip from the local watering hole has anything to say." Abby's voice was muffled as she was turned completely around in the chair with her back to them, looking at the movies stacked in a small bookcase behind her.

"Aunt Abs, that chair twists. You can just sit and turn if you want."

Abby wiggled her butt in the air. "That's no fun."

Maggie's worried gaze fell on Skyler. Abby seemed to be doing her best to lighten the mood, but her mom was never one for letting big feelings go. She was staring at Skyler the way Skyler stared at Cam when she knew there was more to be said.

Exhaling through her nose caused a bubble to form, and Skyler reached over to the end table to grab a tissue. "Cam's not sure what she wants. It's a big step for me to move to Sitka when we haven't even dated. And I get that, up here." Skyler brought two fingers to her temple. "But in here is screaming something else." She held a palm over her heart and rubbed the ache away.

Maggie and Abby exchanged twin glances as her mom pulled her into an embrace. "I think this is one where you have to give it some time." Maggie's low voice washed over her frayed nerves.

"We have it on pretty good authority that she feels things for you, but you also can't force it. I was always a battering ram, and it scared everyone away." Abby's soft tones were so similar to her mom's that Skyler had to look up to see the spoken words were indeed coming out of Abby's mouth.

"What are your plans?" Maggie asked again, sweeping a piece of hair out of Skyler's eyes.

"My plane leaves tomorrow morning—the super early flight. I've got a few things to do in Portland, plus I miss Raven. I'll grab our cats, and they can stay with me. What about you?"

"Abby and I are dividing and conquering. She will look at buying a house while I start tying up a few things in Portland. She's starting to look for a place to rent, but I'll want to come back up to help Lily, or there might be a homicide at the house." Maggie's shoulders displaced Skyler's head when she laughed.

Skyler felt a pang of jealousy at their ability to just up and move like that. "You can stay here, Abs, if you want. I'm not sure what I'm doing with it yet." She looked around at the first house she felt was a home. If she couldn't stay in it for now, at least someone she trusted would be here.

"Thank you. That's sweet. I know what this house means to everybody and will do my best to honor Winnie's memory." Abby could be extremely thoughtful when she wanted to be.

"Knock, knock." A voice came from the door as it opened. "Shit, I'm sorry." Cam stood in the doorway. "I'm so used to just barging into this house." She brought her hand to the back of her neck, rubbing it gently.

Goose lifted his head and stood, wobbling towards his pack leader. The meds had worn off long ago, but the inflatable pillow created a balancing issue that he hadn't figured out yet.

"I guess we'll either have to start locking doors, or I'll just have to get used to putting on pants if people are going to barge into the house," Abby said, slapping the chair. "I'm going to check out my room."

Cam looked at her, blinking as she tried to decipher what Abby had meant. Skyler came to her rescue. "Abby is going to stay here for a bit while she looks for a more permanent place. So, you might want to learn to knock." Skyler smiled and was glad to see the corner of Cam's eyes crinkle in silent mirth.

"Noted. Thanks for the heads up."

Skyler looked around and was surprised her mom was no longer in the room either, having snuck out presumably to give them some privacy to talk. "I'm leaving tomorrow." Skyler ripped the Band-Aid off. "I'll have to be back at some point, but I just wanted to let you know." She looked down at the floor.

"Oh, okay," was all Cam said.

It took everything in Skyler's power to look up, and hope surged in her chest at the teetering indecision she saw in Cam's eyes.

Reality was a cold bitch when nothing more was forthcoming. Skyler was at a loss at what to do, but she wasn't going to force herself on Cam. She had to meet her at least partway. "It's the early flight, so this might be goodbye for now." Skyler dropped to her knees to hug Goose gently. Cam helped her back up and kept hold of her arm as they looked each other in the eyes, searching for something.

"Can I hug you?" Cam asked as she squeezed tighter on Skyler's arm as if she was going to disappear into smoke.

The tentative question made Skyler's knees buckle as she fell into Cam's waiting arms. She wasn't one for painful goodbyes, but it felt good to connect, even if it was for such a short time.

The hug was soothing and heartbreaking at the same time. It felt like there were things left unsaid but were screamed in the physical contact. For now, all Skyler could do was relish the world's greatest hug.

Chapter Nineteen

Cam watched the jet that held Skyler take off as she leaned against a railing where her plane used to be kept. It was two painful reminders wrapped up in one exhausting hour. She stood in the spot where she had spent countless hours fussing with her plane, and now it was just a hole, an empty spot. Rubbing her chest, she tried not to think of the parallels.

Goose kept sniffing the area then looking up at Cam to see if he got the wrong spot. The lack of Plane Jane in the stall was throwing the poor thing for a loop. He tilted his head at her and whined. Cam would have laughed if she hadn't felt the exact same way.

The thought that she would feel better once Skyler's plane took off was almost laughable. Her eyeballs felt like they were too big for her head after no sleep and no midnight visitors. Staring at the water gently lapping at the dock, she wondered where to go from there.

Knowing she'd done the right thing in asking for time to process and living with that decision were two vastly different things. In her head, she knew they needed to talk things over and not make any rash decisions, especially since they lived in separate states. But tell that to her mind that wanted to sleep but apparently could only find relief when wrapped in a Skyler blanket.

"I thought I'd find you here." Micah's voice floated to her.

Quickly she wiped the errant tear that was threatening to fall before turning to her brother. "I'm surprised you left your wife alone for three minutes." She groaned inwardly at herself, instantly feeling bad for being so snippy. "Sorry, I didn't get much sleep last night."

"I didn't either, but it was because Lily had another bout of cramps." Micah glared at her.

"Is she okay?" Cam asked quietly, wishing a tsunami would come to swallow her whole. He didn't need her crap on top of everything he was dealing with regarding Lily's pregnancy.

"Yeah, they stopped." Micah came to stand next to her. The jet wasn't even a dot amongst the clouds anymore, and the further Skyler went, the worse she felt. "How are you doing?" he asked, tapping her shoulder with his.

"Oh, peachy. I'm going to work on getting a new plane. I think the insurance should cover some of it."

"You know that's not what I meant. And you're not scared to fly?" Micah turned to her with wide eyes.

She looked at the space that had previously held Plane Jane. She wanted to laugh at the name, but tears sprung up instead. "I'm scared of a lot of things, but flying isn't one of them," was all Cam could say on the matter as she swallowed through her thick throat.

"Come on. I think Maggie is cooking some breakfast back at our house." Micah turned back towards the ramp but waited until Cam was beside him to continue walking.

"It's been great getting to know them over the days. Nothing like an emergency to bring people *closer together*."

Cam could feel Micah's sideways glance when he emphasized the closer together part as if trying to say something without saying it. Cam was tired and didn't want to play into his hand. "I'm glad Maggie has been around to help, and it's been great to get to know Abby," she said diplomatically, rising above the bait.

They reached the top of the ramp. "I'm going to get you to talk about her. You have to process everything that happened, and I'm not going to let you slink back into your lonely life. Now, I'll see you back at the house."

Micah playfully raced her to the car, yelling "Shotgun!" which cracked the first genuine smile on Cam's face. Of course, the race was a moot point since they took separate vehicles, but her goofy little brother always had that effect on her, making her laugh when all she wanted to do was sleep.

Pulling into their driveway, Cam sat in her truck and watched the scene play out in the window. Lily was on the couch, smiling at something Maggie was saying. Abby was dancing in the kitchen as she flung something in the air before it landed back in the pan. Micah had just gone in and kissed his wife on the forehead before going to help Abby in the kitchen.

Seeing all those things made a pit of loneliness open up in her stomach as she wondered if she would always be looking through the window of someone else's story. Practicing a few placating smiles in the mirror, she gave up and walked into the cloud of happiness, fully aware she was bringing the rain.

***

The takeoff had brought a lovely bookend of tears for Skyler's stay in Sitka. Now she was wandering her house with two cats who were happy to see her for a few minutes but then went on with their cat things. After having a near-constant person next to her, the quiet house was hard to handle.

There was a slight discontent that was easy to place. Skyler looked in the fridge and sighed at the fuzzy block of cheese and takeout she had forgotten before she left. Pulling a sweatshirt from her bag, she sucked in a breath when she realized she had taken one of Cam's sweatshirts by mistake. She brought it to her nose, inhaling the summery, sweet scents.

Putting it on was torture. It felt nice to feel Cam near, but also creepy and a little emotionally unhealthy. With slumped shoulders, she went to look for some groceries.

As the fluorescent lights of the grocery store glared down on Skyler, and everything seemed to be louder and more aggressive, she kept finding herself, thinking, *how do you come back from a plane crash and being stuck on an island for ten days? How do you go back to normal after something like that?*

The flight had been surprisingly easy, but she wasn't ready for anything smaller than a jet anytime soon. Flying brought thoughts of Cam. *Would it be weird to text? Or do I wait for her? If I wait, would I be waiting forever?*

When she got home, she tried to ignore the loneliness barreling down on her as she put the groceries away, which only consisted of more cheese and crackers and some wine. It sounded fancy until you saw it was Tillamook cheddar and cheap boxed wine.

She checked her phone for the thirtieth time in five minutes and almost dropped it when it lit up with Micah's name. Swallowing a slight pang of disappointment of it not being Cam, she looked around the house before deeming it an acceptable state to answer the FaceTime call.

"Heeeeyyyyy. Skyler!!!"

A chorus of yells echoed through the phone, and Skyler had to pull it away from her face with a wince. She ignored the disappointing plummet her stomach was doing currently and instead focused on the blurry blobs bouncing in and out of the frame. It looked like everyone she knew from Sitka was at some point in the frame as she was passed from her mom and Abby to Lily before it landed on

Micah's face. She had only seen a glimpse of Cam's awkward wave as the phone was passed from Abby to Lily, but it was enough to get her heart racing.

"Micah, hi, how's it going?"

She tried not to stare, willing for another glance of Cam. It was going to be fun to try and deal with these emotions.

"We are doing well but miss you already." Micah's pouting face came through. "Why couldn't you have stayed longer?" He looked up and glared at someone. The coughing fit in the background provided a clue as to who was the recipient of the glare, and she just hoped that Cam was alright.

"Miss you too, Mike." Skyler counted in her head before he corrected her. She got to one and a half.

"Don't call me Mike! But seriously, it's not the same without you. So when are you coming up next? How about this weekend?" His puppy dog eyes matched those of Goose, whose head had just popped into the frame.

A large tongue licked the screen, then he whined and searched for a way to get to her. Micah pulled the phone away just as a paw was about to swipe it.

"I don't know when I'll be up next. Still have a few things to take care of, but most of it I can do from here. I promise, though, it won't be as long between trips like last time."

Seeing everyone was making things harder. "Well, I should probably get back to unpacking." She looked behind her like the laundry was tapping her on her shoulder. "Bye, everyone!" she yelled, and Micah twirled the phone so that everyone could wave goodbye.

The screen went dark along with her mood. Should she have done more, stayed longer, grabbed Cam by the shoulders, and shook her, or better yet kissed her passionately until she saw what they could be? None of those things would help, and she knew that. Right now, she had to adjust to glimpses on a tiny screen.

***

The week after Skyler left was becoming more brutal for Cam as she tried to function with ineffective sleep. She thought that if she dove into a project, she'd be able to keep her mind off *things*, but in the dead of night, those were the things she craved. Her heart ached for Skyler's playful banter, her warm arm and her smile that stretched across her face more than Cam thought possible.

It was hard for her, but she could rationalize everything knowing that her decision not to pursue things further right now was, for the moment, the right thing to do. But tell that to her body trying to go to sleep. One of the most heartbreaking things was watching Goose keep looking at the door or wandering rooms. It seemed he was searching for someone, and when he didn't find her, he'd come back to Cam's feet and lay his head down with a sigh. Each time this happened, she wanted to explain her side, why it felt weird to have Skyler move here after only a few days, but explaining that to a dog wouldn't bring more clarity.

She picked up her new phone, happy that the salesperson had transported everything from her old phone from the mysterious cloud and she was able to keep the same number. She created a new text message and sent Skyler a picture of Goose on her foot.

Got a new phone. Someone misses you. Cam sent it without thinking. If she wanted to text at all, the non-thinking texts were the only way she'd communicate. Or the slightly tipsy texts. Other than that, she would overthink and analyze every syllable and potential emoji.

I finally got mine charged :) Awww. It looks like he's healing well <3. Skyler's response was quick.

He is, but I think he's milking the attention at this point. I caught him limping from his good side. Cam looked at

241

Goose, who knew he was the center of attention now and wiggled his body.

The wound was healing well, and the fur was growing back around the claw marks. Her heart stuttered at the thought of how close they had been to losing him that day. If Micah hadn't found them... Cam shook her head at the negative flight path her mind was taking.

Her phone buzzed, and she looked down at a picture of Goose with the inflatable pillow around his neck. The following text said, *Use this photo when he is feeling particularly smug. We can't have him knowing he runs the house now, can we?* An undignified snort shot out of Cam's nose. It was the first sound she had made in a day, and it hurt her throat a little.

Dang it, I already showed him. I will need another picture. Cam sent the text without thinking, but her heart skipped a beat when she reread the words. If she squinted, the words could be flirting adjacent. Was that okay?

The next picture had her rolling her eyes with a chuckle. It was of a black cat against a dark sofa. The text read, *The superior non-bird bird, Raven, seen in its natural habitat of the couch, blending perfectly with its surroundings. The only predator known to Raven is unknowing rumps sitting down or toes hanging over a bed. Feet are known to cause significant damage to mighty Raven, so he launches a counterattack, usually in the dead of night. I'm running out of nature documentary commentary.*

Cam read the message over as her heart pattered along, wanting to reach out for something more. But, instead, the lightness and laughter she felt dissipated in the wind, not knowing where to take the exchange. Skyler was always better at things like carrying a conversation or putting herself out there. She looked down at Goose and they both sighed at the same time.

***

Abby coughed as she pulled over a box that had been left on Winnie's dresser. She had moved the few things she'd taken with her to Sitka and placed them in the master bedroom. She felt a little awkward being in the room, but Maggie and Skyler had insisted since it wasn't currently being used.

In her heart, Abby knew Skyler would be back. She had watched Skyler and Cam dance around each other and was optimistic that she'd be planning their wedding soon. With that in mind, Abby wanted to get the house done. She had put an offer on a new build out on Sawmill Creek, and until she could move in, she'd make this place ready for Skyler and Cam. *SkyCam, or Scam.* She shook her head. Never had two names fit together so perfectly: Skyler, the photographer, and Cam, the pilot. Cam spent time in the *sky* while Skyler played with *cam*eras.

They belonged together, and it put a real bee in her bonnet, knowing they were apart right now. Huffing, Abby grabbed the lid and peeked inside. She gasped and carefully took out the eagle carving packed in the box as a note and photo tumbled to the ground.

She placed the carving on the dresser and picked up the fallen papers. The picture showed that the eagle was part of a pair, and when they were put together, they fit perfectly, creating an image of majestic flight. She rummaged through the box to see if the missing pair was in there, but the mystery was solved when she read the accompanying letter.

Abby tucked everything back in the box but kept the photo out. Something told her she would need it here in Sitka. The note and carving would be packaged with care and sent back to her niece. With an extra pep in her step, Abby went back to the house to resume cleaning.

***

243

The week passed by in a blur. Once Skyler fell back into a routine, it was easy to fake being okay. She had a few photoshoots to get through, clients to contact, and one magazine from LA called asking if they could interview her about the harrowing events—their words, not hers—of her survival story.

The Sitka Sentinel had called, and she and Cam did a joint interview over Zoom. It wasn't the first time she had talked to Cam, but it was still lovely to see her sitting in the designated square. Cam was never one for FaceTime, and most of their interactions had been through text which was fine, but seeing her face was both tremendous and excruciating.

Getting home after a particularly awkward and slightly frightening photoshoot with a man, his cat, and a sword in the woods, Skyler placed the mail on the table. She was balancing a box, but she didn't have the energy to open it yet and left it on the table.

With a fortifying glass of wine in hand, she felt ready to tackle the photos from their time on the island. With the glass already half empty, she took the plunge and put the SD card into her computer, watching the tiny squares of memories fill her device.

There were pictures she didn't even remember taking. Some of Plane Jane before takeoff, to magical photos of the snow capped mountains that protected the town called Sitka. The display on her phone lit up, and Skyler looked down. Cam's name was a ribbon across the screen, almost like a rope tied to her heart. For the first time in a week, she clicked the side of her phone to go back to a black screen without checking the message, just letting it be.

When Skyler reached the photos of the actual island, she was surprised and wanted to pat her back at how well she was handling things. That was until she saw a few photos of Goose. For her sanity, she had to skip over the ones of

Cam, and she found herself clicking the button far more often than she was comfortable with, knowing Cam was like a magnet to the camera. Apparently, she couldn't help herself.

When she got to the photo of Cam in the waterfall, her heart stopped. It was even better on a bigger screen, with the vivid colors and nature at its most crisp. The photo would be great in black and white, so Skyler started messing with the filters after saving an original. When she finished, she couldn't take her eyes off the picture in front of her.

Needing a break, she stretched, and her eyes fell to the package she hadn't gotten around to opening. The box on her table had finally taunted her enough that she broke down and opened it. What was inside broke her even more. With shaking hands, she took out a replica of the eagle that had been on the dashboard of Cam's plane.

She put the carving down on the table, not wanting to damage it with her unsteady hands. Raven curled up in her lap as she looked at the eagle her Nana had painstakingly carved. A sob escaped her chest as she moved the carving to different angles while tears fell into Raven's fur. That only made her think of Goose's fur holding countless tears, and the waterworks were turned up, causing Raven to huff off her lap.

"Goose would have stayed," she said to her cat. At least she thought the blob in her water-soaked eyes was her cat. It could be a load of laundry for all Skyler knew at that moment.

Once the tears stopped, she saw a letter peeking out of the box. With her heart hammering in her ears, she took the note out and smoothed its edges on the tabletop, staring down at Nana's shaky handwriting.

My Dearest Sky-Tie,

I don't believe I'll get the chance to tell you this while I'm alive, but I need you to know, I have only wanted happiness for you. I believe someone here will bring you the ultimate joy, like the kind I found with your grandfather. I don't need to tell you who I see you with. You have known since you all were kids. I hope this carving brings you closer together. Cherish her, Skyler. Forever.

All my love,
Nana Winnie

Skyler looked at the carving for a long time as memories of the island flooded her soul. Keeping the letter, she printed off the photos of their time on the island. Tucking the pictures in an envelope and sealing it with a kiss, she sat down to write a note before placing the photos and carving in one box and trekking to the post office.

As she watched the package get placed in line behind a hundred other boxes, Skyler couldn't help but feel relieved. Relieved that maybe, just maybe, this would be it. Either way, she would have to find some closure.

Chapter Twenty

A blast of frigid air hit Cam's cheeks as someone next to her opened the freezer door in the grocery aisle she was standing in. She was having a hard time concentrating on finding the brand of meatless sausages she liked. Instead, her mind was trying not to think about why Skyler hadn't responded to her. They were still friends, right? Had she moved on already? Did Cam have a leg to stand on being gutted by the thought? Or was she just overthinking things, like usual?

"Are you okay?"

Cam turned at the soft voice behind her. The voice was familiar, but she couldn't place it right away. She blinked at the flickering fluorescent lights overhead and tried to focus on the person in front of her. *Amber. You rescued her and Eric what feels like thirty years ago*, her brain helpfully supplied.

Resisting the urge to look around to see if she could figure out how long she had stared at the frozen foods, Cam tried to work her face into a smile. If Amber's wide eyes and slight step backward were any indication, she missed the mark by a wide margin.

"Amber, hi. How is it going?" Cam had to swallow at the scratchy feel of her throat. How long had it been since she'd spoken out loud? Most of her communication had been texts with Micah to see how Lily was doing.

"Are you okay?" Amber repeated, looking closely at her raccoon eyes and slumped shoulders.

Cam pursed her lips with a nod, crossing her arms over her chest. In a slow breath, she tried to release her tension and relax her arms. "Sure. I'm fine." Her voice cracked at the words, and she had to turn her head towards the freezer to cool her embarrassed cheeks.

"Nope, that's it. Come on." Amber grabbed her arm and led Cam outside.

If she weren't so dumbstruck at the assertiveness that had burst out from the timid woman, Cam would have given more of a protest. But as it stood, she went along with it and found herself in the parking lot. "Now, where do you want to go to lunch? My treat. We are going to sit in a booth, have a cocktail, and you are going to talk to me."

Amber's hands were on her hips, and her jutted chin looked so much like Skyler that Cam almost went in for a hug. "Bossy," was all Cam could manage, as her sleep-addled brain wasn't shooting on all cylinders.

"You've got that right. I'll let you follow me in your truck, so it's not a complete kidnapping, but other than that, we are going to have lunch. Get in." She shooed Cam towards her parked vehicle.

Cam couldn't help but smile as she followed Amber to the restaurant. Amber's eyes kept looking up in the rearview mirror, making sure that Cam was following. As she pulled into the eatery's parking lot, she didn't know if her heart would beat out of its chest when she saw it was the place she and Skyler had brunch. "Talk about outrunning ghosts," she mumbled.

When they got situated in the booth, Cam's eyes kept gazing at the place she and Skyler had sat at a few tables over. She could hear Skyler's laugh, practically feel her fingers as they grazed over Cam's hand a few times while they ate.

"I'm sorry, what?" Cam completely missed what her tablemate was saying, and she tried to focus.

"I was saying, I'm glad you and Skyler are okay. We were all worried. Hank had a rescue team going, and even Eric went out on his boat a few times, but I don't think he went far enough." She looked down as a blush crept up her neck.

"We're thankful for all the people that came out to search for us. We were lucky the weather was okay. I mean, besides a little rain here and there. But there was plenty of water, and of course, the company was great." It was Cam's turn to heat up as she thought of Skyler again. No matter where she turned, her memory wasn't far away.

They ordered some food, and Cam tried to think of something to talk about. She didn't want to talk about Eric and what the heck was going on with that, and she wasn't sure she had the strength to talk about *things*. However, there was a certain appeal in opening up to someone she didn't know that well. It could be helpful to bare her thoughts to someone that wasn't Micah, Lily, or God forbid Maggie, who had tried to coax a conversation out of her.

Just when Cam was debating spilling her guts or going with some inane comment on the weather, Amber straightened in her chair and fiddled with the napkin. "Alright, I just have to ask one more time, because there is something in your eyes that is screaming something. Are you okay?"

Maybe it was the whispered concern of the delivery, or perhaps it was the fact that ghost Skyler was staring at her from three seats over, but something broke loose. "I don't know," she said, her voice cracking at the end as the flood of emotions she had been keeping at bay tumbled out.

"Why isn't Skyler here? You both went through something, and it just seems nuts she isn't here processing the ordeal with you. It seems like a perfect time to have her stay awhile, maybe use the time to see if she would move

249

here." Amber started tapping her pointer finger on the table in evident discomfort from her own outburst.

Cam opened her mouth to retort but before she could respond, the waiter placed their food in front of them. She took a tentative bite of her veggie burger and chewed far longer than necessary before replying. "It's too soon. We're still friends, but it was only ten days. How can I ask her to move here, uproot her whole life, on the possibility of something more? What if it doesn't work out? Where would we be? I'm barely holding on as it is, and we weren't even together." Cam blinked in surprise at her candor.

"I'm sorry, but that's bullshit." Amber looked away, gathering her thoughts. "If I could be out and open with the person I love, I'd hold onto them and make it work." She held out a hand to halt the denial that was about to burst out. "Love evolves as you do. If it doesn't work out, then at least you *tried*. But I'll ask you this, what if it does work out, and you get what you've been searching for? Wouldn't it have been worth it to try?"

Cam's jaw muscles ached as she tried to chew the veggie burger that had become a thick mess in her mouth. Her mind filtered the crucial aspects of what Amber had said. Finally able to swallow, she took a sip of water before eloquently saying, "I just don't know." Never one for quick processing, she needed to sit on what Amber communicated.

"I've said my piece, but just think about it, please." She reached over the table and squeezed Cam's hand.

"You've given me a few things to work through. I don't know if I should be grateful or mad for the added piles in my overloaded brain." Cam smiled in jest.

The rest of lunch was surprisingly fun. They'd run in different groups in high school, and even as adults, Amber was someone she would wave at, but Cam couldn't think of a conversation they had shared. It was nice to open up to someone who wasn't close to the situation.

When they parted in the parking lot, for the first time they parted as potential friends, and the thought warmed Cam. For the first time since she left the island, she felt hopeful.

***

A knock on Skyler's door jerked her away from one of the most important parts in her favorite book. She'd had to buy a new copy since the one she brought to Sitka was destroyed in the cabin fire. Never one to not finish a book, she had to finish what they'd started on the island. Not expecting anyone, she continued with the book, hoping the knocker would go away.

Her phone dinged as her mom's name popped up. *Open up,* was all it said as another knock came from the door.

Groaning as she lifted herself off the couch, Skyler stumbled slightly when her shin hit the coffee table. Looking back at the table to ensure her half glass of wine was still standing, she celebrated that no wine was spilled. Although if her buzzy head was any indication, she should probably stop at that glass.

Opening the door, she hugged her mom quickly before standing aside to let her through.

"I didn't know you were coming back today. You should have told me. I mean, you know I wouldn't have been able to pick you up since I had seizures on the island and Oregon state law says I can't drive for two years after having one, but I could have gotten some things from the grocery store so you'd have food." Skyler automatically grabbed another glass to pour Maggie a glass of wine. She knew she was rambling but was having a hard time stopping.

251

"It's fine. I had a few things to do and didn't want to pester you. I'm sorry you can't drive for a few years. I know how excited you were when you were finally allowed to drive last time," Maggie said softly before adding a "thank you" when Skyler handed her the glass.

"Did Abby come with you?" Skyler asked, getting settled back on the couch and pulling her feet under her.

"No, she's taking care of a few things there. I'll go back up when Lily gets closer to her due date."

Skyler could only smile, loving how close their families had gotten while she and Cam were stuck. "Need any help?" she asked, taking a sip of her drink.

"Yeah, I need to pack up some of Abby's things and ship them back to Sitka." Maggie's eyes narrowed when she got a complete look at her daughter. "Are you okay?"

Smoothing down her hair, as if that was the sole cause for concern and not the bloodshot eyes of sleepless nights, Skyler just shrugged. "Waiting sucks."

Maggie nodded, knowing full well what Skyler was waiting for. "If I thought it would do any good, I would have smacked her upside the head a long time ago. Maybe knocked some sense into her."

Skyler smiled into her wine glass. "Wouldn't have done any good. With Camryn Porter, it's better to approach her like she's a spooked horse. Slow, hands up, and soothing voices. Although what do I know? I'm here, stuck in limbo—not able to move forward, unwilling to budge, afraid to spook the damn horse."

"I'm sorry, sweetie. I wish there were something more I could do." Maggie ran her hand through her hair.

"It's alright. I just have to learn how to become a horse master. Is that a thing? Horse wrangler? I don't know. My brain is pickled." She tapped the side of the glass. "Three deep in. Shh, don't tell my mom I might be tipsy." Skyler put a finger on Maggie's lips before slumping sideways onto her mom's shoulder with a sigh.

***

Maggie could only chuckle as she tucked her daughter in on the couch after a night of laughing and catching up. She watched as the bundle of tension smoothed out on her forehead as her daughter slept. It was hard seeing her only kid hold so much pain in her heart, especially when she saw Cam struggling with the same thing.

She had watched as Cam tried to hold everything together after losing her parents, as she learned to keep everyone at arm's length away, lest she get hurt. One of her regrets as an adult was taking Skyler away from Sitka. It was necessary at the time, but she hadn't realized the guilt or impact on the Porter children and the lasting effects it would have on them.

She would do anything to right this wrong as she watched two people struggle with their decisions. They belonged together, and if it were the last thing she did, she'd make sure nothing was standing in their way this time.

***

Cam held the package in her lap as she pushed Goose's nose out of the way. Traffic was clear, and she was trying hard not to speed as she worked her way from the post office. She had seen the notice that a package was waiting for pick-up but kept getting sidetracked with tasks for the insurance on the plane. Assuming Goose smelled Skyler and was trying to see if she had shipped herself, she pushed him back again.

"Come on, buddy, I'm driving here. We'll open it when we get home." She briefly looked at his wagging body while stuck at one of the red lights. "I miss her too," she whispered to him as he scooted forward on the seat and placed his head down on the box.

Pulling into her driveway, she tried to relax. A few steps and she'd be able to see what was in the package. Her heart thudded, trying to hurry her along, but first, she needed to help Goose out of the truck. Not willing to part for very long with the package, she put it on the roof before bending into the cabin of the truck and gathering Goose in her arms. As she gently placed him on the ground, she said, "Hope you're not going to get used to that elevator ride, Mister." Turning back, she grabbed the package and walked up to the porch, stopping halfway when she saw Abby waiting on the steps.

Holding back a groan at a further delay, she tried to smile, but it probably looked somewhere between a grimace and a look of constipation. "Hey, Abby." At least her words didn't scream *rude*. "Come on in."

No, go away. Let me open this package. I need to know what Skyler sent. I'm dying here.

"Can I get you anything?" She opened the door and let Abby go in first, which wasn't a courtesy that Goose extended as he shot past them and claimed his bed near the couch.

"You can get me scissors because we are busting open this package. Don't think I don't recognize my niece's handwriting. You must be bursting to open it up." Abby went to the small kitchen, and like she had been living there for years, picked up scissors from the first drawer she opened. "It's a gift." She shrugged at Cam's bewildered expression, not giving anything more away.

Shaking her head, Cam wrapped her fingers around the cold handle with unsteady hands. Abby grabbed the package and put it on the table, where they both hovered over it. She was having a hard time taking the last step in actually opening the box for some reason.

"Go on, I think I know what it is, and I think you'll want to see it." Abby put a gentle hand on her shoulder.

Abby's support became a source of strength for Cam, which was something that had been missing since Nana Winnie had passed. There was something to be said about having someone older who could impart wisdom in funny stories. Abby had a gift, instinctively knowing when to impart a story from her past, release tension in a self-deprecating manner, or just hold a shoulder and be a solid presence to lean on while Cam processed.

Cam reached for the package and cut the tape with scissors before opening the flaps. She had to let out the breath she was holding as the room started spinning. The first thing she saw was the photos of their time on the island. Goose jumping in the water, a few animals, but when she got to the one where she was in the pool near the waterfall, all air left her lungs. It was magnetic, and she couldn't look away. A practical part of her brain niggled that it was her bare back that was in the picture, but she couldn't find the will to care much. The image was artistic, beautiful, and sensual in a way that took her breath away.

There was a slight rustling then the front door closed, which she didn't even register as her eyes kept going back to the picture. Biting her lip, Cam pulled the bubble-wrapped object out of a box that was stuffed full of paper. Her hand shook as she undid the wrapping. Goose came over to inspect when a bubble popped.

Placing the wooden carving on the table, Cam could hardly blink for fear it would disappear. Looking around, she saw Abby had put a picture down on the table and left, leaving her alone to process the box's contents. With her eyes flooding with tears, it was hard to see that there was a neon green envelope buried in the bottom of the box.

Not knowing what to open first, she set the envelope aside and picked up Abby's photo on the table. The sob deep in her chest burst forth with the new round of tears. In the picture was her eagle that had been attached to the dashboard of her plane, connected with the carving that was just sent. The photo showed that they were a perfect match. Their outstretched wings could be slotted into each other, looking as if they were one bird.

Cam saw the eagle's chests were slightly different, bringing her nose closer to the photo and trailing a thumb on the detail. Cam picked up the one Skyler had sent and studied it closely. Where hers had a medallion with a camera carved on the chest, this one had a floatplane. Shaking her head, she wanted to laugh at Nana Winnie's blatant message. With all the pieces of the picture, it became glaringly obvious.

Fighting the urge to laugh and cry, Cam picked up the envelope and slid her finger under the flap. Her hands had stopped shaking, and the tears at seeing something that meant everything to her had finally dried. Goose had fallen asleep on her foot after snuggling up with the bubble wrap. Cam could only assume the material still had the scent of Skyler lingering.

Opening the letter, she smoothed it out on the table and started reading:

Cam,

It looks like this was the last thing Nana Winnie made, and I want you to have it.

I'm sitting here thinking of our stint on the island, and there were a few times you mentioned the eagle that was lost to the crash (or hard landing, as you like to say). I don't know what will happen. What I do know is what I want. I shudder to think that we won't be able to give this a chance, but I know you deserve this carving, and I would love for you to have it. As for the pictures, I'll leave it up to you. I know you weren't comfortable with one, and I want you to know I won't do anything with the pictures without your permission. They are beautiful, and I hope you enjoy them.

Cam, I've been in love with you since I was fourteen. That might seem drastic, but there were times my heart pattered out of its chest just being in the same room as you. My point in saying that is I have known how I feel about you for years, and you just started developing these feelings. I realize we are at different points in this journey, but my biggest fear is that you have always been so content in your ways that you'll never leap.

Please don't blame me if I'm not a great friend while getting my heart in the right place. I'm content waiting right now, but I can't promise I'll wait forever.

With all my love,
Skyler

After finishing the letter, Cam glanced at her watch then back at the photo, unable to keep her eyes away from it for very long before scrambling up from the table. Spinning around like Goose when he was trying to find a comfortable position in a bed, Cam tried to put her thoughts in order. She had already been close to jumping on a plane to see Skyler face to face, but the letter pushed everything forward.

With pure panic at needing to see Skyler, she reached for her phone to call Abby to see if she would watch Goose. Usually, she'd contact Micah, but his hands were full with Lily. Abby quickly agreed before randomly adding a tidbit about Portland weather and possibly packing a sweatshirt. Cam, who hadn't said anything about where she was going, would have laughed if she wasn't so frantic to get to her heart.

Chapter Twenty-One

Skyler leaned back in the chair in her home office and stretched her hands over her head. Her neck was stiff from looking through hundreds of photos but she figured the cat and sword guy would be happy with the results.

Needing some semblance of sanity, she had left her phone in the living room, or else she would have been tempted to check it incessantly, and that just wasn't healthy. She had gone to the opposite side of the spectrum and had left it on the counter for a few days without charging it as she threw herself entirely into work.

At the blank screen, she smiled sadly, seeing her reflection in the black void. She still wasn't getting sleep, but steady work had helped keep her mind off of other things. The lightning bolt came on the phone, indicating the phone had started to charge. Leaving the device to do its thing, she lumbered to the kitchen and browsed the limited contents of the fridge. Not seeing anything call out to her, she walked back to the counter and saw her phone light up with messages.

That never happens, she thought as she clicked on the first message.

It was a voicemail from Cam. She debated for a good two seconds before hitting play.

"Skyler? Damn, where are you?"

That was all the message said before texts started popping up. Micah, Lily, Abby, and multiple texts from Cam had her heart clenching. What if something had happened to Lily? Surely her mom would have said something, right?

Not sure who to contact first, she walked back to the kitchen for some water when there was a light knock on her door. Hurrying to open it, thinking maybe it would be her mom and they could talk about what could be going on, Skyler didn't look through the peephole and just yanked the door open.

Expecting her mom and seeing Cam instead was doing some interesting things to her body. Cam had her fist poised for another knock, and when Skyler tugged the door wide, they both stood blinking at each other. When it registered that they were staring, matching smiles grew on their faces.

"Skyler," Cam whispered. Skyler's whole body seemed to turn to putty as she just stood there, gaping. Cam looked around, then leaned in, asking, "Can I come in?" Her hands were in front of her rubbing together like she didn't know what the answer would be. Like Skyler would ever say no.

"Sorry, of course." She shook her head and stepped aside, letting Cam walk into her sanctuary.

As Skyler closed the door, she tried to think of something to say but drew a blank. Cam pulled her into a hug, and Skyler melted into her arms as she relished the contact. Then, trying to wrangle her heart back to a respectable beat, she stepped back, placing her hands on Cam's shoulders, searching her eyes for some clue as to why she was standing in her living room.

Raven rubbed along her sweatpants, the ones that had paint splatter on them, and Skyler had to sigh. Of course Cam would choose one of the six days out of the week she wasn't dressed for company. Pulling her hands from Cam's, she tugged the threadbare sleeping shirt lower over

259

her torso. Not that it was showing any skin, but she needed it to cover more of her while Cam was standing in her living room.

"What are you doing here?" Skyler's squeaky voice broke the quiet of the room, and she winced.

Cam stepped back to look at her bookshelf, pulling the book they had started in Sitka from the shelf and opened it reverently. "Did you get a new copy?" She waved the book back and forth.

Skyler wanted to throw the object across the room. It was causing a distraction, and she demanded an answer. "Cam, what are you doing here?" She just barely refrained from a foot stomp, but one was waiting in the wings if she didn't get an answer soon.

"I, umm…" Cam turned to look at Skyler while her hand went to massage her neck. Skyler knew this was usually her indicator of being uncomfortable. "I got your letter and the carving."

Skyler tried not to lean into the low volume but didn't want to miss a thing. She had spent a few days trying to distance herself and coming to terms with only being friends. Tell that to her stupid skipping heart. "Oh, nice. Umm, you could have called. I didn't know you were coming." She looked down at her outfit, fidgeting with the edge of the shirt.

"I tried calling, but it doesn't matter. Skyler…" Cam grabbed her arms and pulled Skyler closer. She whimpered and relaxed into Cam's arms. Her body and soul finally soothed after weeks of being in turmoil.

"I love you, and life is meaningless if we can't make this work because you are it for me. What I'm trying to say, Skyler" —she pulled her in closer to whisper into the shell of her ear— "I want you as my co-pilot in life, and I'm sorry it took so long for me to get to the finish line, but I'm here if you'll still have me."

Skyler's heart radiated a tingly warmth as she tried to swallow. The only working part on her body was the nodding feature of her head as she bobbed up and down, not able to come up with anything more eloquently than cupping Cam's face and leaning in for a passionate embrace. This was the first time she had initiated a kiss, having allowed Cam to set the pace up until this moment before she reluctantly broke the kiss and pulled her into a tight hug, letting all her emotions flow into the contact.

As they stood looking at each other with matching bright eyes, Skyler responded, "You have no idea how long I've craved hearing those words. Let's talk." Skyler dragged Cam to the couch. When she got to the edge, she stopped and looked down. "Raven, this is Camryn. Cam, this is Raven."

Cam leaned down and grabbed a paw. "Nice to meet you, Raven."

Skyler grinned at the display. "Goof," she whispered before shooing Raven to the ground so they could sit down on the couch. Cam sat close with a knee tucked under her so she could be face to face with Skyler. Cam reached out to grab Skyler's hand to keep a connection to her.

"So." She was having a hard time coming up with something to say. There was still so much to discuss. She struggled with where to start when they had to talk about everything. "How have you been?" She shook her head with a sheepish grin.

Chuckling, Cam slid her hand to Skyler's leg, and she cursed the fact that sweats were so thick—great for lounging days of comfort, but horrible when she wanted to feel the caress of wandering fingers. "I've been okay. You know, just having a few epiphanies, like figuring out I'm in love with my brother's best friend." Cam grinned at her.

"That's quite the epiphany. I can't say I'm upset about this new trajectory. But I have to ask—what changed?" Skyler kept her head down, but she almost wanted to look around for the other shoe to drop. They could have had this discussion in Sitka.

Cam leaned over and tentatively placed her fingers under Skyler's chin to lift her head up gently so they were eye to eye. Once there was an established connection, Cam didn't hesitate. "I don't think there was one specific thing that changed my mind. It was more the patience you afforded me and coming to the realization that you were right. I might never have found the courage to take a chance on love. I was protecting myself, but from what? The carving reminded me that flying doesn't mean as much to me without you, Skyler." She finished in a whisper.

Skyler's eyes blinked back her happy tears as she sat dumbfounded. "That was. Wow. Cam…" Skyler grabbed Cam's hand and held it close to her heart. "I've been waiting so long to hear these words, and I want you to know I love you too. This isn't news to you, I realize, but I want you to hear it and know I'm so excited to take the next step and to move home."

Cam's eyes softened at the words, her eyes bright. "Wait, so are we doing this?" Cam leaned forward on the couch, looking intently at Skyler. "We're giving this a try, for real?" She indicated between them.

Skyler could only laugh at the slight bounce in Cam's body, which was practically trembling with excitement, knowing it was mirrored in her own body.

***

Cam was trying to keep her eyes open. Weeks of not getting adequate sleep, the terrors of traveling, and not knowing what was going to meet her in Portland had taken their toll. However, she was now comfortable, excited, and best of all, snuggled up in Skyler's bed.

She wasn't sure what was keeping her up. Maybe it was the thought that it would all disappear when she closed her eyes. Lifting her head, she looked into Skyler's eyes but found they were closed. Putting her head on Skyler's chest, she felt the deep inhale of sleep. Skyler's body relaxed under her, and with that, Cam felt pulled under to dreamland.

Cam slept for the first time in weeks, a deep and relaxing sleep that regenerates cells and replenishes energy. Not sure how long she was out, she was slowly being pulled up through the levels of awareness with a gentle caress on her back.

Fluttering her eyes, she was disoriented when the view wasn't of her room like she was expecting. However, Skyler's scent filled her senses, so it didn't matter where she was if Skyler was still there, a solid presence of comfort and home. She turned and saw Skyler's hair fanning her pillow, a smile playing at her lips. The darkness under her eyes had dissipated slightly.

Sitting up, Cam watched one of Skyler's eyes peek open at the movement. "Morning. How long were we out?" Rubbing her eyes, she looked around to see if there was a clock somewhere.

"It's still early afternoon, but I think we both needed that nap." Skyler yawned and stretched out her arms.

Cam tried not to stare at the strip of belly exposed with the stretch, but it was as if her eye was magnetized to that spot. She felt her pulse quickening, feeling Skyler's body shift as a light kiss brushed across her neck, making the little hairs stand up.

She felt Skyler's hand sweep her hair away from her neck as she nipped and licked the sensitive skin. A particularly sensual dart of her tongue on the pressure point on her neck had Cam dizzy. Turning slightly in the bed, she captured Skyler's mouth in a passionate kiss that left them breathless. She pressed forward as Skyler leaned back on the pillow.

Lying on top of her, Cam ground down when Skyler's hands wandered up through her shirt and caressed the skin on her back. "Want to take a shower?" Skyler mumbled into Cam's lips.

"I took one at the hotel, but if I stink, I can hop in." Cam playfully bit at Skyler's shoulder.

"You got a hotel?" Cam felt Skyler's hands tighten around her back as if she was scared she would up and leave. Like that was going to happen.

"Yeah, I didn't want to presume, plus I needed a second to gather my wits." Cam leaned down and kissed Skyler on the neck.

"Umm, you don't have to stay in a hotel. You can stay right here and, mmm yeah, do that."

Cam had found a spot by Skyler's ear that pulled a sharp intake of air out of her. She was so intent on getting Skyler to create sensual sounds she hadn't realized that Skyler's hands had been busy until she felt the tug on her sports bra and heard a delightfully frustrated huff from Skyler.

"You're not wearing a bra that's easily snapped open." Her face was flushed.

Cam sat back up on her knees, giving herself and Skyler room to remove their shirts. Her hand hovered on the hem of her own shirt, but she was enthralled watching the shirt and pants come off Skyler. Each inch of exposed skin shot Cam's heart rate spiraling, which was how she ended up still fully clothed while Skyler was almost nude.

Skyler's eyes widened when she saw Cam still had everything on, and she scrambled to cover up with a blanket. Cam tore off her shirt to try and soothe the panic she saw in Skyler's eyes, but it got caught on her head and tangled up in her arms. Trying to find the end only ensured a deeper twist into the fabric. Through the material, she could hear Skyler's husky chuckle, which calmed her nerves a little.

"Hold on, stop moving, or you'll get stuck further." Cam felt the warm fingers of Skyler's hands as she maneuvered and twisted the fabric over her head.

Free of the material, she tried to meet Skyler's eyes, but she was feasting on the view of newly exposed skin. "Are you sure you want to do this?" Cam placed her hands near Skyler's shoulders as she leaned back into her.

Skyler's answer was to rip off Cam's sports bra before pulling her into a deep kiss. The feel of Skyler's body on her bare nipples caused a shudder that seemed to start somewhere deep in her heart.

A gasp escaped from Cam when she felt Skyler's hands wandering to her breasts. Skyler swiped her thumb over Cam's nipple and watched with hungry eyes as it pebbled beneath her touch. Cam's hips ground down as she unconsciously chased friction. Her heart pounded as she looked into Skyler's eyes and only saw love radiating out of them.

"I've wanted this forever," Skyler whispered as their tongues stroked each other.

Cam caressed the silky material of Skyler's bra and moaned at the ripple of muscles she felt under her when Skyler sat up slightly to provide better access at the clasp behind her back. Then, with a flick of her wrist, Cam freed the bra and gently pulled the straps down Skyler's arm. The task was proving difficult when Skyler replaced her fingers with her mouth and started stroking Cam's nipple with her tongue.

Cam wanted to take her time and sensually remove the fabric one tantalizing inch at a time, but Skyler had other ideas as she shrugged out of the straps and threw the bra across the room before kicking her underwear off. Cam watched the realization hit Skyler's face that she was now fully naked in bed with Cam. Cam wiggled out of her briefs, relishing in the contact as their bodies melted together as one.

265

Skyler wrapped her legs around Cam's waist and was grinding into her. Cam could feel their slick wetness mixing, and Skyler's flushed face showing signs of intense arousal. She maneuvered her hand between them, and with a final look into Skyler's eyes, Cam slid her middle finger into Skyler's dripping wet folds, gently teasing her clit.

Grabbing Cam's arm, Skyler moaned. "More. Slip another finger in. Fill me up, Cam."

Not one to ignore a request, Cam slowly sank two fingers as deep inside of Skyler as they would go.

Skyler's eyes fluttered closed with a look of rapture on her face. Cam had never seen anything so beautiful. She relished hearing the deep moans as Cam's fingers worked Skyler. They found a quick rhythm where Cam allowed Skyler to set the pace. She rolled her thumb repeatedly over her clit, causing Skyler's body to quake.

"Don't stop. Right there, Cam. Yes. God, a little more pressure." The rest of the words were drowned out as Skyler's orgasm ripped through her, lifting her off the bed slightly into Cam's waiting lips. Skyler wrapped her arms around Cam's neck, riding out the rest of the wave before they both stilled.

After a minute, Skyler looked impishly at Cam. "It's my turn." Her voice was deep with arousal.

Cam felt like she'd come home.

Chapter Twenty-Two

Skyler leaned against the window of the plane, thinking of the past couple of weeks since Cam had shown up on her doorstep.

Skyler had a lot to do to get ready for her big move and had offered to meet Cam back up in Alaska, but Cam had gripped her tight, replying, "Nah, I can help you get things ready. Abby is fine watching Goose, and where you go, I go." Cam had kissed her on her nose then grabbed another box to load up more books.

A few days ago, they had dropped off Skyler's car with Maggie's help, along with a few boxes of personal effects that wouldn't fit in their suitcases, and placed them on a barge cargo ship that they would pick up in Sitka in a few weeks. Skyler couldn't drive for a few months, but Alaska's epilepsy driving law was more relaxed than Portland's, only needing to be seizure-free for six months. Seeing her life packed up made Skyler excited for her future. She couldn't believe Cam was next to her, ready to take the step. It was everything she had wanted, and she couldn't believe it was finally happening.

Maggie had dropped them off at the airport that morning, and the fact they would see each other in a few weeks made the ordeal of saying goodbye much more palatable.

Once at the airport, they took turns going to the restroom while the other watched over Raven's cat carrier. He kept his nose to the mesh screen, trying to see everything, but didn't seem nearly as freaked out as Skyler.

She'd had a minor panic attack before the flight, but as Cam had so lovingly pointed out, "The plane wants to stay in the air. You'll be fine." She had rubbed Skyler's back, and it felt great but still didn't dissipate the anxiety. "Why is this one harder? You already flew once." Cam's question came near her ear, and she shivered.

"I think I was too tired to think about it for very long." Skyler had shrugged, leaning into Cam's touch, although she could still feel her muscles jumping with tension.

When that didn't work, Cam had gone to plan B, which was booze. She had stopped at one of the airport bars, and Cam piled on some vodka sodas. She might have to roll her to the gate, but Skyler had found her strength to get on the plane.

Once the alcohol dissolved a little, she could relax and enjoy the snow capped mountain peaks. She lifted her head to look at Cam. The noise was too loud for conversation, but she hoped the hand squeeze conveyed all her emotions.

Her heart started thumping in excitement when the flight attendant came down the aisle one last time to pick up the garbage. She pulled Raven into her lap to ensure he was still doing okay and got a wide-eyed response. He kept pacing in the carrier, and she told him they were almost home while she stroked the side. It probably wasn't providing any comfort, but it soothed her for a minute. She returned him to under her seat and leaned against the window.

Cam's hand started playing with hers, and she smiled into the reflection of the windowpane. They started descending, and the feelings she'd had when she'd flown into Sitka all those weeks ago were there, but instead of sadness, she felt lighter with a dash of gratitude.

Skyler's head slammed forward as they landed. It always jarred her with how fast they had to put on the brakes. When the plane started turning, Cam leaned over to her and, at the shell of her ear, whispered, "Welcome home, Skyler."

Turning in her seat, she placed a light kiss on Cam's lips, ignoring the sideways look from 17A. "I was home as soon as you said you were at the finish line."

Skyler could feel the smile on Cam's lips as they both sighed contentedly. Then, finally, the ding of the seat belt alert went off, and it was off to the races to see who could disembark the plane fastest. Skyler didn't care if it took them five hours to get off the plane as long as she had Cam's hand in hers. She found she no longer cared about any minor inconveniences of life.

Hand in hand, they walked off the plane. Skyler had Raven strapped over her shoulder and struggled with his shifting weight as he prowled the small area of the carrier. Skyler stopped to adjust the straps while Cam greeted Micah with an enthusiastic back slap.

Skyler had forgotten about Cam's aversion to hugs because she didn't seem to have an issue hugging her. She flushed at her flashback from the morning back in Portland, when they'd said goodbye to the first place they lived together, even if it had only been for a few weeks. She had just gotten off the phone with Nicole, her ex, who had called to ask if she would be the photographer at her wedding. It was impressive how quickly Nicole mentioned an article she'd read about Skyler's island adventure. When Skyler said she was moving to Sitka to be with Cam, she could hear the disappointment that they'd have to find another photographer, but they left the call on civil terms. Cam had waited patiently for her to get off the phone before lifting Skyler onto the counter and kissing her deeply. She definitely didn't have a problem holding her close.

"Skyler, as I live and breathe! Aren't you famous now? With your unplanned camping trip on the island and some amazing photos being published in National Geographic!" Micah's booming voice cut through the crowd, pulling her back to the present. He wasn't tall, but dang, his voice could carry.

Her face flushed for an entirely different reason as people looked over to her, wondering if it was true and she was famous. "Micah. Come on. It's just an article."

"And a podcast, news segment, and multiple articles. We're trending." Cam grinned at her as she added the various news formats that had picked up on their story.

"This must be our fifteen minutes," Skyler said, giving Micah a bear hug. As they parted, she looked at her best friend. He seemed a little more at ease since the last time they had been in the same room. "How's Lily?" she asked as she picked up her bag.

He was peering in the cat carrier. "Raven, I've only ever seen you on a screen." His face was lit with delight as he twitched his fingers in front of the carrier. "Lily is doing better. She's had a couple scares, and I think I've found the balance of overbearing and helpful, which I know has helped with her stress."

Micah grabbed a bag from each of them and started walking to the car, catching up on the trip and the move. He was bouncing like a kid. Skyler and Cam walked hand in hand, providing tidbits from the past couple of weeks.

During a three-way conversation a couple days ago, they were able to plan the living arrangement prior to them coming up. Abby wanted to offer Winnie's house, but since she couldn't get the keys to her new house until later that month, it made more sense for Skyler to stay with Cam while the house Abby bought was getting ready. With an asterisk, it wasn't *moving in together*, in case it was too soon, but rather a temporary plan until things were settled. Skyler ignored the scoff her brain kept trying to insert. The thought of not sleeping in the same bed with Cam held as much appeal as sleeping in a field filled with no-see-ums.

Micah and Cam both went to Skyler's door to open it for her. Cam won and gave a victory punch to Micah's arm while leaning in to kiss Skyler. When they parted, she caught Cam sticking her tongue out at her brother, causing everyone to laugh.

"Oh boy, this should be fun getting to know the Porter siblings again." Skyler chuckled as she climbed into the car.

The drive to Micah and Lily's house was full of laughter. Deciding to leave the bags in the car until they got to Cam's house, Skyler grabbed Raven and bounded up the steps to the house.

Her ears perked up when she heard a bark at the door. She turned to Cam and whispered that she should go first, just curious to see how Goose would react when he saw her. Cam picked up right away, taking Raven's carrier, and hurried ahead while Skyler retreated to the bottom of the steps.

Looking back once, Cam winked and opened the door. Goose took one sniff at her and burst down the stairs in a full-body wiggle, his front paws bouncing in front of Skyler before he stretched on his hind legs, trying to reach every part of her. Muddy footprints stained her shirt and pants, and Skyler didn't care one bit as she crouched down to get a slobbering hug from the dog she'd bonded with on the island.

"You're looking so good, Goose! Good boy." Now that she was at eye level, he pushed his nose in her face and licked her face. The pure excitement radiating from his body was impressive. Skyler didn't think she had ever been this excited about something before. Her face hurt from smiling and whispering sweet things to Goose's ear.

"I raised that boy from a pup, and it's like I'm Sally Stranger," Skyler heard Cam tell Micah at the top of the stairs, the laughter in her voice clear even with a barking dog in Skyler's ear.

"You're old news. There's someone new and shiny." Skyler stood up and brushed her pants off. "Come on, Goose. Let's say hi to everyone else."

Goose followed closely behind with his tail stuck in the air as if he was on a mission. Skyler's chest expanded with the love she felt at that moment.

Getting into the house, the first thing Skyler noticed was Lily's belly as she laid on the couch. She tried to swing her legs to the floor, but the Porter siblings were both quick to stop her from getting up.

Skyler caught a glance of Abby in the kitchen, and wanting to give Cam a moment, along with not wanting to overwhelm Lily, Skyler practically skipped to say hi to her aunt.

"Thanks for watching Goose. It's so good to see you." She squeezed her aunt but had to issue an apology when she heard a pained grunt.

"Oh, please, it was a pleasure. If there were a way I could have smuggled him away without you asking where he went, I probably would have tried. He's trained extremely well, although this is the most emotion I've seen since you left. I think he missed you." She nudged her side with her elbow. "He wasn't the only one, either."

Skyler's eyes found Cam's, and she noticed they were trained on her. The look made her want to drag her back to the house pronto.

"It's good to be home." Skyler shook her head, trying to reform her body that apparently had turned to goo. "Need any help?" She looked around at the ingredients but was unsure where to start.

"Nope, I got this. Go say hi to Lily."

Skyler kept glancing back to the kitchen. There was something calmer about her aunt. She couldn't put her finger on what it was, but it seemed Sitka agreed with her.

Sitting towards the end of the couch, she put a hand on Lily's leg. Micah had dragged Cam to the garage to show off some engine project he was working on, leaving a quiet peace with Lily. Goose had settled at her feet, basically taking up the duties of ensuring she never left again, which was A-OK with Skyler.

Turning towards Lily, she tried not to stare at the protuberance of a belly that seemed to have grown exponentially since the last time she saw her. "It's good to have you two home. I'm sure Goose is ready to have you both here." Lily was rubbing her stomach with the glow only an expectant mother could have.

Skyler looked down at Goose, who had barely lifted his head at the mention of his name. She tried to capture the feeling of warmth her body radiated at hearing the word *home*.

"We're excited to be back," Skyler replied. "How are you feeling?"

"It was touch and go for a bit. I'm on bed rest for the duration of the pregnancy, but this little bean is a fighter."

"Wouldn't expect anything less, considering his parents. I don't think I properly thanked you for all you did for us when we were lost."

Lily shook her head and stretched slightly. "No need to thank us, it's what we do for each other." Lily grabbed her hand and squeezed. "I'm so happy for you two. Nana Winnie and I had been talking for years, trying to come up with a plan on how to get you together."

"Really?" Cam asked as she walked back into the room. "Why am I always the last person to know things?"

"Because you're hard headed and if you don't come up with an idea, you reject it right away. So if they had told you point blank that we would be good together, you would have balked at the idea and run away," Skyler teased as she stood up to sit in Cam's lap. Goose was instantly alert but settled when she sat back down.

"Dinner's ready." Abby's voice floated from the kitchen. "Micah, Skyler, and Cam, you are on table-setting duties. Lily, you are on protecting that precious bundle and not moving duty."

Skyler climbed out of Cam's lap and helped her stand up before stepping up to Cam's side and putting a hand around her waist. Skyler was pretty sure water would boil if placed between their heated looks as they made their way to the dining room.

"We'll have to make this dinner quick. I'm not sure how much longer they will be able to wait before tearing off each others' clothes." Micah gave Lily a knowing look and gagged, making them all giggle.

Skyler's cheeks could have reheated the dinner. Micah gently helped Lily up as she slowly walked to the table. As Skyler looked around the table, her eyes landed on Cam's next to her, and she sent a silent thanks to Nana Winnie. It was everything she'd ever wanted since she was a kid, come to life at the table.

***

Like Goose, Cam felt she was following Skyler everywhere with her eyes. It would have caused her anxiety, but she caught Skyler's eye more times than not, meaning Skyler was looking for her just as much. Currently, it looked like Skyler was about to cry, but if it was anything like the feelings bubbling up in her, they were good tears.

"You realize we're keeping Nana Winnie's tradition of Saturday dinner, right?" Micah said once everyone sat down.

A small tear threatened to bubble over, and Cam tried to wipe it away discreetly. In her peripheral vision, a white square slowly inched under her nose, and she looked up to

Skyler handing her half of a paper towel, the other half already in use to wipe Skyler's own eyes.

Goose was still near Skyler underneath the table, but Raven was currently rubbing up against Cam's legs. The few weeks in Portland had brought them closer. When they first got to the house and she let Raven out of the carrier, Cam had been nervous that the pets wouldn't get along. The feeling was quickly replaced with warmth when Goose sniffed the cat and Raven allowed the action before walking away. They had a bit to go before they were friends, but at least they weren't fighting.

"Let's toast." Lily lifted her sparkling apple cider while everyone else grabbed their wine glasses. "To Nana Winnie. The one person that brought us all together."

"To Winnie," everyone echoed.

Cam couldn't believe the journey they'd had to endure to get to this place. She looked down when she felt Skyler's hand land on her thigh. There was nowhere she would rather be.

Once everyone helped clean up dinner, Micah dropped them off with their luggage at Cam's trailer. She had been itching to get Skyler alone, ready to replenish her introvert-levels with a fire in the backyard, or something, anything if it had Skyler by her side.

After putting their bags in the room, Cam pulled Skyler outside. A few years ago, she had built a fire pit in her backyard. She was a smidge worried that Skyler would be sick of sitting out by a campfire, but Skyler's slight squeal of excitement warmed the kindling in her heart.

It was a perfect time to sit by the flames, Cam thought as she settled Skyler on a chair near the pit. The bugs had gone to bed a half hour ago, and they were alone under the Sitka sky. Once the fire was burning nicely, she tried to sit in the chair next to Skyler, but she wasn't having any of it and pulled Cam onto her lap.

If she was honest with herself, she didn't like the vulnerable feeling she felt sitting like that, but Skyler's wandering hands along her back, stomach, and thighs quickly shook any vulnerabilities out of her mind. Cam laid her head on Skyler's shoulder as her arms wrapped around her middle, creating a seat belt hug.

"I love you." Skyler's words wrapped around her mind as her lips found the sensitive part behind her ear. A shiver tapped along her spine, and Cam felt a light kiss on her neck.

"I love you, too," Cam whispered into the night as Skyler captured the words with her lips.

Under the canopy of the stars, their moans filled the symphony of the night.

Epilogue: One year later

Nothing had gone right, and Cam was trying not to cry. She still had a few things to get together, and being rear-ended wasn't on the list—she had checked. The only silver lining was that she had dropped her nephew back to Micah and Lily, and he wasn't sitting in the car seat when it happened.

Skyler was handling things like a pro but gave her concerned looks, meaning she was picking up on Cam's frantic mood. There wasn't much damage to either vehicle, so they exchanged information with the thought that nothing more would be needed. Getting back in the car, Cam shook her head and pulled back out to the street.

"I can't believe we got into a crash today of all days," Cam growled, gripping the steering wheel so tight her knuckles were turning white.

Skyler laughed, and Cam gave her the stink eye, which only made her laugh harder. "Why are you calling that a crash when we were in a literal plane crash, and you keep calling it a hard landing? Maybe you should just start saying fender bender. At least that would be consistent."

That laugh did it, and just like that, Cam's mood had flipped around, and she was ready to take on the world again—or at least the rest of the day.

Cam and Skyler had officially moved into Nana Winnie's place once the construction on Abby's house had finished. Maggie was thinking of moving in with Abby, but a budding relationship between Abby and Hank, the pilot, had made her rethink the idea, and Cam suggested her trailer. The families continued with the Saturday dinner tradition in Nana Winnie's honor. The hosts rotated each week, and laughter filled each house.

It had taken a lot of coaxing, and a few test runs, but Skyler was finally comfortable enough with going on a flight that lasted more than ten minutes, which was necessary for the five-step plan Cam had come up with three months ago. Today was the final step, which first entailed getting Skyler on the plane.

Getting to the dock, Cam reached out to Skyler and pulled her close, kissing her cheek. "Sorry, I guess I was wound a little tight."

"A little," Skyler scoffed, but all was forgiven as she wrapped her arm around and landed her hand on Cam's hip.

Goose led the way, his nose inspecting every plank on their way to the new plane. The insurance money had come through, and Cam instantly bought a new plane. It was her source of income, after all. Skyler was terrified of her going up for the longest time, but slowly she was able to ease her fears and had even gone with Cam on a few runs, nothing like where they were going now.

After everyone was strapped in and the flight was underway, Cam felt her shoulders relax. She pointed out animals and different camping sights to Skyler while practicing what she would say in her mind.

The landing was smooth as Cam maneuvered to the beach. When she cut the engine, she looked over at Skyler to see if she recognized the beach. Her eyes scanned the area and widened when she saw the familiar opening leading to their campsite.

Skyler's head turned quickly to meet Cam's eyes, which were bright with what was to come.

"It's our island," Skyler said in awe.

Cam could only nod. "Hold on, let me help you get out." She pet the carved eagle Skyler had given her that was again on the dash of the plane. She let Goose out to explore the beach before hurrying over to Skyler's side.

Opening the door, she held out her hand. "M'dear." She dipped her head and grasped Skyler's hand to help her down.

On solid ground, Skyler leaned in and placed a gentle kiss on her lips that caused a tingle throughout her body. Cam loved that after more than a year, Skyler still could do that.

Once Skyler cleared the plane, Cam leaned in and grabbed her backpack. Before leaving, she had checked four times that a particular object was there. She had also told Skyler to bring her camera, which was hanging low on her neck.

They didn't say much as they explored the area while taking pictures. When they got to the tree that Cam had spent a lot of time leaning against, Skyler's fingers caressed the bark, and it was something Cam swore she could feel. Cam let Skyler lead, and she made her way to the trail that led to the cabin, just like Cam expected her to.

"When do you hear back on the pictures?" Cam asked, breaking the silence as they walked the overgrown trail, more because she wanted to hide her huffing breath.

"In a few weeks," Skyler responded but didn't elaborate.

Skyler had entered a series of photos from their adventure in a contest. They were mostly of wildlife, but one specific picture stood out amongst the rest: The silhouette of her at the waterfall. Cam had hidden a bottle of champagne at Micah's house, knowing Skyler would win. It was just a feeling she had, and Cam knew the award would mean a lot.

After stumbling through the final hill, they got their first glimpse of the burnt-down cabin.

"Do you think the person who built it ever found out that it burned down?" Skyler asked as they walked along the camp, taking pictures of the pot that had held so many meals still sitting near the fire pit.

"I don't know. I'd think some of it would have been cleared up if they had." Cam shrugged. She called Goose, who had wandered too far for Cam's liking, as memories of their final hours there took over.

"Let's go see the waterfall." Skyler turned and grabbed Cam's hand.

It had been taking everything in Cam not to drag Skyler that way and she let out an exhale in relief that they were finally going in that direction. "Sure, yeah, let's go," she said casually. Inside she was giving herself a high-five at how calm she sounded when all she could feel was her heart pounding out of her chest.

The timing was a little suspect because it needed to be dusk when they got to the waterfall. But after going over different scenarios, Cam just chalked it up to chance. A lot of things could go wrong, but if she was with Skyler, it didn't matter.

When the waterfall came into view, Skyler pulled up to a stop, her eyes roving around the new campsite Cam had set up yesterday. There was a tent already set up, a fire pit with wood cut, and a few camping chairs already around the circle with sticks already shaved and ready for some roasting.

Cam placed the backpack on one of the chairs and slipped her hand in the side pocket, pulling out the small box and slipping it into her sweatshirt pocket.

Skyler still hadn't said a word as she took in the setup. In the fading light, Cam saw her chest heave up and down with quick breaths. She still hadn't seen the best part, but Cam could tell she was working her way close to it. The sharp inhale of breath told Cam she had found the message. Showtime.

Cam was nervous until this moment, but when Skyler turned around to seek her out, Cam was on one knee with the ring held out in front of her, her hands steady and her voice clear. Along the waterfall's edge was the question 'Will you marry me?' in fairy lights that were powered by sunlight. The lights reflected off Skyler's unshed tears. Cam wasn't sure they would get enough charge but was excited that the words were visible in the dusky light.

"Skyler, I've been told I'm stubborn and hardheaded, most often by you." Cam chuckled, losing the thread a little. "Well, that's not how I wanted to start. Umm, my love for you has changed over the years. For a long time, I only saw you as my brother's best friend, but you've been there patiently waiting for me to open my eyes. They are open and only looking at you. You told me once that you would wait for me at the finish line. I'm here. Now I'll wait for your answer. Will you marry me?"

Towards the end, Cam had a hard time getting the words out, but Skyler's sob helped as she nodded through her tears. Cam scrambled off her knees and waited a millimeter away from Skyler's mouth.

"It's all I've ever wanted, yes. Of course. Yes!"

Their lips met as Goose barked his approval at their kiss under the twinkling lights of the Sitka sky.

Made in the USA
Monee, IL
20 April 2022